Macarons and Murder

A Yolanda's Yummery Cozy Mystery

Book 4

By
Lisa Maliga

LISA
MALIGA

Yolanda's Yummery Cozy Mystery Series

The Great Brownie Taste-off, Book 1
The Missing Sea Captain, Book 2
A Pie to Die For, Book 3
Macarons and Murder, Book 4
Title and date to be announced, Book 5

Other Works of Fiction

Diary of a Hollywood Nobody
Hollywood After Dark: 3 Tales of Terror
I Almost Married a Narcissist
I WANT YOU: Seduction Emails from a
Narcissist
Love Me, Need Me: A Narcissist's Tale
The Narcissist Chronicles: The WHOLE
Story
North of Sunset
Notes from Nadir
Out of the Blue
Satan's Casting Call
September Harvest
South of Sunset
Sweet Dreams

COOKBOOKS

Baking Chocolate Cupcakes and Brownies:
A Beginner's Guide
Baking French Macarons: A Beginner's
Guide

Baking Macarons: The Swiss Meringue
Method
Dessert Cookbook Series: A Beginner's
Guide
Ruby Chocolate: A Beginner's Guide

Table of Contents

PREFACE.. 1

CHAPTER 1... 3

CHAPTER 2... 42

CHAPTER 3... 74

CHAPTER 4... 109

CHAPTER 5... 143

CHAPTER 6... 158

CHAPTER 7... 164

CHAPTER 8... 175

CHAPTER 9... 184

CHAPTER 10.. 232

CHAPTER 11.. 277

CHAPTER 12.. 285

THE RECIPES 299

ABOUT THE AUTHOR 308

PREFACE

Back in 2016, I wrote about learning how to bake macarons to better understand my characters and story. After struggling to make my first batch, I didn't know that I'd become so obsessed with the French pastries. I had no idea that I'd end up making almost 100 batches and writing two cookbooks about these little cookies.

I'm returning to the land of macarons – where I first began back in 2013 when I wrote my novella, *Sweet Dreams*. Book number four, which was originally titled *Macarons of Love,* took longer to write than any of the other books in this series. After I completed the first draft, I wanted to make macarons for myself to evaluate the process and get an original cover photo.

I bought all the ingredients to bake those dainty French cookies. It was quite a learning experience. I had confectioners' sugar spill out of a mixing bowl, egg yolks fell into whites, under-mixed macaron batter, and incorrect measuring of ingredients. As a piping novice, the batter and filling oozed onto my hands and the counter. A couple of batches were so bad they had to be thrown away. Fortunately, most of the batches made it into the oven and were baked for various amounts of time. The resulting cookies cracked, had no feet, were rustic looking, and formed shapes ranging from miraculously round to *avant-garde*. No matter what they looked like, they still tasted incredibly sweet – thanks to confectioners' sugar and granulated sugar.

I immersed myself in the process of making these sugary delicacies. Unlike using a mix, yes there are macaron mixes, all nine batches that I baked before this book was published, were made from scratch. I usually took pictures and always made detailed notes. It got a bit easier and faster every time and I learned from my numerous mistakes. I'm happy to include my tested recipe in this book.

CHAPTER 1

Wednesday, February 13

Yolanda Carter had finally fallen asleep after working a fourteen-hour shift at her yummery. In her mind, she saw a white dry erase board in her Brentwood store's office. The heart-shaped bullet points and neat red printing highlighted the variety of goodies, the baking schedule, along with her other duties as owner and baker. A floating pink and red heart pirouetted and flipped in her mind and then she saw them, one highlighted after the other like a stage show of events:

- ♥ 2-14 appearance on Dessert Network's *America's Best Bakeries* show @ 9 PM
- ♥ Valentine's Day
- ♥ Macaron class
- ♥ Train Rusty & Suzie
- ♥ 2/28 Yummery Anniversary

The pink and red heart faded and vanished. Dozing had changed to sleep as her two feline companions heard her gentle snores. Cuddling up to her lay the classic tuxedo cat, Miss Chef. The medium-sized cat had a white stripe down her face and a lovely curved white smile. Her paws resembled white boots and a wide white stripe covered the front of her body. Mr. Whisker sported plush black fur and the larger cat had a single white whisker amidst his black whiskers. He was Miss Chef's adopted younger brother and someone who appreciated resting next to his young owner on soft flannel sheets rather than in a small and lonely cage. Yolanda found him two years ago when she was an employee at the Crown Street Cat Shelter.

The Sherman Oaks cottage had been willed to her after her grandmother's death several years ago. The bedroom was furnished in a Shabby Chic style that was a combination of her own taste and that of her predecessors' homey style. Due to a cold snap of near freezing temperatures, Yolanda had made the queen-sized bed with new flannel sheets along with an electric blanket. The cold-blooded young woman had turned her cottage's thermostat up to seventy to help ward off the chill.

Mr. Whisker sneezed and tightened his tail around his body. Atop the nightstand sat a clock. The red numbers read 2:17.

As she slept, Yolanda was unaware of someone lurking outside her yellow cottage on the corner of Dove Drive and Willowbrook Street. A house that was bought and paid for with Easter eggs. Yolanda loved her artisan family, a glassblower father, an artist and Pilates teacher mother, and her grandparents had made wooden Easter egg trees. Mostly her grandfather, Lukas. Her grandmother, Ingrid, decorated real eggs. She also strung colorful plastic eggs in an array of pastel colors that brightened up the trees and bushes on the corner property. An ornate hand carved tree was always on the front porch advertising Lukas Carter's craftsmanship. Lukas and Ingrid were the proud owners of Sunshine Easter Eggs, Inc.

Yolanda dreamt about wedding bells and a large Mission style church on a bright sunny afternoon. She approached the church, radiating intense happiness, clutching the pink and white bouquet of gardenias, garden roses and tulips. The sweet fragrance soothed her, and she silently thanked her mother, Abby, for suggesting it. Her beloved father, Frederick, would be waiting to walk her down the aisle. Inside the church were gathered all the people she loved and cherished, and as she passed a blooming rosebush, a sudden cold wind gusted down, scattering the crimson petals in the wind, blowing her hair loose from her chignon, so it was streaming in the wind like a flag. Her white chiffon trumpet sleeves and veil billowed around her, obscuring her vision. The sky went from pale blue to dark sapphire. Her head bent down, she struggled against the high winds, the veil pressing against her face, and pellets of hail showered over her, as the pealing church bells changed to a strident ringing noise.

She sat up abruptly, heart loudly pounding; the feel of cold sweat on her neck and tangled chestnut brown hair. The cats blinked and raised their heads from beneath the tunnel of bed coverings, both with indignant stares as though she was responsible for the noise. For a second it stopped, and then it began again, the sound of recorded bells; not church bells— it was the front doorbell.

Her hazel eyes were wide in fright as she looked around, noticing the time. Far too early to leave for her job fifteen miles away. Adding another layer of warmth on top of the bed was her fleecy pink housecoat. She hastily pulled it on as she got up, feeling around on the carpet for her matching slippers. Tying the sash around her narrow waist, she stumbled across the floor, tripping on the edge of the woven rug, and catching herself on the wall next to the half open bedroom door. Fumbling for the light switch, the sudden brightness made her squint. *I shouldn't have gotten rid of the security system*, she thought. If it were functional, a glance at the bedroom monitor would have shown her who was at the door.

However, Mr. Whisker had taken an active dislike of anything connected to the motion sensors in the living room and hallway. He triggered it four times in one week and she finally took the hint and retired the surveillance stuff. The oval sticker with the name of the company remained on the front hall and living room windows.

The doorbell echoed throughout the two-bedroom; two-bathroom cottage built in 1932. She raced down the hallway, through the darkened kitchen, almost crashing into the center island, and burst into the living room. The curtain near the couch was half-open, allowing muted street lighting and natural moonlight to emit enough light for her to see the rest of the way to the front door. Yolanda's slippers slid on the parquet foyer, and she again reached out and leaned on the wall. To her right was the light switch, but instead of flicking it on, she approached the door's peephole and looked out. The porch light was on. In the area above the doorway was installed a faux security camera with a battery-operated blinking red light. She saw a man standing on the ceramic tiled porch; a sight that caused her to step back for an instant.

The tall man stood there with his finger poking the lit doorbell, looking over his shoulder, radiating paranoia. She froze as she stared at him, shocked at how much he'd changed since she saw him just before Christmas. Mike O'Neill, the multimillionaire from Texas had moved out to Los Angeles to become a movie producer. She unlocked both locks and unfastened the chain, opening the front door, the almost freezing night air further awakening her.

"Hey, Mike," she said as her teeth began to chatter. "Why don't you come in and warm up?"

He nodded, pulling a banged up hardsided suitcase covered with black duct tape. One of the crooked wheels made a clattering sound on the floor.

She flipped on the light and shut the door behind him, noticing how unkempt Mike looked. The man used to sport custom made cowboy boots and expensive shirts worn with ornate bola ties. Later that year, Mike's wardrobe changed into conventional business attire and his charming Texas twang vanished.

The man who monopolized the floor space in front of the door was in a different wardrobe incarnation—down and out. Loose-fitting jeans with frayed bottoms, filthy sneakers. The windbreaker was too lightweight for the weather and his hair was longer and thinner than she remembered. The stench of cigarette smoke made her eyes water.

"Hey, Yolanda, it's been a while..." he smiled, showing off stained teeth. A swollen bruise on his cheekbone and bloodshot eyes completed his rugged transformation.

"Yes it has," Yolanda said, still shocked at the sight of him so bedraggled looking. He'd never been to her house before. She couldn't imagine her grandparents Old World reaction to some homeless-looking guy showing up unannounced in the middle of the night.

This was the man who had whisked her off in his Bugatti and they'd dined at his Malibu Beach house on a super expensive dinner. That was last summer, but it seemed like it had been years ago.

"Yo! Yolanda!" he laughed at his lame greeting. "Look, I gotta ask you a big favor."

Biting her lip, she gazed at his bruise, then back down at his shoes. Charity was important to her, and he looked like he needed all he could get.

"Did you want to stay in my guest room, Mike?"

"Thanks, but no thanks. I just need to store this bag in your guest room. Or wherever is safe. I'll be back for it on Friday." He paused, looking at his wrist—only he wasn't wearing a watch. "Friday afternoon. I promise."

She nodded. "Okay. Look, I'm forgetting my manners. Would you like some coffee or tea or hot chocolate?"

Mike leaned over and peered through the peephole, "No, I really gotta go now." He looked back at her and then grabbed the suitcase, pulling the wobbly-wheeled thing across the foyer. "If you could..."

"Yes, of course," she said, accepting the handle. "By the way, where's your car?"

"I parked on Ventura Boulevard."

"Mike, what's going on?"

"It's a long story." He went over to the door and looked through the peephole again. "Gotta go. No overnight parking on Ventura."

He reached for the doorknob. She sensed that he had somewhere to go.

"Mike, what's in here?" She let the suitcase stand on the floor.

Turning the doorknob, he gave her a sly grin. "Some important business documents, that's all. I'll be back for them on Friday."

"Okay then." Her words were as reluctant as her feeling about the situation in the foyer made colder as he opened the door and quickly fled down the trio of steps. She shut the door and stood in front of the peephole, watching the lanky man disappear into the night.

She made sure the door was locked and the chain was on and stepped back into the living room, reluctant to bring the duct-taped piece of luggage into her home. It looked like it had endured many baggage handlers in a multitude of airports and bus stations.

The silence of the house returned, and she knew her cats had gone back to sleep in her warm bed. She was tempted to leave the smelly thing standing in her living room but decided to wheel it back into the spare bedroom and park it in the closet until he reclaimed it two days later.

Yolanda wheeled the suitcase into the spare bedroom, which had a pair of twin-sized beds and an old-fashioned white oak roll top computer desk. Next to that was the small closet. Opening the closet door, she moved the old upright vacuum cleaner aside and put the suitcase inside, so it wasn't hidden but easily accessible. She shut the door and returned to her room where she promptly slid back into bed next to her feline companions.

Troubled by the handsome man's disheveled appearance, she remembered how he'd suggested her ex-boyfriend, Zac Field, should audition for a reality show. He had also helped promote the yummery's launching of pies back in December and while he never admitted it, she suspected that new pop star sensations, Knick and Knack, had announced their engagement in her yummery, which led to even more business. What had caused Mike to fall onto hard times?

Just as she was dozing off, the doorbell rang. *Not again,* she thought, unwilling to leave her warm bed. Both cats were still asleep. The bedside clock read 4:20. The noise stopped. It was the alarm clock, not the doorbell. She turned it off and sat up, hearing the wind rustling through the trees. A storm was approaching. It was the day before the biggest and busiest day of the month, namely Valentine's Day. The cats glared at her and remained unmoving, then shut their eyes and returned to sleep. She stumbled out of bed and went into her bathroom, not wanting to bother them with too much light at such an hour. She sighed, knowing they'd probably sleep until seven or so and then stroll into the kitchen for their waiting bowl of breakfast along with a sprinkling of homemade salmon treats. For an instant, she regretted having to get up on a dark winter morning and wished she could sleep in like her feline pals.

Her iPhone and iPad rested on the pink and black tile countertop in the bathroom. They used to be stowed away in a kitchen drawer, but that was before she owned Yolanda's Yummery. Being a twenty-eight-year-old owner of a thriving Brentwood business had earned her way more stress than she could've imagined. Only two years ago, she was an employee at the Crown Street Cat Shelter in nearby Van Nuys. Now, her daily commute took her over the hill and ate up about forty to fifty minutes each way. She activated her iPhone's screen, noting the number of messages, missed calls, and went straight to her daily to do list. In fact, she should have gotten up an hour earlier if she wanted to tackle more than just arriving at work before five o'clock.

Instead of one of the standard pastel yummery colored shirts of yellow, pink and seafoam green, today she pulled on the new red and pink polo shirt that would usher in Valentine's Day. The T-shirts and polo shirts had arrived on Monday, and she had distributed them to all the employees with instructions to wear them on the "big day" of the year. Yolanda saw it as Valentine's Day Eve and was looking forward to seeing her boyfriend, Nigel Garvey, that day. He was the owner of the adjoining Beverage Bar and while he still hadn't popped the question, she thought that he might get romantic enough on the fourteenth.

****

As she drove to work, images of her and Nigel kissing over a bubbly glass of champagne and a plateful of heart-shaped macarons made her smile. *It's almost like Christmas*, she thought, when she pulled up behind the yummery and popped open the Honda's trunk.

A white van with the company's logo adorning both sides sat next to her parking space. She grinned upon seeing the van with the prominently featured yummery's logo.

Another vehicle was parked by the dumpster in the other employee parking spot, Quinn Hendrickson's red Toyota Camry. He opened his car door and got out as soon as she pulled up. The young man from Wisconsin managed the Beverage Bar and was a friend of Nigel's. He had extensive barista and bakery experience and specialized in baking the yummery's mini-Bundt coffee cakes. An unzipped windbreaker was worn over his red polo shirt. Yolanda noticed his customary pinstripe chef pants.

"'Morning Yolanda," he greeted her as he walked over to the back. He clicked open the trunk lid and inside was a large box.

He lifted it out and walked towards the yummery's back door. She rushed ahead of the man and unlocked it. He hurried inside and set the bulky box down, returning to his car to shut the trunk and retrieve his briefcase. Then they walked over to her car and began unloading all the boxes from her car's trunk.

Quinn and Yolanda assembled the five-foot tall pastel pink tree with the embedded pink and white miniature lights. Once it was assembled in front of the main window, Yolanda began hanging up the brightly colored heart shaped ornaments. The array of glass and wooden hearts ranged in size and color from plain wood to sparkly rhinestones and crystals. The loud knock on the front door startled her as she turned.

A roundish young woman in an oversized cherry red ski jacket waved at her as she approached the door. Yolanda smiled upon seeing the pastry chef, BB

Gustafson. Frizzy natural blonde curls peeked out from the edge of the hood.

"Hey Yolanda, it's still really cold out," BB announced, rubbing her gloved hands together.

"Hey BB," Yolanda said as she unlocked the door to allow BB to enter. She glanced at the cupcake shaped clock above the door that read 5:35. "You're right, I could see my breath. Did it get this cold in Oklahoma?"

BB nodded. "Yeah. And sometimes it even snowed."

"Snow, I only see it on the mountains..." she shook her head and went over to the tree that was festooned with dozens of hearts. Several boxes of ornaments were still on the floor. "Well, I've got to check on the ingredients for the macarons. Suzie should be here any minute. Could you please finish hanging these ornaments and then meet me back in the kitchen?"

"Okay, Yo. I've just got to hang up my jacket and I'll be right back."

Yolanda went behind the counter and into the kitchen, pushing aside the striped cloth covering. There was a knock on the front door. She looked past the Gift Corner to her left. A spiral clothes rack featured colorful aprons, T-shirts, and sweatshirts bearing the cute logo. Shelves behind the clothes rack boasted a half dozen colored and clear glass pedestal cake and cupcake stands with domed lids. They were designed by her father, Frederick Carter.

The middle and lower glass shelves held rows of bottles, advertising Heather Hathaway's Lotions & More ~ The Yolanda's Yummery Collection. Each fragrance had a small tester size available. There were also some realistic looking cupcake shaped soaps in bakery aromas and colors, along with heart shaped soaps.

A pale-yellow china cabinet stood in the Gift Corner. The mirrored back was softly lit, and all the glass shelves contained her mother's batik creations, a dozen mugs sporting the yummery's logo and vivid yellow, pink, and green batik designs. ABC, Abby's Batik Creations, was her mother's company and she had created the logo seen on all the items for sale at the yummery. On other shelves of varying heights were tea and coffee cups with matching saucers. Plush white teddy bears holding red satin hearts decorated the ends of the main shelves.

BB returned wearing a red and pink T-shirt covered by a pink apron. Lately, she wore baggy black chef's pants to look more professional, although Yolanda suspected it was to hide the fact that she was naturally heavyset. BB went over to the tree and began hanging the colorful ornaments on it. She noted a gold and red rhinestone studded heart that was larger than the others. "Is this a tree topper?" she asked, holding it up.

Yolanda nodded. "Yes it is. I just got it. If you can't reach it, use the stepstool."

"Okay, Yo." BB went behind the counter and picked up the small folding stepstool. She plunked it down in front of the tree and climbed up it, gently adding the beautiful heart topper. "Just like on a Christmas tree, only it's not a star," BB observed.

She stepped down and began adding the rest of the ornaments. Within minutes the task was done. "I used to decorate my family and church Christmas trees every year," she explained to Yolanda as they gazed up at the glittering tree.

"Fifty shades of fuchsia," Yolanda said.

BB giggled. "I love fuchsia and anything in the pink color family."

"I've noticed. But so do I," the yummery owner said. "I love the fact that the tree has miniature lights in the branches just like the Christmas tree does."

A quick, loud tap on the door startled her. She rushed over to open it for the newest employee, Suzie Palmer. Suzie was a tall woman with short platinum spiky hair and shoulder-length filigree earrings.

"Hey, Suzie," Yolanda greeted the woman as she held open the door for her.

"Good morning, Yolanda," Suzie said in a quiet voice.

Yolanda shut and locked the door. "Quinn's getting the coffee started. I know you're not a big morning person."

The woman unbuttoned her black coat and nodded, heading back to the break room.

Just as she was about to step away from the door, a tentative knocking sounded. She turned to see a slender man wearing a denim jacket. Rusty McFadden had a smile on his thin face. "Hey Miss Yolanda," he greeted the much younger woman as he entered the yummery. The man paused, looking at the shimmery pink tree, covered with heart-shaped ornaments and the large sparkly gold and red heart topper. "I've never ever seen a tree like that before!"

"Well, Rusty, it's our first official Yummery Valentine's Day tree," said Yolanda, proudly gazing up at it.

She looked over at the smiling older man. Out of the corner of her eye, she noticed Suzie hesitating for an instant before stepping out into the yummery.

Not observing the fact that the woman was uncomfortable around Rusty, Yolanda's attention was drawn to the recently installed long menu spanning the area above the counter. The special of the day needed to be written in bright yellow chalk, but for the next two days, Yolanda thought that pink was a more appropriate color choice. As she was about to get the chalk out of the storage area behind the counter, she noticed that Rusty was still rooted to the spot looking up at the tree.

"Rusty, would you like to help put the boxes away?"

"Why yes ma'am, I sure will."

He looked down at the empty boxes and walked over to them. "Where would you like me to put them, Miss Yolanda?"

She smiled as she returned holding a piece of chalk. "Just put them in the back room near the door for now. Thanks."

Rusty began gathering them up. "Want me to break them down for you, Miss Yolanda?"

"No thanks, Rusty."

He nodded and picked all of them up and hurried towards the back room just as Suzie walked around the counter and into the yummery. She wore a red and pink French cut polo shirt and a color-coordinated apron. Her skintight white leggings emphasized her thin figure. She stood nearly six feet tall with her pink pumps.

If the man hadn't been wearing glasses, Yolanda thought his eyes might have popped out of his head and rolled to the floor, so intently did he watch as she strode out into the storefront. Yolanda sighed, feeling so much fatter than her newest employee. She lugged an extra ten pounds of fat, all of it around her hips. Her once daily Pilates practice was mostly weekend Pilates practice. And lately, not even then.

A tapping on the glass and Yolanda saw Jeannie Stanton, an older woman wearing a sequined headband that matched her shirt and pink Yolanda's Yummery tote bag. Yolanda unlocked the door, letting the employee in. "Good morning, Jeannie," she said warmly.

Jeannie stepped inside and inhaled deeply. "Good morning, Yolanda, it smells heavenly in here." She looked up and saw BB walking in holding a tray of raspberry chocolate cupcakes. "Good morning, BB! Good morning, Suzie!" The older woman looked at the shimmering tree. "Oh, Yolanda, that Valentine's Day tree is so beautiful!"

Suzie nodded and leaned against the immaculate glass case, which BB was filling with colorful creations. The Magical Cakes of Love were the first products anyone saw--smaller than normal nine-or ten-inch round cakes that most bakeries carried. Yolanda and BB baked the signature cakes in six-inch round pans. The cakes were large enough for one or two people. They were often shared, a fact that the employees had learned. As the special was raspberry chocolate, there were several of those lovely bright pink and brown cakes along with decadent chocolate, fancy vanilla buttercream, red velvet, and the newest flavor: Crazy 4 Coconut. In the next display case was the selection of brownies, which ranged from the prizewinning plain to those filled with chopped California walnuts or topped with a rich German chocolate frosting. There was also peanut butter brownies and chocolate mint brownies. For the month of February, the two new bestselling brownie flavors were strawberry chocolate and cherry chocolate. There were also the latest additions to the yummery: apple and cherry pies. An entire case contained a variety of oversized cookies and shelves of cupcakes.

"I just can't wait to see you on *America's Best Bakeries* tomorrow night. Milton and I have the DVD set up to record it so we won't miss a second! Milton knows so much about DVDs and cable and satellite and all kinds of high-tech TV and even computer things!" She giggled. "I'm so lucky to have met him—especially at my age."

"You're just a year or two older than me," BB said as she added the last cake and went back to the kitchen to get another tray.

"Oh, BB, you're such a dear!" Jeannie giggled.

****

Suzie stood behind the large stainless steel counter in the kitchen. All the employees were on the other side, each of them held a yellow folder with the yummery's logo. Rusty set his down on the counter. Jeannie opened hers, looking at the flyer and colorful brochure with photos of macarons. Yolanda had done her research and included a list of selling points for everyone behind the counter to memorize. They were encouraged to sample each flavor of macaron to describe it to the appreciated guests. Whether they would help with the macaron making or not, the employees watched how they were made.

A new red stand mixer was whipping up a frothy batch of meringue. Suzie switched the machine off. "These egg whites have peaked," she said, removing the whisk attachment and holding it upside down. See how the egg whites have clumped near the bottom. Yet the peaks, which are now the top, are evident?"

"Like a mountain?" asked Rusty.

Suzie nodded. "Yes, that's one way of describing it." Returning the whisk, she picked up a plastic container and measured out a small amount of bright pink powder. "Raspberry macarons will be bright pink, of course." She flipped the switch and the white turned to bright pink within seconds. "But the most important part of this process is the macaronage—mixing the meringue with the almond flour and sugar mixture. If it's not properly blended the macarons won't get feet during the baking process."

"Then they won't walk away," Rusty said.

Everyone in the kitchen from Quinn to Jeannie to BB laughed. Suzie rolled her eyes and looked at the pink meringue. She nodded and shut off the mixer. "Very funny. After the blending, I want to show you how to load a piping bag. The macaronage was taught to me by Bertrand Larouche when I was at *Le Cordon Bleu* in Paris."

****

After the store opened at seven o'clock, Jeannie was training Rusty to operate the cash register and box or bag the sold yummery items. Before she went to the kitchen, Yolanda stepped towards the far end of the counter, away from Jeannie, and discussed the day's schedule with the man. "Now as soon as Nick comes in at ten I'll need you to load up the goodies in the van and drive to the Beverage Bar on the Third Street Promenade. Park in the loading zone behind the place and Nigel will be there to sign the order. Then when you come back I'll need to you to help with the macarons as we'll need 1200 macarons in five different flavors." She paused. "Well, that's all for now, and I want you to know that I appreciate your work and I'm so glad you're here with us."

The man beamed at his boss. "Thank you so kindly, Miss Yolanda. You're a wonderful boss. This yummery is the best place I've ever worked."

She noticed his posture straightened as he returned to the front of the store and waited on a mother with a pair of sleeping

23

twins in a stroller. A bearded older man carrying a laptop case strode in and made his way over to the last of the eight round white vintage ice cream parlor tables. They lined the wall from back to front on the other side of the cookies and cupcakes display case. The pastel striped seat cushions of the chairs matched the pink, lemon yellow and seafoam green wallpaper.

As the sun had finally shown its rays and brightened the day, she was about to return to the kitchen when the front door opened. There stood a handsome young man in his mid-twenties wearing an elegant hunter green jacket and tan corduroys. He beamed upon seeing her and she noticed that he was the one to initiate the first move by rushing across the store and behind the counter, where he greeted her with a big hug and kissed her gently on the lips. She felt the strong attraction and stared into his penetrating dark eyes. Beneath the light of the shelving units filled with bagged and boxed sweets, she saw that his natural golden brown wavy hair had more gold than brown. He had been in Miami for three days, which explained the difference.

"I missed you, Nigel," she said as a way of greeting her boyfriend.

"Darling, you know I missed you. But I can't wait to spend tomorrow night with you. There's something very important I want to discuss with you—after we see ourselves on *America's Best Bakeries*, of course!"

Surely, he heard her heartbeat increasing in tempo. She steadily gazed into his eyes, as though trying to gauge what he would say to her in twenty-four hours. Well, not what exactly, but how would he phrase it? What kind of engagement ring would he present to her? Where would he pop the question—in her house? In his house? At a romantic restaurant? Or at her parents' house down in Laguna Beach?

Their reverie was interrupted by his cell phone and he quickly removed it from his jacket pocket and glanced at the screen. "Must take this call. We'll talk later." He connected to the caller and walked into the kitchen. She followed him because she was desperately needed there.

Crystal Irwin had arrived just as the Beverage Bar and yummery were opening for the day. The young woman mumbled a greeting and even nodding her head took a bit of effort. Now, after finishing a small cup of imported Jamaican coffee, she was smiling, and her face had more color to it. Quinn, who was the expert mini-Bundt coffee cake baker, removed a tray of cakes from the oven and set them down on the last available space atop the crowded cooling rack. Everyone else was in the midst of the macaron making frenzy.

Aside from the usual cakes, cupcakes, energy bars and cookies, the large kitchen looked like a Parisian patisserie. Additional mixing bowls and two new stand mixers were on tables and countertops. Suzie was scraping the sides of a stainless steel bowl with a plastic scraper. She picked the scraper up and watched a stream of chocolate batter flowing back into the bowl. Suzie grabbed a pastry bag and poured the batter into it, twisting the top and expertly gripping it as she piped the circles of macaron batter onto a silicone mat placed on top of a cookie sheet.

BB stood in one corner piping batter onto a parchment covered baking sheet, each perfectly round disc a crimson red macaron shell in the making. To her left stood a stack of empty stainless steel baking trays and several large sheets of white parchment paper. She piped the last disc, placed the parchment paper on a cookie sheet, and lifted it up, dropping it back down on the countertop a few times. She looked at all the batter-filled circles and saw no air bubbles and the center peaks that had formed from the piping had vanished. She slid the tray into the five-foot tall baking rack along one wall. BB returned to her little corner of the kitchen and picked up the half-full piping bag.

Suzie's apron had splotches of powdered sugar on it from where she'd wiped her hands. She strode over to BB's area and watched the younger woman piping batter onto a parchment sheet. "*Mon Dieu!* BB you stupid cow, put that parchment onto a tray right now!"

BB's hands shook and she nearly dropped the piping bag. She stopped what she was doing so she wouldn't make a mess of the batter. "Um, okay..."

Yolanda flicked off the Hobart stand mixer with the fluffy peaks of meringue and just stared at Suzie for an instant before going over to the older woman. As she stood within a couple of feet away from her newest employee, she kept her voice low. "Um, Suzie, can I see you in my office ... please?" Adding that last word was difficult, but she knew that all the employees were focusing more on her and less on the sweets. "Everyone, please get back to work. We have 1200 macarons to make by tomorrow! We have no time to lose!"

Yolanda closed the door behind Suzie once they were in her small office. She kept everything organized in the labeled in and out bins and the color-coded filing system was helpful for her visually. Unlike the white dry erase board with the red hearts in her dream, she had a large old-fashioned cork bulletin board next to her desk. It was covered with rows of index cards and neon green sticky notes. She sat down behind her desk and pointed to one of the two guest chairs. Suzie sat at the edge of the chair, hands folded in her lap, her back straight as she stared down at Yolanda, thin lips pursed.

"Suzie, I know you used to be co-owner of a patisserie in San Francisco that went under due to circumstances beyond your control. I know you have your own show online—well, that's how I found you and hired you. With your personality and expertise along with attending *Cordon Bleu* in Paris..."

"It's *Le Cordon Bleu*," the woman said, smirking.

Yolanda rolled her eyes, noticing the woman's pinched nose. "Yes, fine it's *Le Cordon Bleu*. However, I don't know what they taught you about working with other employees, but we don't call them stupid cows. Especially since BB has been baking for most of her life."

"If that's the case, then she couldn't have been taught how to bake macarons because I was taught that you must pipe the filling onto the parchment paper which is already placed on the cookie sheet. She was doing it wrong."

"Maybe she was but you still don't call her, or any of the employees, names like that. She has feelings, you know. That'll be all."

Suzie immediately got up and left, slamming the door behind her. Yolanda jumped, not used to aggressive employees. That type of behavior hadn't happened at the yummery before. Everyone was courteous to one another. Yolanda considered all the yummery employees as friends and vice versa. Everyone worked harmoniously together—and it was a highly unusual phenomenon. Even at the cat shelter there had been employees that were lazy or combative around each other or potential adoptees. She knew that Suzie was being nitpicky as BB was doing her best. It was more challenging for everyone due to it being more crowded than usual in the kitchen.

The framed photo of her and Nigel beaming at each other was a nice addition to her desk, but she wished they were more than boyfriend and girlfriend. Next to that, was a photo cube filled with pictures of her two cats. For an instant, it looked like Mr. Whisker winked at her with his coppery green eyes. She sighed, feeling like an old maid or a spinster, an even uglier word. Staring at cat photos when she was supposed to be making macarons for the busiest day of the year wasn't very helpful. She got up and went into the kitchen.

Quinn walked by pushing a dolly loaded with boxes that contained coffees and teas, on his way through the kitchen and to the back door. Nigel hurried in, holding a box and smiled upon seeing her. "Off to headquarters. Just wanted to say that Rusty's working out very well."

She beamed. "Thank you, but it's my mom you want to thank. She's the one who found him through that new program she saw on the news. Oh, how many macarons will you need tomorrow?"

"I guess about 200 or so. And several extra gift boxes. If we need more, Rusty will be able to deliver them, yes?"

"That's why I bought the van and hired him," she said.

"And it's so nice to have a second Beverage Bar location only three blocks from the beach. Lots of foot traffic on the Third Street Promenade equates to lots of business. And we need to keep more of those mini Bundt cakes in the store because they sell out quickly. We've also been getting more requests for muffins as well as more energy bars." He handed her a file. "I offer a free small beverage of their choice for anyone who completes an online survey."

"Yeah, I've been meaning to do that too. Last month I had a free energy bar day and it seemed to help a little."

"Which reminds me—the spring cleansing juices will be launching in late March or early April? We want to attract more vegetarians and vegans who drink only fresh juice. Plus, sometimes they like a little extra sugar pick-me-up. And the macarons are all vegetarian, so there's that..."

Yolanda laughed. "I think that's a great idea. We'll have complete health food to complete fun food."

He leaned over and gave her a quick kiss. "You're right, well, must dash." He turned and headed for the back door.

She went into the yummery. *Oh no, what about the sample trays*, she thought, noticing the pair of custom-made glass trays on the countertop—one near the point-of-sale area and the other farther down, were almost empty. Where was Nick? Glancing at the clock, she saw it was 10:45. It was Nick's job to replenish them especially as Jeannie was the only counter help at the moment. She also knew that they would have to be moved to another area near the Valentine's Day tree where she would set up a small table because the countertops would contain trays of macarons. Good thing she had foreseen that when she had planned the big macaron launch last month. While her father hadn't had time to make special macaron-sized display cases, she had found some at an online auction site.

At eleven o'clock, Nick Delany hurried in, his broad face red with exertion. "My new used car broke down. My fault for trusting some guy in Arleta selling his junker on SaveBuxBoard.com," he explained. "It ran fine when I first got it." Nick was still grumbling as he dashed into the back room to clock in and put away his knapsack.

When he returned a couple of minutes later wearing a red polo shirt and matching apron, he smiled upon seeing the half-full tips jar. There already was a colorful heart shaped sign:

FEBRUARY 14 IS ALL ABOUT LOVE -- BUT SO IS FEBRUARY 13!

Late that afternoon, Suzie was going through the pantry storage cupboard in the back of the kitchen where all the crystal sugar, colorants and other decorations were stored. She had opened the door and was leaning inside. "I thought the rose petals were kept back here?" Suzie pushed aside a row of small containers of powdered and gel colorants, knocking some to the floor.

Yolanda rushed over and bent down to retrieve the fallen jars. "No," she said, moving over to the area, leaning in to replace the colorants as the older woman sidestepped her.

"Really, Suzie, it's not necessary to add dried rose petals."

"I'm so glad to know that" Suzie replied. "After all, I've only been making French macarons since 1999, or before most people in America even heard of them. And now suddenly you with no culinary school degree and with about four batches of baking macarons under your belt, are telling me we DON'T need a certain garnish? A garnish that was first added back in 1862 by Louis Ladurée, himself?"

Yolanda stood there with her mouth open, unable to say what was coursing through her mind. Having an employee speaking disrespectfully to her hadn't happened since she worked at the Crown Street Cat Shelter more than two years ago. And that was by a short-term college student volunteer who wasn't liked by anyone – including the cats.

This is my business and I'm letting a new hire talk like that to me. A woman who's almost as old as my mother?

She took a couple of deep breaths before responding, remembering her Pilates training. Her mother had been teaching Pilates since the late 1980s. "Yes, Suzie, I'm sure you know more about macarons than me or any of the other bakers at the yummery. That's why I hired you, because you're an expert. But I don't think that rose petals on top of 100 macarons will make that much of a difference. The main flavors will be vanilla, strawberry, raspberry, red velvet and chocolate. Americans aren't that huge on the rose flavor—I've tried it in the past and the results haven't been as successful as more conventional flavors like strawberry and chocolate."

"You're only doing 100 rose flavored macarons?" Suzie's gray eyes widened, and Yolanda noticed the thick webbing of mascara and fake eyelashes that the woman wore. If one of those lashes fell onto a macaron it would resemble a spider leg.

"Yes, I'm sure you've seen the order form. After all, YOU are in charge of everything to do with the macarons..." Yolanda glanced at her watch. "But let's call it a night and I'll see you tomorrow morning at five?" Yolanda remembered to smile and edged away from the pantry, but she closed the door first.

Suzie nodded, "Yes, but I don't have a key. Are you sure that you or Quinn will be here at five?"

Yolanda struggled to avoid rolling her eyes. "Yes, I'm certain that someone will be here at five on the busiest day of the year."

"Good." The woman turned and walked into the break room to clock out and retrieve her coat and handbag.

By 7:30, Yolanda still hadn't left the yummery. She was sitting behind her desk going over the next day's schedule. The phone rang, causing her to jump. She quickly answered it and smiled when she heard the voice on the other end. It was her best friend and counter employee/sample giver extraordinaire, Teagan Mishkin.

"Yo, my cold is over now so I'll definitely be there on the big V'Day at seven – maybe even a quarter till if I get up in time."

Yolanda laughed. "Great. You were really missed today. Suzie is nuttier than a grove of almond trees. She had a major freak-out about no rose petals on the rose macarons. And she called BB a stupid cow."

"Wow, that woman is nutso. How could anyone call BB that? She's always so nice and she's the best baker around other than you."

"Thanks, but I think Suzie has some personality issues. Her internet show still hasn't led to anything on a network so she's taking it way too hard."

"Whatever. Sean called me last night. He wants to get back together."

"Oh no."

"I'm not worried about it. It's not like he's shown up at work and I think he knows that I'm not interested in riding around in his blue and white minivan with hundreds of *GO Georgia Gamecocks* flags stuck on the roof. It was sooo embarrassing. Even after that endless football season he just goes from football to basketball to baseball, so it never ends." She sighed. "I was so embarrassed at all the jokes people were making about his van and the flags. And the rude comments about the name of the team – it was worse than when I was working at the gentlemen's club. At least there, Rocky always made sure everything was respectable."

"I get that you're done with Sean." Yolanda stifled a yawn, looking at the clock on the wall above the bulletin board. On a napkin beside her keyboard sat a half-eaten lemon coconut energy bar. *I'm just low on energy today*, she thought.

The call ended and Yolanda got up, grabbed her purse out of her desk drawer and slipped on her coat. As no one was around, she locked the back door behind her and hurried over to her car, feeling the bone chilling cold wind ruffling her hair. Inside her car, she switched on the heat, glad that it worked quickly to warm her up. Thoughts of tomorrow night's events were occupying her as she drove down San Vicente Boulevard. *Will Nigel ask me out to dinner at his place or will he come over to mine? Nine o'clock is when the show will be on.* She found herself getting drowsy and opened the window, allowing the night air to wake her up enough to drive home safely.

Pulling up into the driveway, she saw the house next door was dark. Ever since she'd been visiting her grandparents when they were still alive, Mrs. Steele and her vibrant rosebushes had been a topic of admiration for Ingrid and Lukas. Her parents admired them, too. Mrs. Steele was a large woman who enjoyed talking on the phone when watering her beloved flowers. Drought or no drought, her roses were always in blooming good health and her grass was the greenest on the block. The two-story slate blue and white Cape Cod style house was twice the size of her cottage and a little newer. There was a FOR SALE sign in front of it and every time Yolanda saw it, she felt sad. Just after Christmas,

Mrs. Steele had a stroke, and her daughter put her in an assisted living facility in Pasadena.

As soon as Yolanda walked into the kitchen, both cats rushed up to greet her, meowing loudly. Miss Chef's jade green eyes and Mr. Whisker's coppery green eyes were bright as they welcomed her home. Rubbing themselves around her legs in figure eights, she thought they were telling her about their day. The TV was on, providing visuals and noise for them. After petting them and hearing their purrs, she filled their almost empty food bowls with wet and dry food. Going to the cupboard where she stored their treats, she removed a bag of little brown heart-shaped goodies, doling out an even number to each eager cat.

After a light dinner of sushi that was about to expire the next day, she returned to the kitchen and sat on the floor in front of the quartz-top island. She opened a lower cabinet and took stock of her private inventory of edible decorations. She began pulling out tiny containers of luster dust. Behind them were orderly rows of sparkling sugar, glitter dust, dragees and pearls in a rainbow of colors ranging in order from darkest to lightest. In the very back was a large jar of 24-karat edible gold leaf flakes. She pulled it out and held it up to the light, admiring the gold glimmering in the overhead light. "Who needs rose petals when you have real gold?"

It jogged a memory about her friend and investigative blogger, The Other Patrick Stewart. The young man had visited Golda's Golden Goodies bakery in Beverly Hills. The new bakery was in the Golden Triangle, and they sold cakes and brownies sprinkled with edible gold dust. However, Patrick had found bags of commercial brownie mix in their dumpster. He had two separate lab analyses done on five of the brownies and cupcakes and he shared the results: the gold dust was tainted because it contained a high percentage of copper. Golda's business wasn't booming after that discovery. However, The Other Patrick Stewart was in negotiations with Channel 10 to become a reporter after breaking the story.

The cats wandered over and sniffed the jar, looking at it. Miss Chef swatted a jar of neon pink edible glitter, and it skidded to a stop in front of the stove. Mr. Whisker immediately raced after it, nudging it into the living room with his nose.

Yolanda jumped up, "hey kids, this isn't a toy!" She ran into the living room and picked up the small jar, holding it under the light from the table lamp.

"Bright pink edible glitter will also work. Thanks for the idea!"

Just as she was about to return to the kitchen, she stopped in front of the TV and saw Vern Hess, the veteran newscaster on Channel 12 Action Street News. The older man wore a spiky brown wig. His mustache was dyed to match. He stood next to a sign for the Hardy Henz Chicken Farm. Behind him was a small, corrugated tin building with a gaudy yellow and red logo featuring a smiling cartoon hen. There were no chickens in sight.

"This is Vern Hess at Channel 12 Action Street News. I'm here in Pomona outside the Hardy Henz Chicken Farm." He gestured widely, indicating the building. "Well, viewers, it looks like the supposed pasture-range eggs from this farm aren't free to range at all. It turns out that the hens are NOT allowed to go outdoors and must stay in CAGES in that little building. Basically, it's a tin shack with no windows, no air conditioning, and no heating. That's where your 'farm fresh pasture-range eggs' are coming from..."

The camera panned a little closer to the building.

"But I'm not allowed to interview the owner, Harold Bernett. In fact, I've been told I'm trespassing. That's why I have to stand on the road..."

A grainy photograph flashed on the screen showing a cluster of mangy looking hens crowded in stacks of cages.

"We have pictures from a former employee." Vern narrated as another photo was shown, a close-up that was even more disturbing. "Chickens never see the light of day," Vern announced. Yolanda looked away from the TV.

"I can't watch this," she said, picking up the remote control and shutting it off. "I know that I'm done doing business with them. I thought they were organic pasture-range eggs. I thought the chickens had freedom to move about. I'll need to find a new supplier stat," she said more to herself than the cats.

She walked into the kitchen and placed the sugar container next to the 24-karat gold container. "I'll have some very elegant looking macarons for Valentine's Day, at least." She paused. "I'll need to find the certificate of authenticity."

Instead of getting ready for bed, Yolanda opened her iPad and thumbed through the listing of organic chicken farms within a 200-mile radius of L.A. She found an organic farm that only sold eggs from pasture-range chickens. They were all laying hens, meaning that none were killed for their meat. She looked at the photos of chickens poking around the long grass and scrubby areas. No crowded conditions, plenty of space. The indoor area featured roosts and sunlight streamed in through windows and a skylight. The various colored chickens had all their feathers and body parts and plenty of room to spread their wings and walk about. The chickens were fed an all-natural GMO-free diet of organic wheat sprouts, peas, corn, barley, flaxseed oil, fish meal and oyster shells. They also pecked the ground for worms and grubs as chickens weren't natural vegetarians.

She sent the company an email expressing her interest and wanting to know about bulk pricing. Yolanda checked her email once more and decided that anything that needed answering could wait until tomorrow. She had to go to bed early if she wanted to be at the yummery at five o'clock. Tempted as she was to leave her iPad in the kitchen drawer like she used to do, she carried it with her back to her bedroom and put it on the bathroom counter.

I'll shower in the morning, she thought, forgetting to check to make sure the doors and windows were locked.

CHAPTER 2

By the time Yolanda parked in the employee parking area behind the yummery at 5:05 on Valentine's Day, she was surprised to see only the company van. Suzie was supposed to be there to get the macarons out of the walk-in refrigerator. They needed time to get to room temperature. The buttercream frosting had to be made for the most recent batches, plus the gold and sugar crystals needed...Yolanda took a deep breath, just as she'd been taught by her mother many years ago. "One breath at a time, one step at a time," Abby had told her.

An old red Volvo puttered into the parking lot and as the car stopped next to her white Honda, the engine was switched off. Only it didn't stop right away as a rattling noise from under the hood continued for several seconds. Suzie got out of her car holding a canvas pink yummery-issued tote bag in one hand and a large Neiman Marcus shopping bag in the other, along with her designer handbag. Kicking the door shut with her pointy toe boot, the stylish woman mumbled something that resembled good morning.

"I think you're the first one to arrive today," Yolanda said, trying to sound cheerful. She headed towards the back door and unlocked it. "Biggest day of the year!"

If there was an affirmation, it was done with an unseen nod. Suzie followed Yolanda through the back door, her heels making clickety-clacking noises when they hit the tile floor.

Yolanda's sneakered feet were silent as she went to her office.

A loud banging on the just-closed back door startled them. Yolanda turned around, rushed back, and looked through the peephole. She opened the door and let in Rusty who was carrying his beige canvas tote.

"Hey boss, sorry I'm late. My bike got a flat tire just before I got to downtown." He sniffed loudly, wiping his runny nose with the back of his jacket sleeve. Suzie grimaced and Yolanda's eyes widened in surprise.

"Rusty, you know my name. Now why don't you get changed and start a pot of coffee? I think we can all use some caffeine!"

He nodded. "Yes, Miss Yolanda. It sure 'nough is windy out there—I lost my baseball cap." He ran his hands through his messy hair.

"No problem, Rusty. I'll get you a new baseball cap."

****

All the employees had arrived. Everyone was in the process of gearing up for the big day. Suzie oversaw baking the macarons and per Yolanda's request had added bits of gold flakes to some of the rose and chocolate-flavored macarons. Others were getting sparkling pink glitter sprinkled on top.

The Beverage Bar was running a Two-for-One special and lots of flavors of hot chocolate and mochacchinos were featured. Nigel and Yolanda were alone in her office with the door closed. A platter of heart-shaped macarons, some festooned with lovely golden flakes, sat on her desk. Yolanda picked up her phone and took photographs of the platter for the website. She put the phone down and stood close to Nigel. He wore a red and white Beverage Bar polo shirt, and she was festive in her pink and red Yummery polo shirt and red skinny jeans. They began sampling the macarons. Nigel grinned after the first bite, not hesitating to admit, "I'm not much for sweets before seven but this is exquisite!" He finished the rest of the chewy cookie with the rich chocolate ganache filling.

She had a vanilla one with bright pink sugar sparkles and smiled as she ate it in four dainty bites. "Nigel, I'm so nervous about tonight. I know my parents and me will be recording *America's Best Bakeries* and watching it at the same time, but still, I just can't wait to see it!"

He grinned and leaned over, tenderly kissing her sugary lips. They tasted such sweetness from the sugary breakfast. The attractive young couple pulled away from each other very reluctantly. "I wish we could go back to my place," she said.

"I know, my love." He glanced at his watch. "In twelve hours, we can be there."

She giggled. "I'm so looking forward to it, Nige. I'm planning to have..."

There was a knock on the door. "Yo? You there?" asked a female voice.

Yolanda recognized the voice of her best friend and part time coworker/part time model/actress, Teagan Miskin. "Yeah, Teagan, the door's unlocked."

Teagan slunk in, already dressed for work in a pink and red French cut T-shirt paired with matching leggings. She barely glanced at either Yolanda or Nigel. "Hey guys...um, Yo, can I talk to you privately?"

Nigel nodded and quickly left the office, gently closing the door behind him.

"Sean's been stalking me," Teagan began, looking down at the floor. "I'm glad I'm here because I'll be safe. But last night he...well, let's just say that I almost called the police."

"Why didn't you?"

"Because they'd never believe me. It's not like I have a great reputation, I worked as an exotic dancer and I'm …"

"Worked as in past tense. And even then it wouldn't matter. Stalking's against the law. Besides, you work here now, and you do modeling."

Teagan shook her head. "All he did was park outside my apartment building for like, well, all night. He finally left at five. He probably had to go to work."

"That's not normal behavior," Yolanda said.

"Neither is being a super crazy sports fan." Teagan sighed. "I didn't mean to start off your day so negatively, Yo. Plus, you and Nigel are so close. Think he'll pop the question tonight?"

Yolanda smiled, looking down at the tile floor. "It would be perfect. But I'm not going to hold my breath."

There was a knock on the office door. "Um, Yolanda?"

"Yes, BB?" She walked over to the door and opened it. BB stood there holding a tray of burnt goodies, thick smoke coiling from twelve overdone mini cherry pies. For a few seconds, all they could do was stare at the blackened baked pies.

"How long did you leave them in the oven?" Yolanda finally asked.

"The usual amount of time, Yolanda. This has never happened to me before. You know how I always check the temperature."

Yolanda went over to the tray and looked at the burnt pies. "Well, I guess these are a total loss." She took the tray from BB and walked out of the office, followed by BB who was nervously wiping her hands on her apron.

She emptied the scorched mini pies into the garbage bin at the back of the kitchen. She went over to the first oven, leaning over to check the temperature. The gauge read 475. Instead of saying anything, Yolanda just pointed the number out to BB.

BB stood there, staring at the number for an instant, and shook her head. "That can't be right. I always set it at 425."

"Don't worry about it, BB. Everyone makes mistakes," Yolanda said.

"Of course, I know that. But I also know that I checked the temperature. It's something I've always done—you know that. But, well, today's been so hectic and I was making raspberry buttercream filling for the macarons..."

"So, you got distracted?"

BB nodded. "Yes, Suzie said that she needed the filling right away because she had to..."

Yolanda was staring at the newest employee who wore a red apron over her white polo shirt and black leggings. The woman was piping the filling onto a tray of chocolate heart-shaped macarons. *Did she change the oven's temperature? I wish I had a surveillance system because I'd know for sure.* She turned away and went back to her office.

****

Rusty ambled out into the yummery lugging a stepstool in one hand and a red string of jingle bells in the other. Each step was marked with a pleasant ringing noise.

"Jingle bells, jingle bells it's Valentine's Day," he sang, enjoying the laughter of those around him. "Time to ringy dingy now," he improvised, laughing at his tuneless but merry singing. *Last year at this time, I was NOT enjoying breakfast of fake scrambled eggs and hash browns with a pat of margarine and skim milk. Here Yolanda insists on using only the freshest kind of butter and whole milk or even real cream—and those eggs are so good I could eat a ten-egg omelet! I think things are looking up!* He unfolded the stepstool and quickly hung up the bells, giving them one more jingle as he stepped down. He picked up the stool and returned it to the kitchen. Yolanda thanked him.

"Make sure you help invite all the appreciated guests inside when I unlock the door at seven."

"Yes, Miss Yolanda, I'll be there with bells on!" He gave the bells an extra jingle and laughed as loudly as all the others who overheard his corny joke.

Just before the yummery opened, the last tray of macarons was slid into place, the neat rows showing off the perky Valentine's Day colors. Elegant gold topped pastries next to glittery pink next to plain pink, red or white macarons: all perfectly round and festive. Plus, two rows featuring heart-shaped chocolate and red velvet macarons -- clearly the work of Suzie's artistry. Nigel stopped by to have a look at the display. He pulled out his iPhone and took several photographs, as did Yolanda.

BB added a tray full of mini cherry pies that were baked to golden brown perfection. She paused to admire the full shelves. Smiling, the young woman turned to look at the lovely tree in the corner and just then, Yolanda shot more photos. There was a knock on the front door.

Vern Hess stood there, waving at her. She rushed to open the door, noticing that it was exactly seven o'clock.

Yolanda unlocked the door and paused to admire the lengthy line of appreciated guests. Many wore Valentine's Day red and she waved and stepped outside in the cold dusky morning and shouted "Happy Valentine's Day! Welcome to my yummery! Come on in and warm up. Free coffee, tea and hot chocolate! Free macarons and other Valentine's treats!"

She laughed at the sound of people returning her greeting and cheers, all beautiful noises resounding in her ears, warming her up as she held open the door and watched Vern stepping into the yummery and deeply inhaled. "It smells wonderful, as usual. Sorry I'm late but there was an accident on the 405."

"Good morning, Vern. Glad you made it and you're right on time. I hope you're in the mood to try some authentic French macarons!"

Rusty took over and held open the door for all the appreciated guests, cheerfully greeting everyone who walked past him.

Vern followed Yolanda as she went back to the Beverage Bar. "I'm going to be serving free coffee, tea and hot chocolate. Let me know what kind of coffee you'll want with your macarons."

"Artie the camera guy will be along in a minute. Thanks, any of the macarons. Oh boy, is that real gold?" he pointed to the ones in the display case.

She nodded, gesturing toward a row of chocolate with gold-topped macarons. "I'll get you one." Yolanda went behind the counter and used waxed tissue paper to gently take the shiny macaron and put it on a colorful heart motif napkin. She gently handed it to the reporter. "24-karat edible gold leaf. I'm sure you understand why I have the certificates of authenticity from the FDA, MSDS, and the AOAC lab report, in case anyone questions the authenticity. Unlike that other, ahem, bakery in Beverly Hills."

Vern laughed and sniffed the intense chocolate aroma of the macaron. "There goes my diet!" He bit into it and paused, looking at the delicacy. "First time eating gold!" He popped the rest of the sweet into his mouth. "Oh, darn, this is the best I've ever had! It makes me feel so … wealthy!"

"Gold contains zero calories and is sugar-free and gluten-free," Yolanda said as she pulled off the top to the sample tray. "Try one of the raspberry buttercream ones. Unlike many bakeries, we actually use cream instead of milk or even water, and butter instead of shortening so we have true buttercream filling in our macarons—and our cupcakes and Magical Cakes of Love have buttercream frosting."

"What's the difference between a frosting and a filling?"

Vern's tossing a softball question, she thought. "Filling goes inside the macarons. Frosting coats the outside of cakes and cupcakes. No real difference," Yolanda replied.

Artie arrived toting his camera. The stocky bearded man glanced at the array of macarons. Then he began filming each row. "These are so sexy!" he said.

"Artie, as soon as you're done filming, please help yourself," Yolanda said. "And don't forget to have some of your favorite beverage."

"Thank you so much, Yolanda," Artie said, stopping to give her a big smile.

Vern bit into the raspberry buttercream, chewing it so quickly she thought he'd want another one. There were only so many samples that had been made. As she accepted his accolades and watched him film his segment, she quickly consulted her iPad and made a note to check on the number of macarons that were in the process of being made and the status of the ingredients.

Vern leaned over and put the microphone in her direction. "So, Yolanda, I understand that you're going to be on *America's Best Bakeries* tonight?"

The grin that spread across her face and the flush of nervous excitement was captured on camera. She nodded and continued with the interview as behind her the appreciated guests continued entering the shop.

Suzie handed Teagan a sample tray filled with chocolate, strawberry and vanilla macarons. "So many customers this early in the day."

"Appreciated guests," Teagan said. "Yolanda prefers we call them that."

Suzie rolled her eyes. "Right, I forgot." She turned and strode back into the kitchen, making sure the curtain behind her was closed.

Vern was handed a coffee and he sampled a strawberry macaron on camera accompanied by lots of lip smacking. He did his usual reporting of how the yummery made the finest sweets in Los Angeles. The camera focused closely on the extra bins of macaron-filled magnificence. Artie's camera lens homed in, close enough to show off the perfection of each row of goodies, aimed at enticing the viewers.

Al and Hilda Goldberg rushed over to the counter. They were celebrating the holiday by wearing color-coordinated designer tracksuits. Al stood in front of the cash register located between the two main display cases. He removed his platinum bankcard from his pocket and passed it to his wife.

"Good morning, Yolanda, I was wondering about the strawberry energy bars..." He looked up and saw Vern stuffing another macaron in his mouth as the camera filmed him chewing it with his eyes closed.

Hilda leaned closer to the display, pointing her finger at the case and tapping it. "Yolanda dear, which flavor would you recommend to someone who's doctor told them to eat only sugar-free desserts?" She turned and glared at her husband. "Even though it's our forty-seventh wedding anniversary today!"

Yolanda grinned and reached behind the counter, grabbing an elegant Lont pastel striped box with a red satin ribbon. "Happy Anniversary!" She rushed around the counter and handed it to Mrs. Goldberg, and they all exchanged hugs. "Half dozen variety macarons—all with edible 24-karat gold because it's your anniversary," Yolanda said.

Mrs. Goldberg immediately removed the ribbon and lifted the lid, parting the pink tissue paper and admiring the colorful French delicacies. "Oh my, these look so, so elegant! I've never eaten gold before!" She leaned forward and took a big sniff. "I have to share these I know, but I could eat all of them in..."

Her husband reached over and gently took the box from her. "I think I need to hold onto these for safekeeping. Dr. Cohen warned her about cutting down on her sugar intake."

"It's our wedding anniversary, Al. I think we're entitled to have some sugar! That doctor has told me about eating fruits and vegetables and whole grains and staying away from pastries, steak, dairy products and it doesn't end. I've never been given a list of so many food no-no's in my life. If I listened to him, I could never set foot in this yummery."

Yolanda shook her head. "I know your doctor means well but we do have the energy bars that are very nutritious."

"I know they are, Yolanda. They're very good too, but I love my sugar, especially chocolate. And I'm pleased to see two chocolate macarons!"

"Made with healthy dark chocolate imported from France. And all macarons are gluten-free!" Yolanda decided to keep the fact that the ganache filling also contained heavy cream and butter with 85 percent butter fat content.

Jade Wilson, the owner of the Shimla Yoga Studio at the other end of the mall, entered the yummery. She wore a tight orange T-shirt and matching yoga pants. Teagan approached with the tray of macarons arranged in enticing rows but had included a row of cut up energy bars for appreciated guests who were avoiding sugar. Jade smiled as she took a piece of energy bar and slowly chewed it. The slender young woman nodded. "These are excellent gluten-free energy bars."

"I like them, too," Teagan said. "Care to try a macaron?"

Jade almost reached for one but stopped, pulling her hand back as though avoiding an electric shock. "They may be gluten-free but they're certainly not sugar-free. Thanks, I'm picking up my usual order of energy bars."

Teagan laughed. "You're consistent!" She walked over to another area just as the bells above the door jingled, announcing the arrival of business executive Dani Kramer. Her thin figure was emphasized with a short faux fur jacket and skinny black jeans. "Hello everyone. I need my brownie fix...oh no wait a minute, make that macarons! I'll need three dozen in all varieties. Plus, six mini cherry pies and a dozen brownies."

Yolanda greeted her with a wave as she passed Jeannie and Nick behind the counter. Not for the first time, she wondered what Dani did for a living. All she knew was that Dani was always impeccably dressed, lived in Marina del Rey, or had a boat docked there, and worked in an office on the border of West L.A. and Santa Monica. She loved a variety of coffee and preferred brownies to cookies. The woman loved pies so much that last year she had asked why she never baked and sold pies. So, Dani was responsible for the yummery now selling pies and BB turned out to be an expert pie baker. Yolanda knew that Dani was married, yet nothing had ever been mentioned about her husband. Just as she was about to return to the kitchen, she looked at the front door and saw a trio of young professionally dressed people. Behind them was Captain Angus Prescott, the multimillionaire who lived aboard his yacht in Marina del Rey. He again looked the part of a wealthy man with a new yacht hat and uniform fit for any respectable captain. His white deck shoes were so new they gleamed. Even his hair was combed. But the captain was sporting black and grey stubble.

"Greetings, Yolanda!" He gave her a salute as he walked over to her. "I have to say that I've been using the lotion from here and my skin has never looked better. He rolled up his jacket sleeve. His skin was pale and freckled but there wasn't any of the blotchiness of eczema that he used to have when he had been dating Teagan over the summer. Teagan confided in Yolanda that his arms and legs were covered with weeping eczema that he ignored—but she couldn't. The over-the-counter medicated cream never relieved the itching or the red blotches. He grinned and saw the tips jar with the sign reading:

HAVE THE SWEETEST VALENTINE'S DAY!

A pudgy man wearing oil and grease-stained overalls hesitantly walked in, admiring the decorated tree, and then surveyed the rest of the shop. Teagan went over and offered him a free chocolate macaron from the tray she was holding. His smile was genuine as he admired the pretty young woman in the tight-fitting outfit. As he reached for the delicacy, his grimy hands made her flinch and almost drop the tray. Two well-dressed office workers suddenly moved away, the older woman's face crinkling in disgust.

"My wife wants to try the macaroons," he said. "She gave me a list of flavors she likes..." he reached into his jacket pocket, finding nothing, then tried his overall's pocket and pulled out a folded sheet of paper. He opened it up and began reading aloud. "Chocolate, strawberry or raspberry, orange, coffee, Key lime…"

Teagan smiled patiently at the man. "I'm sorry, sir, we only have five flavors. I'd recommend the gift box with six – and that includes two chocolate."

The man nodded and followed her over to the counter where he joined the growing line of appreciated guests. His cell phone went off and he picked it up. "Yeah dude, I'll be there by eleven. I'm in this bakery with these fancy dancy French cookies and let me tell you it's snooty McSnootsville!"

A tall, balding man in a green sweatshirt advertising Gymnastics & Fitness Training Center stood in line, smiling at Teagan as she offered him a raspberry chocolate macaron.

"Thank you so much, Teagan. Jeannie's mentioned how much work goes into making these." He took a small bite, his face brightening. "Darlin', whoever makes these is a culinary genius!" He looked at the small cookie. "I wish I had the time to make these." He popped the rest in his mouth and saw it was his turn. He smiled at Jeannie. "Just the lady I want to see." He beamed at her and she was just as happy to see the younger man.

"Milton, I'm so looking forward to seeing you tonight."

"As I am you, m'lady. All I need is a peanut butter brownie and, well, that's all I can say for now!" He pulled out some money, stuffing a ten-dollar bill in the tips jar right after he was handed his dessert.

Nick grinned at the latest addition and smiled at Milton Knight. The older man winked as he took his brownie and left the yummery. For an instant, Jeannie stared at the man, her fingers on the glass counter. "He's just so handsome," she said, mostly to herself. Suddenly she looked to her left and noticed an empty space in one of the trays. "Nick, see how many raspberry chocolate cupcakes we have in the fridge."

"Sure will, Jeannie." Nick hurried back to the kitchen.

Yolanda was in her office going over the schedule and she absently pulled on her apron string as she double-checked the chart. She glanced at the clock and frowned. *Where's Rusty?*

****

Rusty McFadden was pulling into the parking space reserved for the van. The clock on the dashboard read 10:13. He glanced in the rearview mirror and saw the box he had to unload...just some yummery supplies, nothing heavyweight. Rusty ran his hand through his thinning hair and took off his glasses, wiping the lenses on his shirt. "I wish to heck I could afford that laser surgery." He sighed and put them back on, turning to see the large coffee cup in the cup holder. "Better pitch it so no one yells at me about messin' up the van."

As he got out of the van, a strong gust of wind almost knocked him over. "Whoa, where'd that come from?" The man looked up at the darkening sky. "It's almost as cold as it used to get back east in February." He stepped over to the nearby dumpster that was directly behind the vacant shop next to the yummery and Beverage Bar. Past the vacant store was the tiny Antonia's Dancewear Shop that had opened last month.

Approaching the dumpster, he lifted the top and was about to toss in his half-empty cup when the overpowering stench hit him. It was unlike anything he'd smelled in his job of being around delicious sweets and a medley of beverages ranging from sharp and robust coffee to imported tea and hot chocolate. The stink emanating from that dumpster was something he hadn't smelled before and at that instant he wished he had left the cup in the vehicle. The man stepped backwards as though punched in the stomach. His cup fell to the ground, the top dislodged, and the black contents dripped onto the concrete. But his curiosity was stirred; what had died in there? Someone's pet? A wild animal? A dead body?

Hell no! Not a dead body, he thought. That was the worst-case scenario for someone like him who was on probation and just starting a new job. His fingerprints were on the dumpster, and obviously on the fallen coffee cup. He picked it up and marched over to the offensive smelling trash receptacle and decided to throw it out and not do anything because what could he do? Rusty flipped up the top, tossed in the cup, and heard a beeping sound. His cell phone. He reached for it and saw a blank screen. The beeping continued. It was coming from the dumpster.

This ain't good, he thought. Leaning forward, he was unable to stop himself from peering inside the half-full bin. There was a muddy sneaker and pushed down sock and as his eyes scanned the sight, taking in each segment of an unmoving human being lying on a cushion of boxes and discarded bags and fast-food containers. In disbelief, he realized that the jeans and windbreaker were blood-soaked. The cell phone's noise stopped. The yummery employee stood immobile as he stared at a figure lying in a pile of trash. The beeping noise began again, and he saw a pinpoint of light amidst the trash and the blood.

He began mumbling as if talking to himself was a habit. "So, I pick up the phone and say dead corpse guy outside Yolanda's Yummery? Nah, I need to call the cops. Like any ex-con wants to call 'em. No, I tell Yolanda first. It's outside her place. I'm at work, well, if I didn't stop off here I'd already be at work and I wouldn't know about this dead guy...I think it's a guy."

Rusty let the lid fall with a thud and turned away, reluctantly returning to his job that up until a few minutes ago he liked. He had to tell a naïve young person about a corpse in a dumpster behind her dream bakery. Breaking news like that wouldn't be welcome any day of the year, let alone the busiest day of the year, the most romantic day...*hey, Yolanda, there's a corpse in your dumpster. No, I don't know who it is, and I didn't do it even though I spent nineteen years in a federal penitentiary. Even though your mother got me this job.*

Sighing, he left the area, looking down at the asphalt, noticing the fallen lid from his coffee cup. The free Beverage Bar coffee he was given by Nigel, his other boss. A nice British bloke who had inherited the family business that dated back to 1901.

Back in the yummery, he went to the break room to hang up his jacket. The sight of the body was disturbing but the thought of telling Yolanda about it was gnawing at him. Could he pretend he didn't see it? Then what? Eventually, someone else would. Especially when it really got stinky. The dancewear store two doors down also shared the same dumpster and even if none of the employees saw the body, eventually the workers who picked up the trash would. Or would they? He shut his locker and shuffled over to the door, preparing himself mentally for delivering the news, concentrating on his breathing. Walking out into the kitchen, he almost collided with Suzie who was holding a tray of red macaron shells that had just come out of the oven.

"Watch it, you klutz," she said.

"Excuse me, ma'am," he replied, still noticing the now dreaded red color of the French cookie shells. *Maybe she did it*, he thought. *I bet we're all gonna be suspects.*

****

Yolanda went to her office to check on a report, flipping through her filing cabinet. She heard a quiet tap on the doorframe of the open door and saw Rusty standing there. The man's furrowed brow and the deep lines on either side of his mouth warned her that he wasn't there to shoot the breeze.

"Hey Rusty, what's up?"

"Well, miss, I wish I could say nothing, but, uh, um, well..." the man was twisting the bottom of his T-shirt. "It's just when I got back I found a body in the dumpster."

She closed the file drawer and leaned against the tall metal filing cabinet. "The dumpster out back?"

He nodded. "Yes ma'am, that very one. I was throwing out my coffee cup when I saw it, I mean um, the, you know, the body."

Yolanda walked over to her desk and reached for the phone. "I'll call the L.A.P.D., of course. I happen to know Detective Churchill and I think he'd be the best one for you to talk to. That is, if he's available." She paused. "You haven't called it in or told anyone else about this?"

He shook his head. "No ma'am, I wasn't sure what to do having never seen or found a dead body before. But since you're my boss and the owner, I thought maybe I should tell you."

Yolanda hit a button on the speed dial. "You did the right thing, Rusty. I just hope the detective answers instead of you having to leave a voicemail." Her shoulders were tense with the latest information on top of the extremely busy day. Out in the kitchen, Quinn was taking care of his mini Bundt cakes and she saw that BB was alternating between making pies, cookies and she'd just frosted another half dozen decadent chocolate Magical Cakes of Love. Suzie was frantically filling macarons.

"Churchie, you there?" Yolanda smiled as she listened. "Great, and a Happy Valentine's Day to you, too. What? Oh, busy, of course...yeah." She nodded, smiling and turning away from Rusty's scrutiny. "Right. Well, I may have a case for you. Our newest employee, Rusty McFadden, just told me he found a body in the dumpster."

Both overheard the detective's exclamation about the discovery behind the yummery. She handed Rusty the phone.

Yolanda watched as Rusty greeted the detective. She knew about his time spent in a minimum-security federal prison for embezzlement and how he'd only done it to pay for his mother's cancer treatment.

Rusty nodded and handed the phone back to her. She hung up the receiver.

"Detective Churchill's on his way and he said that he'll be interviewing you. In the meantime, if you could, um, sift more almond flour, that'd be great."

"I'll be glad to, Yolanda," he scurried out of her office and into the kitchen.

Yolanda stood in the middle of her office, stunned. "I can't believe this is happening on Valentine's Day of all days." She went over to her desk and hit the speed dial button. Tapping her sneakered foot impatiently on the floor, she waited for him to answer his phone.

"Yes?" Nigel answered abruptly.

"Hey, Nigel. I didn't want to bother you but um, we have a situation here."

"Don't make me guess...I'm in Santa Monica..." the loud noise of an espresso machine along with audible background music and talking customers was apparent.

She knew he meant the new Beverage Bar location, which was always busy. "Yes, I know. But we have a corpse in the dumpster behind the shop."

The only noise she heard was his sharp intake of breath.

"Nigel?"

"I'm here."

"I know that. I can hear you breathing. Um, when are you coming back?"

"So I can be interviewed as a suspect? I haven't seen a thing."

"Never mind. I'll take care of it. Detective Churchill's on his way over."

"I'll be there shortly." He disconnected the call.

Yolanda hung up the phone and returned to work, not wanting to think about what had happened outside -- and what was about to happen when Churchill and his coworkers showed up. Would she have to close the shop? How would it be kept out of the news? She shook her head, knowing that question was futile. Although Vern had already left for the day, it wouldn't take much for him to return along with all the other newscasters in the area. A dead body found behind the yummery was news – and not good news.

She surveyed the bustling kitchen and thought of how, except for Rusty, none of them knew about the shocking news that was about to descend upon their place of employment.

Twenty minutes later, Detective Winston Churchill strode into the yummery. He had short wavy hair and wore a navy suit. She approached him from behind the counter and the first thing she noticed was his greenish grey eyes, thick eyebrows, and a serious gaze. More serious than usual. If he'd noticed the festive decorations or the free macaron and cookie samples, he didn't let on. Instead, he followed her back into her office and watched as she closed the door behind them.

Without a word, he sat down on the guest chair in front of her desk, pulling out his notebook and pen.

"I'm sorry we have to meet like this, Yolanda."

"So am I, Winston."

"Where's the witness—Rusty McFadden? Can I interview him in your office?"

"Of course. I'll get him." She bustled off.

After checking the kitchen, the yummery, and glancing into the Beverage Bar, she couldn't locate the man. The only other place was the break room and the restroom at the back of the Beverage Bar. She tested the handle, and it was locked. Nothing was said, as she didn't want to bother the man. Being a free man for only a month, Rusty must have been terrified of doing something wrong to land him back in prison. *Not as if I can stand here waiting for the guy to come out...*she backed away, about to return to the kitchen.

Just then, the door was flung open, almost hitting Yolanda's foot. Rusty glared at her, "Can't I even use the crapper in peace? This isn't Pelican Bay last I checked."

She stood there with her mouth open. First Suzie had been rude to her and now

Rusty. What was going on? Did older employees resent her because she was only twenty-eight? No, Jeannie was the oldest employee by far, as she was retired from a career as an executive administrative assistant. She was always courteous.

Detective Churchill walked into the Beverage Bar and waved at the pair.

"Yolanda, can I speak to you for a moment please?" He grinned tightly, then turned and walked back towards the yummery.

"Yes, of course, detective." Yolanda followed the young man in the new suit.

Once in the yummery, Churchill leaned over and whispered in her ear. Feeling his hot breath made her temporarily forget about Nigel as he quietly told her about inspecting the crime scene first and then interviewing the witness in her office. She nodded as he started to leave.

"Excuse me, detective, you've forgotten something!" Her smile returned and she walked over to a sample tray that was left unattended on the counter. For an instant, her smile vanished. Who had done such a thing? Unattended samples were always supposed to be covered. If a health department inspector happened to show up that wouldn't help her business. Teagan was in charge of handing out samples. She glanced around the yummery and didn't see her tall friend. "Before you go out there, I thought you might like to try a chocolate macaron?" She picked up the tray and extended it towards him.

The handsome young detective paused upon seeing the rows of chocolate and raspberry macarons. His nose twitched as he deeply inhaled the aroma of chocolatey goodness. "What type of filling is that?" He pointed to one with a slightly oozing red jamlike substance. "The bloody looking one?"

"Ha ha, you're so funny. That's raspberry jam. We also have raspberry buttercream." she pointed to one with a medium pink filling. "Your choice, Detective Churchill. Though, I think you'll like both kinds."

He smiled as his hand wavered above his two preferences and after a few seconds, he gently picked up the one with the buttercream filling. "My first macaron!" He smelled it for an instant, and then bit into the chewy cookie. The grin that lit up his face told her that he was enjoying his sample.

"Suzie trained at the *Cordon Bleu* in Paris and has been making macarons for many years," she said.

"I wouldn't doubt it." He popped the rest into his mouth and turned to exit the yummery through the front door. "I've got a job to do – but thank you for making it a little sweeter."

"Thank you." She paused as he stepped away. "Don't you want to go through the back door?"

He shook his head. "No. I want to check out the area around the site first." The detective glanced at his watch. "Won't take much longer but it allows me to see the whole scene." Already he was at the door, and the man she saw had slipped into the role of L.A.P.D. detective, someone who was dedicated to doing his job right; someone who would find out who or what had killed the corpse in the dumpster.

Yolanda and the detective were good friends. So good, they had seen a movie together and she had even been to his house in Hollywood. She smiled, remembering the visit just before Christmas when they were working on the cold case of the murdered pie baker, and she had given him a special edition cake stand from the Christmas Collection. It was chosen because the pattern of green holly leaves with clusters of crimson berry centers was appropriate for a man who lived only four blocks away from Hollywood Boulevard.

She was on her way back to the kitchen when Jeannie stopped her. "Hi Yolanda, it's been so busy today," Jeannie straightened her red velvet headband and leaned against the counter. "I got this phone order for cupcakes to be delivered to Beverly Hills." She handed her boss the order form.

"Thanks so much, Jeannie. You're doing great. Got any plans for tonight?"

"You betcha. I'm watching *America's Best Bakeries*!"

Yolanda chuckled. "I thought you might. But what about...?"

"Oh, I think Milton and me might have a very special dinner and dessert!" Jeannie's cheeks grew pinker, and the woman bit her lower lip. She was about to say something else when a couple of teenagers walked up to the counter.

Returning to the kitchen, Yolanda saw that Rusty was standing in front of the sink washing pie pans and cookie sheets. Suzie was filling a piping bag and BB was rolling out pie dough. She felt a wave of sadness come over her as she thought about the ex-con having to wash dishes and sift almond flour. The man had a degree from the University of Virginia. A man who had spent most of his adult life locked away in prison. *Well, the dishes can't clean themselves, nor can the almond flour sift itself,* she thought, going over to the walk-in fridge to check on the cupcakes for the order. There were only four red velvet cupcakes on the shelf. She glanced at her watch. Oh no, BB was going to have to whip up a dozen in the next hour. Wait, how many were in the display case? She rushed back into the yummery and noticed there was only one left. Why hadn't she spotted that earlier? She wanted to question

Jeannie about it, but the woman was packing up a big sale and four more appreciated guests just walked in.

Returning to the kitchen, Yolanda conferred with BB and then began rounding up the ingredients herself. She put the order on the rack next to the oven so no one would miss it.

"BB, we'll also need more cream cheese frosting for the red velvet cupcakes. The order must be delivered to the Beverly Hills address by four- thirty."

BB nodded. "Don't worry, Yo, I have some extra cream cheese frosting in the fridge. I figured we can always use it, especially with the red velvet cakes and cupcakes."

Yolanda laughed. "Thank you, BB. You sure know how to think ahead."

"You taught me that. You said to have extra frosting on hand. But it can't be more than a day old. I made the cream cheese today so it'll still be fresh enough."

"BB, I don't know what I'd do without you!"

BB grinned. "You're always so nice, Yo. Thank you."

Suddenly, Detective Churchill rushed into the kitchen from the back hallway.

"Yolanda, I need to talk to you now!"

"Of course, detective, what's..." she saw his tense expression and turned, hurrying back to her office.

He shut the door behind him and sat down on the nearest chair in front of her desk. "Yolanda, I can't believe what I saw out there. I mean, who I saw..."

She clasped her hands together nervously, staring at the man. His scuffed black loafer was tapping on the tile floor. She couldn't remember ever seeing him look that agitated.

"What? Who?" Yolanda leaned forward, still standing near the desk, too tense to sit down.

"Yolanda, the dead body is someone you know. It's Mike O'Neill."

CHAPTER 3

Yolanda leaned against the wall to steady herself, scarcely breathing, staring at the handsome detective across from her.

He jumped from his chair and gallantly escorted her the few feet to her executive chair, the puffy cushioning absorbing her slender frame. She clutched the padded armrests.

"Mike O'Neill? The movie producer that I went out with?" She shook her head, staring numbly at her desk, which was almost covered with papers and a variety of multi-colored file folders.

"That Mike O'Neill, yes, I'm afraid so." Detective Churchill eyed her for a few seconds, and then returned to his chair. He quickly pulled out his notebook and pen. "I'm going to have to ask you some questions. And there will be an autopsy and we'll have to contact next of kin, but for now..."

"How did he die?"

"CSI is out there investigating. Too early to tell. I can say there aren't any obvious bullet wounds. And that he was dumped out there several hours before your yummery opened."

Her fingers were digging into the armrests. "Um, Win, there's something I need to tell you."

His pen froze just above the notebook. "Yes?"

"Mike showed up in the middle of the night and wanted me to keep his suitcase for him until Thursday."

The detective's eyes widened. "When? Do you have his suitcase?"

She nodded, looking at his surprised expression. "I didn't look inside, it's locked. And right now, it's in..."

The man looked around the room. "Can anyone hear us?"

"No. this office is soundproof."

He scooted the chair as close to the desk as possible and leaned forward.

"Okay, so tell me."

She mentioned the early Wednesday morning interruption and how Mike's face was bruised, his clothing was dirty and torn, and he looked very thin.

The detective was hastily scribbling his notes. "But the suitcase..."

"It's in the guest room. The weird thing is that it was completely wrapped in duct tape."

He continued to make notes. "The suitcase was wrapped in duct tape?"

"Yes. I thought that was really weird. Or maybe it was falling apart. It smelled bad."

"Like what?"

She shrugged. "I don't know. Dirty. Maybe like a little burnt. Like it had been in a fire. He said it contained important business documents."

He stopped writing. "We'll find out soon. Yolanda, was Mike inside your house?"

"Just the foyer. I really didn't even want him inside. I know that sounds mean, but he just seemed so – different. Like there was something really wrong. Oh yeah, he also said his car was parked on Ventura."

The detective made a quick note of that. "Right. So, we'll only dust for fingerprints on the front door and your main entrance area. You took the suitcase back to the guest room, right? Did it have wheels? Did it seem heavy?"

"Yeah, it had wheels. One of the wheels wobbled. I don't know about heavy, not real heavy I don't think. I didn't lift it. I put it in the closet on the floor and closed the door and basically forgot about it. I don't use the room that much."

"Okay. Now here's what must happen. Me and a small team will go to your house and retrieve the suitcase as evidence. The sooner we go there, the sooner we can get this case solved."

"I understand." She glanced at her watch. "It's just so sad, but it's also so...you know, busy. Plus, I need to call..." she trailed off. "I hope I don't sound too selfish but..."

"No, this is the last thing you need today. From a business perspective, I understand." He stood up.

"Okay, I'll tell everyone that I have to run an errand...no wait, I can't because I'm sure it'll get into the news. It's not like we can keep this a secret, can we?"

Churchill managed a half smile. "Yolanda, I think you're the best baker in the world. Those macarons were definitely in that category. Maybe even out of this world. But stick to baking, please. This is a matter of public record. We want to know if it was a murder or a suicide."

"You think Mike just killed himself and jumped into the dumpster?"

"I don't know at this time. I know I need to look at that evidence and we need to determine the exact cause of death and of course we must notify the next of kin."

"So, I don't have to see the body?"

"Only if we don't find the next of kin. Did he mention his parents or anyone in his family?"

"No." She shook her head. "I know his parents died when he was in high school."

There was a hesitant knock on the door. Yolanda rushed over and opened it. "Hey BB."

BB stood in the doorway and wrung her hands. "Um, Yolanda, can I come in?" She looked over, saw the detective, and immediately sensed he wasn't there for a social visit.

"Um, it can wait." She backed away.

"Are you sure, BB?"

The young woman nodded. "Yeah, we have tons to do before closing." She sighed and hurried back into the kitchen.

"Okay, detective, why don't you go and we'll meet at my place." She shook her head. "Of all the days..."

****

An hour later, she drove up the driveway and saw the detective's black Kia sedan along with a police cruiser and a generic beige sedan.

Massive thunderclouds loomed overhead. The wind was rustling through the trees; those with leaves and the ones without looked like they were shivering.

Churchill rushed over to greet her. He was followed by a slender man wearing round wire rimmed glasses. "This is Tim Edsen, our CSI guy. He's already dusted the front door for prints and he wants to see the suitcase."

"Right, of course. Hey Tim."

"Hey Yolanda. My aunt lives in Santa Monica, and she loves your brownies."

She beamed. "Why thank you, Tim, I..."

"I'm allergic to nuts so I have to be really careful what I eat, and I don't eat meat or dairy either."

Churchill laughed. "Which explains why you weigh 94 pounds."

The man scowled. "I weigh 138."

"And at six feet I'd say…"

A loud thunderclap interrupted the banter. Yolanda jumped and then giggled. "I haven't heard the sound of thunder in a long time."

"Same here," Tim said. "I wish it'd rain. The drought is so bad for us. My water bill almost doubled last month, and I haven't even been watering my lawn."

Yolanda pointed to the vacant house. A gardener was watering the vibrant rosebushes. "I'd hate to see that water bill. Mrs. Steele's daughter hired a gardener who waters every single day."

Tim was gazing at the yellow and red rose bushes. "I can see that. They look so healthy." He turned back and focused on Yolanda. "I understand you're holding the evidence?"

"No, I'm not holding it. But I have Mike's suitcase in my guest room closet. I'll go get it or do you need to see it first?"

Churchill shook his head. "See, Tim, Yolanda likes being an amateur detective and she's been helpful in the past."

She smiled. "It's something I like doing. I want to help." She walked up to the kitchen door and unlocked it.

"So why do you have a fake security camera?" Tim asked.

"Because my cats kept triggering the alarm system."

"I've heard about that happening. How many cats do you have?"

She unlocked the door and swung it open. "Two." Yolanda walked into her kitchen and looked for the cats, but they weren't anywhere in sight. "I think they're taking a nap." She glanced behind her and saw the men wipe their feet on the doormat before entering.

"Thank you, guys!"

Yolanda hurried through the kitchen and down the hallway to the second room on the left, pushing the door open. The detective and Tim entered and walked over to the closet. Churchill opened the door.

"Weren't you curious about what was in suitcase?"

"At first I was, but today I forgot about it—until you mentioned Mike."

She watched as the skinny man pulled on a pair of blue latex gloves. He reached for the suitcase's handle and pulled it out of the closet. "Whatever's in here is kind of heavy. But it'll take extra time opening it with all this duct tape. He must've used up about four or five rolls."

"Why would he do that?" she asked.

"To protect the suitcase—looks like it's falling apart. Also, as a cheap theft deterrent." The man shrugged. "And if it contains drugs it helps mask the smell. I'm going to test it at the lab. I hope it has more clues other than a driver's license with an address in Hawthorne."

"I thought he lived in Malibu," Yolanda said.

"Yolanda, you've lived out here long enough to know that this city is filled with fruits, nuts and flakes. If I had a dime for everyone that claimed to live in the 90210 ZIP code, well, let's just say I'd be able to live there myself."

"Me too!" said Tim. They all chuckled.

Yolanda led the way out of the guest room. Her bedroom door was open, as usual. *At least I made the bed today.* She saw the end of a black tail poking out from beneath the lacy white bedspread. One or both cats were hidden underneath – they had dashed under there as soon as they heard Tim's voice, as he was a stranger.

Her phone rang and she quickly answered it, noting the caller was Suzie from the yummery.

"Yolanda we're having an emergency here!" the woman's voice was shrill. "The newscasters are running amok, and we have police everywhere and they want to shut us down! Where are you?"

"I'm taking care of things. I'll be back there ASAP." She disconnected the call. "I've got to get back to the yummery right away," she said. "One of my employees was saying that the police are trying to shut us down?"

Both men glanced at each other as they approached her kitchen. Churchill was the first to respond. "I don't think that's true. The body was found outside the yummery in a dumpster that can be used by any tenant in the mall—or even the public. Maybe she misunderstood what someone said." He picked up his phone. "I'll see what Detective Rodman has to say. He's my boss."

Tim wheeled the suitcase over to his car as Yolanda turned around and shut the door behind them, making sure it was locked. As she was heading back to her car, the detective approached her. "I left him a message. You'll have to park in the parking lot instead of the back as that's now a crime scene."

"Okay, Churchie, see you later." She gave him a wan smiled and got into her car.

After a stress-filled journey back to the yummery in the endless stream of bumper-to-bumper vehicles, Yolanda arrived to find the parking lot was full. She drove around until an SUV backed out of a space near the yoga studio at the other end of the mall. She was disheartened to notice a pair of news vans occupying the red zone in front of the yummery. As she slunk out of her car, the strong wind was gusting around her in the quickly descending dusk.

Just as she scurried around the corner to approach the store from the back, she recalled Churchill's warning about not going near the dumpster. There was a crowd of people and a news team in the vicinity. "What a Valentine's Day," she mumbled to herself.

Yolanda returned to the front of the strip mall and walked past the shops, towards her own. Several people stood outside the front, and she recognized a black-clad young woman with dark hair pulled into a bun. "This is Tabby Flynn Channel 55 Live at 5 News, and we have a murder in Brentwood to report. The body of Mike O'Neill, producer of the upcoming reality TV show for entrepreneurs called *Start Me UP!* The identity of a body found in a dumpster behind Yolanda's Yummery on Thursday morning was just confirmed by the L.A.P.D. today.

"Mr. O'Neill was thirty-eight-years old. His last known address is Plainfield Drive in the city of Hawthorne.

"Detective Churchill has said that an autopsy has been scheduled for Friday to determine O'Neill's cause of death. The L.A.P.D. is investigating the circumstances of the incident."

Yolanda hurried past the news reporter, hoping to escape detection. It was supposed to be the most romantic night of the year and she was dealing with the knowledge that a friend had died right behind her yummery. Hawthorne? When did he live there? She thought he lived in Malibu but after that single visit to the beach house, he never mentioned it again and their only other date was at a restaurant.

Inside the yummery, business was still bustling and a glance at the clock showed that there was an hour left until closing. Jeannie looked flustered and even BB was helping bag goodies for the appreciated guests.

Suzie held a tray that contained a few macaron halves. "These macarons are baked right here in our kitchen," she told a woman with a purple designer handbag that matched her coat and shoes. "I learned to make these at *Le Cordon Bleu* in Paris. I like to present them in this fashion so that you may see there are no large air pockets. Oftentimes, you'll see macarons that look perfectly fine, but you bite into them and they crumble because they have air pockets the size of a nickel."

"I wouldn't know what a nickel looks like anymore. It's plastic all the way," the purple-clad woman said as she bit into a chocolate macaron. "But you're right, you have no air pockets, and this is very good. I'll take four boxes."

Yolanda grinned at the woman and nodded at Suzie as she rushed back to her office. As soon as she got inside, she shut the door. Just as she sat down, there was a loud knock on the door. "Come in," she said wearily.

Nigel strode in and slammed the door behind him. His face almost matched one of the raspberry macarons. "How in the bloody hell did Mike O'Neill wind up dead in the dumpster?"

"That's what I'd like to know." Yolanda said.

"Do you know what will happen to your business and to my business when the news gets out?"

"Tabby Flynn's standing right in front of the yummery and she didn't ask me any questions, I'd say that's not an issue."

"No, Yolanda, when they find out that you knew Mike O'Neill, it will be a huge issue."

She slumped over, staring at the pile of folders and papers on her desk. "IF they find out, Nigel. I have no intention of telling anyone."

He shook his head. "Nor do I. But it's quite possible it will get leaked. You have enemies. And another thing, by adding golden macarons, Golda of Beverly Hills is not going to be chuffed. She'd love to see you go out of business. Now she thinks you're imitating her."

"I'm not imitating her. It was an impulse. I found the gold when I was looking for sugar sprinkles."

"You'll need to call your lawyer if word gets out that you knew Mike. Finding a friend dead in a dumpster outside your yummery on Valentine's Day isn't the type of publicity that's needed."

"No kidding, Nige! It's not like this hasn't been bothering me since I found out."

"I'm beginning to think you attract a lot of bad luck," he said, turning to leave.

"And a great big Happy Valentine's Day to you too, Nigel." She shoved her chair back from her desk and just as she got up, he was out the door, slamming it behind him.

She sat back down on the chair, gripping the armrests, staring at the computer screen with a newscast showing a suited and now shorthaired version of the Other Patrick Stewart standing at the edge of the parking area near the cordoned off dumpster. Patrick? *Why hadn't he shown up at the yummery today? He was a big fan of her sweets and had actively promoted her in the past.* In fact, she couldn't remember seeing him even once this year. And here he was on the Channel 10 NewsTeam based in Burbank. It was odd seeing him wearing a conservative tan coat and a striped navy necktie.

"The identity of the victim is a former yummery appreciated guest, Mike O'Neill, age thirty-eight, single, his last known address being in Hawthorne."

"Oh no, he's tying Mike to the yummery which isn't going to help at all."

She got up and left the office, not bothering to close the door behind her. Even though it was cold outside, she didn't put on her coat. She stormed out the back door and was in the middle of the Police Line – Do Not Cross yellow-taped crime scene. Churchill approached and gallantly hooked his arm around hers as he gently walked her back inside the yummery.

Back in her office, with the door closed, he kept her up to date on the events unfolding outside. She nodded as she listened to his vague news, revealing nothing new, just that the investigation would continue for several more hours but suggesting that she park in the front parking lot the next day.

"Did you see the Other Patrick Stewart?" Yolanda asked the detective.

"No matter which Patrick Stewart he won't be a movie star. But I applaud him for landing a TV station gig."

"I didn't know you were a critic!"

The flicker of a smile made him look younger. "I think I have critical thinking ability."

"Yes, you're right," she said somewhat absently. She thought that Patrick had been ignoring her all year and it was just made obvious to her. "Patrick should be here promoting the yummery not a dead corpse in the dumpster."

"Yolanda, a dead corpse is redundant," Churchill said.

"I know, I know. But I can't believe that Mike's been murdered and thrown in a dumpster. I mean, that's just an awful way to go."

Churchill was looking at his notepad. "We haven't deduced that he was murdered and then thrown into a dumpster. Do you know something that we don't?"

"Of course I don't. Maybe he was in the dumpster when he died, I don't know. All I know is that he stopped by at two in the morning and woke me up from a sound sleep and wanted to stash his suitcase in my closet."

"And I'm very curious as to what was in that suitcase," he said.

"So am I, detective. But I just want to get through the last hour and then watch *America's Best Bakeries.*"

"Is this the show your store's going to be on?"

She felt a flush of pride as she thought of what an honor it was for her small yummery to be featured on such a successful Dessert Network show. Instead of answering, she looked down at the floor and nodded.

"If I'm back in time I'll watch it. If not, I'll call my brother and have him DVR it. He's the techno geek and the foodie in the family and I know he'll be watching."

"I didn't know your brother was a foodie."

"Well, I don't talk about my family...and my brother is a very private individual."

"I know that some people are. Not me. I take after my parents."

"And the world needs more friendly people like you."

"Thanks, Win, that's so sweet." She smiled at him, and the peppy beat of her iPhone's ringtone made them laugh. Detective Churchill waved at her and left the office. She glanced at the screen, and he turned and left with a final wave of his hand. Kyle Newman read the caller ID. Her lawyer was calling, and she felt her shoulders stiffen and her mouth go dry.

"Hey Kyle," she answered with forced cheerfulness. "How are you?"

"Yolanda, I was wondering if you're busy for dinner tonight?"

Why would he call her out of the blue on Valentine's Day? He knew she was dating Nigel. She was supposed to have dinner with Nigel. "Well, I'm only planning to see *America's Best Bakeries* tonight at nine because my yummery's going to be featured..."

"I know that. But we need to get on the same page concerning Mike O'Neill's murder in your dumpster."

"It's not my dumpster it's a shared dumpster."

"Yolanda, we need to talk ASAP. If not tonight, then tomorrow. How about we meet at that Mexican restaurant near your store at one o'clock."

"I can do that."

The call ended and she stared at her computer screen. "I hope Nigel and me are dining together tonight," she said softly, then stopped, not wanting anyone to overhear her. What was the point of Valentine's Day if she was going to be miserable? Wasn't it better for her to drive down to Laguna Beach and be with her parents? She glanced at her clock and went out into the kitchen and almost walked into BB who was carrying a tray of just-piped pink macaron shells. "BB are you working until six or seven?"

"Till I'm done making macarons," BB said with uncustomary terseness. "I never thought I'd dislike macarons." She slammed the tray down on the stainless steel countertop, causing Yolanda to jump in surprise.

BB noticed her boss's reaction and put a hand over her mouth, her blue eyes wide with surprise, round cheeks flushed. "Oh, I'm so sorry, Yolanda, it's..."

She smiled at her friend and pastry chef. "Please, it's okay, I know you've been here since six AM. It's fine, I understand. I just want you to be able to enjoy what's left of a, um, unusual Valentine's Day."

Right after the yummery closed, Jeannie smoothed back her silvery brown hair and buttoned up her long red wool coat. "Oh, Yolanda, I can't wait to see the show tonight. Milton is coming over for dinner and he's going to watch it too."

Yolanda handed her a gift box. "That's great. Here's a variety box of macarons for you and Milton. You're such a wonderful employee, Jeannie, I want you to know that, and I want to always extend goodies to my employee's family and friends."

Jeannie beamed and nodded. "Thank you, Yolanda, you're always so kind to me. I..." she glanced down at her half open purse and saw a flashing light. "Oh, pardon me, I must take this call."

****

Yolanda drove up to her dark and quiet house. She had been expecting to see Nigel's silver Lexus SUV in the driveway or parked on the street. "I hope he shows up," she said as she pulled into the garage and did her precautionary checking to make sure she was safe.

Once inside, the two cats eagerly greeted her. They sensed her downcast mood, meowed, and purred as they rubbed against her jeans. Miss Chef suddenly jumped up on the quartz-topped island, almost knocking over a handcrafted glass cookie jar.

"Miss Chef! Get down from there!" Yolanda's voice was firm. The cat rubbed up against her human friend, not paying any attention to the order. She looked at her beige coat and saw the black cat hairs on it. "Miss Chef!" Her voice was louder, and the cat jumped down on the floor. "Why are you so stubborn?" she asked, though

91

she knew an answer wasn't forthcoming. "I know it's a dumb question." She bent down and stroked her cat's back. "You're just being you." Miss Chef purred in agreement.

Her phone was silent. There weren't any texts or emails. Nigel was ignoring her. He'd never done that before. Looking at the clock wasn't necessary as the cuckoo clock kept her apprised of the time every hour and half hour with a miniature show. She was too nervous to eat anything other than a container of mixed berries yogurt and a bottle of mineral water.

She wanted to bake cat treats but didn't want to get interrupted by Nigel. "If he shows up," she muttered. The unopened garden salad, crispy Scottish salmon, and vegetable lasagna she'd bought at the supermarket sat in the fridge next to the bottle of champagne. Other than some two-day old oatmeal raisin cookies, there was nothing else for dessert. Since the yummery holiday rush, she barely had time to eat, let alone cook or bake. The tuna and salmon cat treats were running low, although she knew that she could substitute some packaged goodies from the Valley Waggin' Tails Bakery near the Sherman Oaks Galleria.

Standing at the island, she paused as the noise of the wind whistling through the trees seemed louder than before. The lights flickered but didn't go out and she sighed in relief. Both cats huddled next to her. The window above the sink showed a jagged flash of lightning. Suddenly it began raining; a sight she hadn't seen in almost a year. The raindrops were splattering against the window and another streak of lightning followed by a loud clap of thunder startled her. The cats took off down the hallway. "Miss Chef, Mr. Whisker, it's okay, it's just a storm. And we need the rain."

Yolanda was about to follow them to her room where she knew they'd be hiding under the bed. A single gunshot sound interrupted her; it was too loud for thunder. The kitchen was plunged into darkness. Another flash of lightning and the pelting rain was blown by wind gusts. The house was still and dark. Her heart was beating loudly as she stood in the shadowy room, hearing the whipping wind outdoors. Her iPad illuminated a small square of countertop. She picked it up, walked over to the end drawer, and pulled out a flashlight and a small glass container with a cinnamon-scented candle. Just as she reached for the book of matches, there was a loud banging on the kitchen door. She froze, until she heard a voice. "Yolanda, it's me, Nigel..."

Grabbing her iPad instead of the flashlight, she stumbled towards the kitchen door. She quickly opened the door and he burst in, his umbrella falling to the floor as his arms were laden with boxes and bags. His dripping trench coat flapped open and she reached for a box before it slid next to the umbrella. He kicked the door closed and let the boxes and bags rest on the floor. "I was on Ventura when the lights went out. I think it's only this immediate vicinity but I'm not …"

"Nigel don't worry about it. I'm so glad you're safe. Now I'm going to light a candle and then find the rest of them."

"Right. Let me get the dinner unloaded and we'll have a romantic candlelight dinner!" They both burst out laughing.

"True!" She lit the red candle, and the flame illuminated the quartz-topped island. "Wait, can I get your coat? Please excuse my manners; I wasn't exactly expecting the power outage."

He shrugged off his coat, she took it, going over to the closet at the edge of the kitchen, and he had picked up a flashlight so she could see to hang it up.

"Right then, I brought a special Valentine dinner of pub grub. I know you wanted a romantic dinner with champagne and violins, but I just grabbed our favorites and even got you a vegetarian shepherd's pie." He pulled a container out of a bag. "I managed to get you these! I know I got a bit riled up earlier but I want you to know that I didn't really mean it when I said you were bad luck."

"Oh Nigel, that's okay."

"Although the power did go out just as I turned down Dove Drive!"

"Very funny, Nige."

"Well, sweetsie, I have something for you on this fourteenth day of February."

Is it a ring? She inhaled sharply, suddenly feeling a little weak in the knees. After all these months, was it finally happening? For what seemed like hours, she stood in the dark kitchen as he unloaded his iPhone from his pocket and set it down on the counter, futilely trying to lighten the kitchen. He reached down, rustled through a paper bag, and stood up, extending a large bouquet of crimson roses. "Happy Valentine's Day, love," he said.

"Thank you so much," she kept her tone perky but felt a wave of disappointment threatening to ruin her mood. *Dinner's not even started yet*, she thought desperately. *There's still time...*

Yolanda inhaled the scent of the fresh roses and set them down on the counter. They stood next to the island and gazed into each other's eyes in the flickering candlelight. He smiled and gently caressed her hair, and moved close to her, putting his arms around her, reaching down, and kissing her. She moved closer to him, feeling his strong body beneath the cable knit sweater. His warmth was spreading over to her as she suddenly realized that there was no heat in the getting chilly cottage. A crash of thunder caused her to jump and even Nigel was startled as he pulled back for an instant.

"Wow, that came out of nowhere," she said. She giggled. "Nigel, I just remembered, I haven't eaten anything but macarons and yogurt today. No wonder I'm so hungry and my stomach just growled but not as loud as that thunder." She paused. "Oh wait, I have to put the flowers in water, let me get a vase."

"Yolanda, the flowers can wait. You're right let's have our romantic *de rigueur* candlelight dinner," Nigel said with his ever so suave voice that she loved hearing.

She laughed as she stumbled over to the bags on the floor and picked them up, setting them on the countertop next to the sink and refrigerator. "I'm so glad you brought hot food as it's really cold out there—and in here. I so wish I had a fireplace."

"Don't you have one of those grills in the backyard?"

"Yeah, funny, I'll just haul in that wet thing and use it to warm up the shepherd's pie and the fish 'n chips. And in the fridge I have garden salad, Scottish salmon and I think there's a quiche in the freezer, but the champagne will be staying nice and cold."

She paused. "I'm going to round up some more candles, get the vase, and then we'll have a proper romantic candlelight dinner in the dining room."

****

They sat at a red linen-covered dining room table with a ring of candles surrounding the rose-filled vase. Outside, the howling wind wasn't as loud and the rain had slowed down. Nigel picked up his phone and shook his head. "Still no bars." He sighed and put his phone back into his pocket. "Never mind, you didn't see that, Yo."

"You're right, Nige. This is our romantic dinner. I even found a scented cranberry candle which is supposed to be for Thanksgiving, but I know how much you love that scent."

"I never smelled it until I came to Los Angeles. Now I love it almost as much as I love you."

She grinned. Was this going to turn into The Question? She decided to say nothing and had another bite of the almost cold shepherd's pie. Between the tensions of the evening, the unheated cottage and the impending start of a show starring her yummery...her watch read 8:54.

"Look love, your parents probably have power, and you know they're DVD'ing it as is everyone else at the yummery...although Rusty doesn't quite know that a DVD isn't a Betamax or VHS tape."

Yolanda giggled. "Poor Rusty. He was locked away for so many years. He just learned how to send a text message. I could've driven to Pomona and back in the time it took him to send one sentence. He knew about cell phones in prison but he couldn't have one, of course, though he mentioned being able to sneak some calls once in a while."

"I can't imagine being in prison for as long as he was—since the early nineties? At any rate, he's out and that's what matters."

She nodded, trying not to glance at her watch. The chatter had veered far from a proposal, and she was fine with that, but the lack of power was bothering her. "Look, Nigel, maybe we should just drive to the nearest place with electricity and watch it on one of our iPads. I just don't think I can wait until..."

There was a noise behind them as a loud voice brayed, "I haven't been told about whipped chocolate buttercream frosting doing..."

The dining room was bathed in light, as was the kitchen. Yolanda stood up and cheered. "Yay, we can watch the show right here! Wait, I must call my parents and tell them!"

Nigel was already sending a text and just then, the phone rang. She spoke to her parents who had finished their dinner. Their TV was loudly playing the Dessert Network, and she overheard a commercial announcing the upcoming show playing while she spoke to her mother who sounded more animated than ever. "Oh, I wish you were here with us. And I hope you and

Nigel are having a..." There was a shriek followed by a laugh.

"You'll have to excuse us dear; your father just brought out the popcorn and has moved his chair right in front of the TV!"

Yolanda smiled and forced herself to emit a laugh. The call ended, the clock was about to do the hourly German cuckoo party, and the couple went into the living room and sat down on the couch.

Yolanda clutched Nigel's hand as soon as the lively theme music signaled the start of the highly anticipated *America's Best Bakeries* show. Host Gavin Jones sported black and red-streaked hair that contrasted nicely with his low-slung yellow jeans and cropped black leather jacket. The young man adjusted his horn-rimmed glasses and waved his hand frantically. "Greetings everyone and welcome to America's BEST Bakeries!" He jumped up and down a few times like a cheerleader. Gavin mentioned a brand new "yummery in the affluent suburb of Los Angeles, namely Brentwood!" There were more jumps and she half expected him to do a back flip. "The man does have cheerleading skills," she noted wryly.

Nigel just sat there staring wordlessly at the screen. The two cats wandered in and jumped on the couch settling next to Yolanda. The immaculate glass cases displayed all the colorful yummery creations on what was a cold, gloomy January day. The next scene showed the busy yummery and she saw herself talking on the phone near the cash register as Jeannie rang up a sale. The next shot was of BB and Quinn in the kitchen. Another scene showed all the ice cream parlor chairs filled as people ate the yummery goodies and Teagan was walking around holding a sample tray as a line of appreciated guests waited to place and pick up their orders.

She gripped her boyfriend's hand as the pleasant images were seen and she was beaming when Nigel strode past. Then her parents were shown restocking a shelf of mugs in the Gift Corner.

Sean Weller, the tall photographer and ex-boyfriend of Teagan Mishkin, appeared in the foreground near the Magical Cakes of Love. The camera focused on him, and Gavin stood next to the man, beaming up at him. "So, Sean, tell me about how you ended up doing publicity for Yolanda's Yummery?"

"I'm a photojournalist and I got my start doing the photo shoot and writing the article about the 'Babes of Brentwood' in the December issue of *Brentwood Monthly Magazine*."

"That's a lie!" she said, letting go of Nigel's hand. "He just lied on camera! All he did was take pictures. He didn't write the article. I've barely even seen him around the yummery! I mean, he didn't even show up at the Christmas party if I remember…"

"Dude, you rock. I'd love to have your job," said Gavin. "I understand you haven't been in L.A. very long?"

"No sir, I've been here a little over a year. And it's been…"

"Why is he even interviewing this guy?"

Nigel was staring at the screen, immobile. He finally shook his head.

"What the hell is going on? Is this some kind of joke? You're right, I only saw him once or twice this year. He was hanging around Teagan, like really being obvious about it, not like he was there for anything to eat or drink."

"I know. She said he was parked outside her apartment all night, that he's a stalker."

"Dead bodies in the dumpster, stalkers, what next?" Nigel said, leaning forward. "And this joker is still talking to that wanker!"

"Hello handsome! I love the photos you took of Teagan Mishkin. Very imaginative placing of the cakes and cupcakes! She is quite divine!" Gavin laughed and lay down on the floor, stretching his hands over his head. "Maybe Teagan can come over here and cover ME with cupcakes!"

"I don't remember seeing any of this being filmed. Was this done on a different day?" Yolanda was resting her elbows on her knees as she keenly watched the events unfolding on the TV. "I know they scheduled two days of filming, but I swear they were only there for one.”

“I think that might be what happened. They filmed the second day when we weren’t there. Is that possible? Because I know I was there, and so were you.”

She shook her head. “Of course I was. As were my parents and all the employees except Nick had to take a few hours off for school.”

There was a commercial break and Yolanda and Nigel were receiving many calls, texts, and emails. Her home phone rang but she let it go to voicemail, along with her cell phone calls.

“If I was a local viewer who didn’t know about the yummery I wouldn’t be too impressed. They’re showing bloody nothing about the yummery and nothing about you!”

She noticed his face was reddening. He was even more wound up as he dug his fingers into the edge of the couch’s cushion. He reminded her of a cat as he kneaded the corner tassel of a pillow, although he wasn’t paying attention to what he was doing. He suddenly got up and went over to the dining room table where he picked up the bottle of champagne, drinking right from it. She almost made a comment about drinking from a glass but decided he didn’t need a lecture.

He returned to the couch along with the bottle and offered it to her. "No thanks. It's back on, Nigel!"

Gavin and Yolanda stood next to the display of Magical Cakes of Love and the host was holding up a Crazy 4 Coconut cake. "Dessert loving darlings, this is the BEST coconut cake ever. It's not just plain shredded coconut, it's toasted and toasted to PERFECTION. And there's tons of it!" He paused, taking a bite right out of the side of the cake, the creamy white frosting and bits of brown and white coconut sticking to his mouth and cheeks. "I'm in coconut heaven here! I see why it's called Crazy 4 Coconut!"

Yolanda giggled as she watched him enjoy the cake.

"My name's Gavin Jones and I'm reliving my first birthday again twenty some years later!"

She handed him a paper napkin and he quickly wiped off his face.

"Thank you, Yolanda of Yolanda's Yummery. I don't think you could've picked a better name. Everything here is yummy including you! Are you single?"

Her face was redder than a strawberry. "Um, no, I have a boyfriend."

Gavin clapped his hands. "Is he as cute as me?"

"No, mate, no one's as cute as you." Nigel winked and went over to Yolanda and gave her a quick kiss.

"You must be Nigel Garvey of the Beverage Bar and grandson of the Garvey Coffee & Tea Merchants founded in London in 1901."

"Great grandson, actually. I'm impressed that you know this."

"It's my job!" He adjusted his glasses. "So, do tell me about the Beverage Bar and how that got started. Sit tight, people, we must cut to commercial break."

Yolanda sighed loudly. "Crap, that means we have to sit through like twenty commercials." She started biting her fingernails. "I can't take this, Nige. And I look so fat and sound so whiny."

"No, you don't! You're not fat and you have a very sexy voice. If I didn't know you I'd be showing up at the yummery tomorrow morning as soon as it opens."

She laughed. "Which you'll be doing anyway!"

For the rest of the show the garrulous host interviewed Yolanda, Nigel and her parents.

Jeannie was happily ringing up appreciated guests' purchases and Gavin went behind the counter and hugged her. "Thank you for all you do, Jeannie. You have such a great personality!" Yolanda grinned and hugged Nigel. "Oh, that's so sweet of him. Look how she's blushing. But it's so true. She's so good with the appreciated guests and she works well with everyone else."

"Right, she's topnotch. Great, finally they're interviewing Quinn."

Quinn was grinning as he expertly blended a mocha latte and then went back to the kitchen to pick up a tray of his mini Bundt cakes and drizzled them with vanilla frosting. He smiled at BB, and she waved at the camera while piping chocolate frosting on a batch of decadent chocolate cupcakes.

Gavin grabbed one and took a large bite. He paused and then swayed back and forth as though he was about to fall over. "This cupcake is almost illegal!"

BB giggled. "Thank you, Mr. Jones. It's one of my favorite flavors. And lots of..."

"You're such a sweetie, BB. You can call me Gavin, I don't mind. How long have you been baking?"

"My mama taught me when I was in second grade 'cause I'd follow her around the kitchen and climb into cupboards and fetch her whatever she needed."

"I bet you were a cute little girl, BB!"

She shrugged as she expertly piped a thick swirl of frosting on the last cupcake. "I just knew my mama was tired from working all day and if I could help her out by grabbing the ingredients I'd be rewarded by helping her cook and bake."

The phone rang again, and Yolanda ignored it. Beside her, the cats slept. Mr. Whisker twitched and then rested his head on her leg.

The address and outside of the yummery was shown and some appreciated guests were briefly interviewed including the Goldbergs and Dani Kramer.

For a few seconds, Yolanda thought about Mike O'Neill and how he'd first walked into the yummery sporting his Texas clothing and hearing his charming twang as he said, "You'd have at least one hundred suitors lined up taking numbers." It was sad that he was dead, and she was determined to help find his killer.

After the show ended, Nigel took one more sip of champagne and belched loudly. "At least they interviewed me and the employees." He yawned and stretched. "Well, my love, I'd like to stay longer but I've got to take care of my communications and get a full night's rest. I'll be there around six tomorrow."

"Me too. Well, probably around five-thirty as I think it'll be crowded." She looked at her iPad. "They're pouring in." she sighed. "I've got to talk to my parents though."

Nigel got up and retrieved his coat from the closet. He put it on as he walked back into the kitchen, buttoning his coat. As he was about to tie the belt, he reached into a pocket and pulled out a small box. "I almost forgot..." he tossed a red satin box at her, and she caught it, almost dropping the box on her lap.

"Nigel!" She shakily removed the white ribbon and pulled off the lid. Inside was a black suede presentation box bearing the name of an expensive jewelry shop. Yolanda got up and went over to the sink, standing next to Nigel. She hesitated before prying open the smaller box that she held in her shaking hand.

Nigel edged over to the counter next to the sink. "Need some help with that, my love?"

"No thanks, I got it!" The lid opened and she paused, noting a rose gold pendant necklace with a miniature golden cupcake studded with tiny pink and blue sapphires. Not exactly a diamond engagement ring, but it was a valuable and gorgeous piece of jewelry. She gleefully pulled out the necklace and Niegel helped her fasten it.

"Now darling, maybe you should look inside the box again..."

Her fingers started to shake. It was now, it was happening, this had to be it. The right box, the right occasion, the right...she peeled open the black suede liner and beneath it sat a tiny red velvet card with a pair of matching rose gold speckled with tiny rubies and sapphires cupcake earrings. They were so dainty, so exquisite. She squealed in delight and carefully, though a bit unsteadily, removed her plain gold earrings, setting them in the box and putting on the new ones. "Thank you so much, Nigel!" She kissed him and he returned her enthusiastic kiss until Mr. Whisker jumped up on the counter between them and hissed. "Mr. Whisker!" Surprised, she pulled away and stared at the angry cat.

Nigel looked at the animal. "What's wrong with him?"

Yolanda fingered her necklace and shook her head. "I have no idea. He's never done this before."

"It has been a very long day. I do need to get some sleep," Nigel said.

Yolanda gave him a quick hug. "I think you're right. And thank you again for such a wonderful evening. *Maybe we should just shake hands*, she thought.

As she walked him to the door, she noticed something sticking off the bottom of his trench coat. Yolanda leaned over and pulled off a small rectangle of black duct tape. *What on earth?* she thought, not saying anything as she watched him leave through the kitchen door. After a quick wave, she made certain the door was double locked. Still sticking to the tip of her index finger was that remnant of duct tape. Should I turn this in as evidence? Or should I just throw it out and pretend that it means nothing?

CHAPTER 4

Yolanda arrived at the yummery at five-thirty and the place was cold and silent. The crime scene tape was still up but no police presence was in the vicinity. Last night's rainstorm was a dim memory, and it hadn't rained as much in Brentwood as it had in the Valley. The power hadn't gone out. She had parked at the far corner of the mall, as an employee was required to do, since her usual parking spot was now adjacent to a crime scene. Despite all that had happened last night with the almost-engagement and the new expensive jewelry she wore, along with the romantic dinner, Yolanda couldn't get rid of the evening's final image--a four-inch strip of duct tape. It was in a plastic baggie in her purse. She'd already left a message for Detective Churchill but knew he wouldn't show up to retrieve it until later. She still didn't know what had been in the suitcase.

Although the yummery had been featured on a national TV show, she was still the first person to arrive to oversee all the opening duties. A cold breeze pushed her inside the door, and she stepped into the quiet yummery with the sparkling Valentine's Day tree. Inside her office, she removed her coat and hung it up on the hook behind her desk. She looked down at the gleaming rose gold necklace with the cupcake motif glittering with specks of precious gems in the overhead lighting. *But why didn't he get me an engagement ring? It's not a money issue, it's a lack of commitment issue.*

She paused, remembering how Mr. Whisker had hissed at Nigel. That wasn't a good sign.

Yolanda sat down at her desk, read the show's reviews by critics, and noticed an abundance of new emails from appreciated guests, fans of the show and even a celebrity: The Knick Knacks. They were a hot young musical duo reminiscent of Sonny and Cher. Knick was the singer, guitarist, songwriter, and Knack claimed to write some of the songs but was mostly known as the singer. Knick had proposed to Knack on bended knee at the yummery late last year but they still hadn't gotten married. *At least they're engaged*, she thought bitterly.

Looking at the emails, the top four had red high priority flags. Clicking on the most recent, she ended up on StinkyBiz.com. The logo was an old-fashioned wooden clothespin clipped over a big nose. The first comment read:

"Yumery sux macroons all taste the same lilke color sugar."

"Worst deserts evah! Bad customer service. Tegan is a stuck up beotch who hates men."

"1 star is too many for this Brentwood dump. Eat here & die!!!! No joke. Mike O'Neill ate here and ended up in the dumpster behind the yummery. O.J. Simpson didn't do it – so who did?"

"The yummery seems nice and then you try a sample and it seems nice. Then you feel really happy. Must be putting drugs in the goodies. Maybe should advertise 420. The way things are priced they could."

"Thumbs down for YY. Yolanda's an airhead who can't bake but that new chick can make some killer macs."

"Drugs served at yummery dude. Go there and you get Hi! High! High!"

"Yolanda and Gavin Jones are dating. Saw them at Hollywood Hotshotz together on Friday and that's how she got on the show."

Yolanda had gotten bad and bizarre reviews before, but these seemed deliberately false. She scanned the rest of the listings and saw a nice five-star: "Great baked goods, especially the Crazy 4 Coconut Magical Cakes of Love. I loved the place and the atmosphere."

She got up to make the coffee and heard a knock on the front door. She rushed over to open it when she saw Jeannie standing there.

Jeannie burst in, resplendent in her pink attire with a matching velvet headband and her left hand held out in front of her for Yolanda to see. On Jeannie's slender finger was a small pear-shaped engagement ring. She glanced at the older woman's face, noticing the heavy amount of makeup that wasn't characteristic of how she'd appeared when she first began working there. Her hair was shorter and darker, the silver covered up with dye. No wonder Jeannie was in a rush to leave yesterday; hair appointment followed by an engagement!

"Milton proposed to me last night over dinner. I found this in the bottom of my champagne glass when we were having dessert – champagne and raspberry chocolate macarons! I'm going to be Mrs. Milton Knight!" The woman sighed. "It was so romantic!"

Yolanda hugged the woman, feeling how thin Jeannie had become. A quick mental calculation indicated that the weight loss had probably started around the time she met Milton. *She's a bag of bones*, Yolanda thought, also noting the large glowing eyes underlined with alabaster concealer and colored a grayish blue that emphasized their size. Trendy thick clumps of mascara completed the youthful image. Yolanda listened as the woman praised Milton and laughed about being seen on TV and complained about being "far too old" and her voice sounded "weak and nasally."

The employees arrived and the flurry of comments and chuckles about the show were discussed, as preparations for opening were underway. Nick added a new sign to the tips jar:

TIP US – WE'RE TV STARS!!!

Yolanda walked past and read it. "Nick, please remove that. I'm sure you can come up with a better sign."

He sheepishly did so, throwing out the piece of paper. "Sorry, Yolanda. I just couldn't help it. It's the first time I've ever been on TV."

"I understand, Nick. It's just that some of our appreciated guests might not."

Although Nigel arrived just before seven, he and Yolanda barely had time to greet each other. A pounding on the door made her turn. Tabby and her camera operator were ready to film. Yolanda opened the door.

The younger woman had a microphone with the number 55 prominently placed on it. The woman stepped inside, pushing past Yolanda. "We're here in Brentwood at Yolanda's Yummery that was featured on last night's Dessert Network show, *America's Best Bakeries.*"

Yolanda smiled at the camera and waved.

"What you're really seeing is the suspect in the murder case of her former boyfriend, movie and TV producer Mike O'Neill. A man that was found outside her yummery on Valentine's Day, dead in a dumpster..."

"That's not true," Yolanda said.

The cameraman was pointing his camera directly at Yolanda, and her employees were backing away from that camera lens. "No, it's not. I went out with him once or twice. That's all. He's never been my boyfriend."

"You knew the man who was found dead directly behind the yummery..."

She shook her head. "No, the dumpster's not directly behind the yummery it's between my shop and the new dancewear store. It's a shared dumpster. Even people walking by can use it..."

"So, what you're saying is your ex-boyfriend just happens to show up in a dumpster behind your yummery?"

For a second she didn't know how to answer the question. Was the reporter really that stupid or just willfully ignorant?

Nigel stepped up and put his arm around his girlfriend. "Miss Flynn, Yolanda has just told you that a. she wasn't his girlfriend or ex-girlfriend. And b, more importantly, she isn't a suspect in the murder of a former appreciated guest of the yummery's. I don't know how much simpler you want me to make it for you."

She sneered at him and then turned back to the camera. "There's nothing simple about the report that I just obtained from the L.A.P.D. citing the time of death within an hour of the victim last being seen at Yolanda's house in Sherman Oaks. Care to comment on that, Miss Carter?"

"Don't say anything," he whispered in her ear. "Call your lawyer."

"No comment," she said, and rushed back into the kitchen and went into her office.

Nigel followed her in there and closed the door. She was standing next to the filing cabinet. "Nigel, that can't be right. Who would've even seen him at my place?" She opened a drawer and shut it again. "I'm meeting my lawyer at one, but I wish it was sooner. And I need to contact Detective Churchill."

There was a knock at the door. "Who is it?"

"It's Detective Churchill," answered the gruff voice.

"Come in, your timing couldn't be better." She walked toward the door and the man entered, closing it firmly behind him.

"Yolanda, we have a...hello Nigel."

Yolanda stared at the detective as she realized the baggie in her purse contained a scrap of duct tape that she'd found on her boyfriend's coat. How was she going to give it to the detective? "Um, Nigel, I need to see Detective Churchill alone for just a minute? I mean..."

Nigel frowned and pushed himself away from the wall where he was leaning and quickly left the office.

"Maybe my timing wasn't that good?" Churchill asked.

Yolanda reached into the desk drawer and pulled out her purse, rifling through it until she found the baggie, handing it to him. He paused as their fingers touched for an instant. She didn't mind. She wasn't engaged. But she was offering evidence of her boyfriend as a suspect in a murder case. All because Nigel had told her that he didn't trust Mike.

As Churchill pocketed the baggie, he offered her a brief smile. "You and your employees and company van can park back there now. We've gathered all the evidence. But we still haven't heard back from any of Mr. O'Neill's relatives. His uncle and cousin both live in Los Angeles. He also has some questionable friends including an investor or producer of some new reality show for people who want to start businesses and need the money."

"That's called *Start Me UP!* My friend Zac's supposed to be a contestant."

The detective shrugged. "If it ever gets started."

She smiled. "Did you ever find out what's in the suitcase?"

He nodded. "If you go by his physical condition you know he was addicted to meth? He had almost ten kilos of the stuff, mostly powdered. It explains why it was duct taped shut. Preventative measure. He didn't want anyone to take his stash. Maybe he was high when he taped it because if he wanted some he could've broken his fingers trying to remove that much tape. Anyway, with that amount, he planned to sell it, but we don't have all the contact info. My guess is that his missing relatives were in on it. Maybe that investor. Whoever it was, they might wind up like him in some dumpster though it better not be this one."

She absently fumbled with her necklace, feeling the ridges of the sapphires. "That would be horrible. I can't take any more of that. I have to check on the yummery. I hope that Tabby's gone! I don't need any bad publicity!"

Yolanda rushed out and saw that the yummery was crowded with appreciated guests and that the news van was still parked outside but no reporters were inside. She saw that Tabby was talking to her lawyer, Kyle Newman. Although it looked as though Kyle was doing all the talking as he pointed his finger at the younger woman and his complexion was redder than Yolanda had ever seen it. She went outside to hear what he was saying.

"Ms. Flynn, you have no case here, just speculation. My client is innocent of any wrongdoing. The body of a former appreciated guest is found in a public dumpster behind the shopping mall. That's it, end of story."

"It's said that she went out with him several times and that he was her boyfriend. It's said that she was involved with him."

"It's said that you don't know what you're talking about. Rumors and speculations are ways to get ratings. And your cable news station's ratings aren't exactly up there with NBC's."

"Don't knock cable TV. Your client was on the Dessert Network show last night which happens to be a cable TV channel," said Tabby.

"Which is headquartered in New York. It's not a local news station. They broadcast internationally." He glanced at his watch. "Thank you, Ms. Flynn. I have clients to represent." He grabbed Yolanda's wrist and they walked quickly into the yummery.

****

Heather Hathaway, the owner of Heather's Lotions & More, strode into the yummery. The gaunt young woman wore an unbuttoned faux fur jacket that showed off her miniskirt and skinny legs. Yolanda went over to her friend, noticing her pallid complexion and lack of makeup. Her strawberry blonde hair was in a loose French twist. Her wedding and engagement rings were gone. Yolanda was all too aware of the pendant around her neck and the matching cupcake earrings. Even though she hadn't received that coveted engagement ring, those two pieces of jewelry indicated that Nigel was interested in her. Heather had removed her symbols of marriage.

"Hey, Heather, great to see you," Yolanda said loudly.

Her friend managed a return greeting and a twinge of a smile. "Yo, can we talk in your office?"

"Sure," Yolanda nodded, and the taller woman stepped around the counter and followed her friend back to her office. She closed the door behind her. The woman sat on the chair in front of the desk.

Heather opened her designer handbag and pulled out an iPad. "I'll come right to the point. I need to rent out the room above the garage. I don't want to run an ad online and deal with a plethora of weirdoes and con artists. I just don't have the time or energy."

Yolanda nodded. "I understand. I think Rusty needs a new place soon. Maybe you can talk to him?"

"He's single, right? Isn't he the one who was in prison for twenty years?"

"That's him. But he's a good guy. Nonviolent crime and so far he's been working out just fine. He's in a halfway house in Monrovia and wants to be closer to the yummery and have his own place, not share a room with three other guys."

"Okay, I'll need to talk to him. How long has he worked here?"

"Almost a week but he's a nice guy," Yolanda said.

"Yeah, well, I need someone who can pay rent on time. I have a big mortgage since Barry moved out."

"I can only imagine. Your house is so big. Rusty made a run to the Santa Monica store, but he should be back soon."

"Have him stop by after work and I can show him the place and see how it goes. I just need to know if he can afford what the last tenant was paying before he returned to Nebraska?"

Yolanda shrugged. "I don't know what the last tenant was paying."

She sighed and entered four digits on her iPad, showing the screen to Yolanda.

"I don't know, that seems kinda steep."

"Yeah, like my mortgage. Well, I can go a little lower if necessary. Just not that much."

"I understand."

"Understand? You were given your place. I'm in a six-bedroom house in Hancock

Park. Do you know how much lotion and soap I have to sell to pay the mortgage, let alone everything else? And I'm opening a store in the Beverly Center in June plus an enormous ad campaign for that and the new Blushing Brides Bouquet line along with the Carnaby Street line. I have a bedroom suite upstairs that if BB wants to rent I'd be happy to rent it to her. Plus, she'd be able to use the kitchen whenever. I almost never get a chance to cook."

"I know she lives near Silver Lake, and I think it's a monthly lease. When do you want to discuss this with her?"

"Whenever she has a few minutes," Heather put away her iPad.

"I'll see Rusty tonight around seven? Oh, and I need two dozen chocolate mint brownies for a meeting."

"I'm sure we have that many in the case and the fridge. Business is going well though, right?"

Heather was on her way toward the door. "Fortunately, yes." She opened the door and Suzie minced into the office holding a tray loaded with chocolate macarons. "No more gold on top?" she asked Yolanda.

For an instant Yolanda couldn't answer, so surprised at the sudden entrance of the older woman in skintight leopard print pants. "Nope, not till Christmas!" she smiled. "Anything else, Suzie?"

Heather glanced at the newest employee, and then left. The woman with the tray of goodies muttered something under her breath and followed Heather out of the office, turning only to shut the door behind them.

"No that's okay, I'm on..." Yolanda went over to the door and opened it, almost smacking Nick in the face. "I'm so sorry, Nick, are you okay?"

He nodded and smiled. "I'm fine. I was bringing you this big box that just got delivered."

Yolanda looked at the return address. "Quinn and Crystal and Nigel will need to see these." Her brow furrowed as she saw the clock. "Hmmm, that's odd, Nigel should be here by now."

Nick was loping away, and Quinn rushed over and grinned when he saw the box. "Look, they're here!" said Crystal.

Yolanda went into her office, grabbed a box cutter from her desk drawer, rushed out to the kitchen, and slit open the box. She lifted out a turquoise and chocolate brown polo shirt for the Beverage Bar with the slogan *Ask me if I know beans about coffee!* She smiled and handed it to him and went back to look through the box. "Oh good, you ordered enough aprons for both stores." She was pulling them out and stacking them on her desk. "I like how some are brown and others are blue—good thinking."

Quinn handed her the plastic wrapped polo shirt. "Not my size. Is there a large?"

She pawed through the contents and handed him a package. "Here it is."

He took it and hurried out of the office. A minute later, he returned, showing off the new turquoise with brown lettering polo.

She nodded at the sight of him in the nicely fitting top.

Crystal received her shirts and bib apron in the color combinations and beamed.

"Thank you so much, I really love these colors. Nothing against pastels, but I'm a Pisces so I love turquoise." She hugged her new uniform to her chest as she left the office.

Teagan walked in and admired the new shirts. "Nice. I wanted to tell you that if Sean comes in looking for me, tell him I'm not here. I just don't want to see him. I'll be back around two."

****

Before Yolanda was about to leave for her lunch meeting with Kyle Newman, Sean Weller entered the yummery. The big man was sporting a blue and white football jersey advertising the *Georgia Gamecocks* along with a matching baseball cap.

"Howdy ma'am, is Teagan here?"

"No, she has the day off."

"Oh." The man paused, looking down at the trays of cookies and energy bars, and then back at the young woman. "Miss Yolanda, I want to apologize for hogging up the TV show last night. I was just joking around about that p.r. thing. But Gavin Jones was asking me all sorts of questions."

"He did? When?"

"When? When they were filming."

"Was that on the first day or the second day of filming?"

He fumbled with his cap, running his fingers along the brim, and then plunging them into the jacket's pockets. "Don't rightly remember, miss. I just remember being here when they had all kinds of people and equipment. Like I said, Gavin was real nice to me. He'd seen my photos in the 'Babes of Brentwood' issue and was really impressed. That's what he said."

"Okay."

"I just went along with it and answered his questions. I didn't think it'd be aired."

"Why didn't you take any pictures at the shoot? Or at any other time between September and now?"

"Well, because my schedule changes every day. I was at the zoo last week and then when they were filming I was told not to take photos because the company didn't authorize me. But Gavin acted like I was this big deal photographer."

"I see."

"Thank you, Miss Yolanda." He paused. "But I'm sorry 'bout all those bad reviews."

She watched as he left, closing the door behind him. "I sure hope that jerk didn't write 'em."

Noticing the yellow folder on top of the pile, she opened it. Inside were all the butter, milk, and cream invoices and information packets for Butter Ridge Creamery. She grinned and looked through the rest of the files, noting the one for the pure cane sugar and organic fine sugar. The orange folder was for the Cute Cluckers Farm—the new egg source that would replace that which was now out of business. Yolanda got up and went into the kitchen. BB slid a tray of pies into the oven and set the timer. "BB, want to help with a podcast?"

BB turned around. "Sure. When?"

"Soon. I want to show our appreciated and potential appreciated guests our natural and organic ingredients. Right down to the different types of pure cane sugar to the free roaming/pasture raised chicken eggs."

"Yolanda, that's such a great idea," BB giggled.

Suzie finished assembling a tray of chocolate ganache macarons. "I think so too, I'd also like to help show that these macarons DON'T come from a mix but are made entirely from scratch. And I think emphasizing the pasture raised chicken eggs is helpful for not only the macarons but for your cookies, cakes, and pies."

"And because of the macarons needing only egg whites, we have loads of extra yolks so I've added them to the pies, cakes and cookies so they taste even better," BB said.

Yolanda was grinning. "Thank you Suzie and BB. It's so important to show this. The bakery show didn't emphasize that at all."

****

Heather lived in a large two-story Spanish-Mediterranean villa. Rusty had taken the bus to Larchmont Boulevard and walked there, staring in dismay at the imposing looking home that had an ample driveway and lots of well-tended trees and foliage. She rushed down the walkway, clutching a set of keys. "Hey Rusty, want to see the apartment?"

"Yes, ma'am. I took the number 121 bus and it's a lot closer than where I live now."

"I see," she said and led the way to the three-car garage on the far-right hand side of the property. "It's above the garage. I can also rent out one of the stalls for your car."

"I'm afraid I don't have one. I just drive the van and take the bus or my bike to get around."

"That's too bad. Well, I'm offering you a great deal, so you'll be able to save for a car."

She went up the concrete steps first and showed him the small one-bedroom

126

apartment. "It's only had one tenant in it and he went back to Nebraska. All the appliances are new as is the carpeting. It's fully furnished." She waved her hand as they stepped into the bedroom and her iPhone chimed. "Have a look around, I need to take this call." She left the room.

****

An hour later, Heather was standing at the center island in her spacious kitchen. BB was across from her and was still in her pink yummery attire. She stood in front of the six-burner Wolf range. "Awesome!"

"This is what I used when I was making my lotions. Now that I have a lab in my warehouse, I create there. You can use this anytime."

"Thanks Heather. This place is so much nicer than where I'm at. I only have a microwave oven. I had to buy a little convection oven but a couple of times it blew a fuse!"

"That's no good. A pastry chef needs to have a real kitchen. I'll be so glad to have you here, but I have to warn you about the rooms."

BB looked at Heather. "Warn me about what?"

"Well, as you know, Barry and I are going through a divorce. For the past few months, he slept in that suite. It has an adjoining sitting room and there's a connecting bathroom. But the weird thing is since he left I've been hearing noises."

BB's eyes widened as they walked up the grand staircase with intricate wrought iron balusters. She hesitated at the top, and then followed Heather down the long hallway.

"It's a nice size, I believe about 1000 square feet for both rooms and the bathroom were refurbished by the former owners so it's very modern but looks like the 1920s when the house was built.

BB nodded, looking around the furnished bedroom that had a picture window overlooking the empty pool. She fingered the elegant beige linen drapes and admired a fireplace across from the king-sized bed. "I can't believe how big this bedroom is and you say there's another room?"

Heather walked out the door and turned right down the hallway. "It was used as a study but there's a bookcase and I found an older TV to put on the table so you..."

"This is great! My current room isn't even half this size and I only have a tiny bathroom with a shower." The young pastry chef was looking at the carpeted room with a newish TV and a wall covered with a row of cabinets topped with six empty bookshelves. "Gee, I don't have enough books to put on even one of the shelves," she said.

"Don't worry about it, neither did Barry. He never read a book once he graduated from college. Always hated to read. Used to store his work files and stuff there—nothing interesting."

BB touched the slate blue leather loveseat. "This is nice," she sat down and sighed. "I've been on my feet all day."

"Yolanda tells me that you're a very hard worker, BB."

"It's something I love to do. I know that lots of people work at jobs they can't stand. I feel bad for them. My mom was a housekeeper in a motel. She hated it, but she couldn't do much else because there weren't many jobs in our little town, and she couldn't type or anything."

"So...you don't feel anything weird about this room?"

BB shook her head and looked around. "No, it's really nice."

Heather walked over to the TV, switched it on, and waited for several seconds before a picture appeared. Both young women stared at the screen as a newscaster appeared, holding a microphone with the number 55 prominently placed on it. "We're here in Brentwood at Yolanda's Yummery that was featured on last night's Dessert Network show, *America's Best Bakeries*."

Yolanda smiled at the camera and waved happily.

"What you're really seeing is the suspect in the murder case of her former boyfriend, movie and TV producer Mike O'Neill. A man that was found outside her yummery on Valentine's Day, covered in blood. Dead in a dumpster..."

"Are they still airing this garbage?" Heather reached over and switched off the TV. "Total nonsense. Yolanda had nothing to do with Mike's death."

"I know that. I wish she wasn't being bothered about it. I hope they find the person who did it," BB said.

"You and me both. I have so much to do with getting ready to open the store this summer, do ad campaigns, and work on production of sugar and salt scrubs and other products. Too much to think about right now."

Heather's smooth jazz ring tone sounded, and she answered it. "No!" She shook her head. "No, that's not right. What? Bye."

"Yolanda just called. Nigel's disappeared."

****

Yolanda pulled out of a parking spot behind the Santa Monica Beverage Bar when a homeless man threw an empty beer can at her car. "Hey, stop you got a flat."

She anxiously glanced into her rearview mirror and saw a short man in a ragged coat in the alley waving his arms. There was a lurching sensation as her car swerved to the right, almost hitting the building. She turned down the nearest cross street and pulled into a parking spot on Eighth Street. Getting out of her car, she saw the shredded back right tire. "I really don't need this," she said as she called AAA for help. Standing on the curb in the dusk, Yolanda contemplated what was going on. "Nigel, this is the fourth time I've called and left a voicemail. Please call me when you get this. I love you." She disconnected the call and stood there, wondering where he was. Should she stop by his house after her tire was fixed?

It was nighttime when she drove to Nigel's house on Pacific Heights Place and parked in front of it. A few outside security lights were on, along with a kitchen light and the one in his upstairs bedroom. The thought of him being at home and intentionally ignoring her made her get out of the car, walk up to his front door and ring the doorbell. There was no answer. She turned and tried calling him again, listening for the sound of his phone and heard nothing other than the noise of neighborhood traffic. Two older women walked by on their evening stroll.

She waved to them as she returned to her car. The chubby woman with a knitted cap gave her a long stare. "You looking for Nigel?"

"Yes, we work together, my name's Yolanda Carter of Yolanda's Yummery."

"I thought you looked familiar. He left maybe fifteen minutes ago. I saw him get in a limo. A rental limo. He had luggage. Maybe he went to the airport."

Yolanda smiled and thanked the woman as she returned to her car and drove off. *I'm wearing fancy gold cupcakes that Nigel bought me and then he disappears without telling me. It doesn't make any sense.*

On the way back to Sherman Oaks, Yolanda talked to her father as Abby was teaching a Pilates class. "Dad, it's never happened that Nigel's just vanished without a trace."

"Dear, he's a guy. He'll get in touch with you, and he'll have a logical explanation."

"Maybe it's taking him a while to think something up," she said just as she pulled into the driveway.

"You're pretty cynical for someone who's just been on a TV show and gotten rave reviews."

"Not all of them are positive. I shouldn't be upset. It's not like he's cheating on me or anything. Well, at least I don't think he is. He bought me this beautiful cupcake necklace and earrings."

"That sounds nice, sweetie." Frederick yawned. "I'm sorry, I don't mean to be rude, but I got up at five and worked on some pieces for an exhibit. Looks like I'll be working long shifts for the next day or two."

They said their goodbyes and she parked in the garage and walked into an eerily dark and quiet house. The timer for the lamps hadn't been activated. A security light was on above the doorway, no lights shone inside except for some appliance lights indicating there was electricity. The temperature was colder than normal. She flicked on the kitchen light switch and both her cats ran down the hall and over to her and greeted her with their usual assortment of meows and purrs and rubbing up against her legs. "Hey there," she said, sitting down on the floor and petting them. "I missed my kitties today." They agreed by cranking up the noise and she saw their food bowls were empty. "Wow, your appetites are really increasing."

She filled their bowls and was about to check the refrigerator for some dinner when the landline phone rang. Yolanda switched off the kitchen light and ran into her spare room to answer it, wondering if Nigel was calling.

"Hello?" She noticed the closet door was open. *How strange*, she thought. It was always kept closed.

"Yolanda? 'Tis me! I'm so glad I finally reached you!"

She exhaled deeply. "Nigel, where are you? Are you okay?"

"I'm in London. I had the flight from hell, and I lost my cell phone on the way to the house. My father's in hospital and is undergoing open heart surgery tomorrow."

"Oh my gosh, Nigel, I'm so sorry to hear that. I hope that your father is…"

"I can scarcely hear you, Yo. Look, I'll text you or call you later. Right now, I need to go to hospital and be with my family."

The call ended abruptly, and she set the receiver down on the old-fashioned phone. *Something's peculiar about the story*, she thought. His father, Roger Garvey, was in his fifties and believed in clean living and eating healthy foods and drinking green tea—he was an expert in the field of green tea. It seemed unlikely that he was a candidate for such a severe operation as open-heart surgery.

She called Churchill's number and got his voicemail. As she left the room, she went over to the closet to look inside. Mulling over the open door, she was about to close it when a movement caught her eye. There was something shadowy in the corner behind the vacuum cleaner. She leaned closer and Mr. Whisker leapt out, startling her. "Oh, you crazy cat, you figured out how to open the closet door." Yolanda laughed.

Just as she shut the door behind her, the sound of pounding on the kitchen door made her jump a few inches off the floor. "What's going on?"

Yolanda turned and rushed into the kitchen and saw a tall figure shrouded in darkness. Then she realized the security light had gone out. Another power failure? What was going on? A quick look around and she saw the appliances' lights in the kitchen and heard the humming of the refrigerator. The security light must have burned out—at the wrong time, though.

Her heart was hammering in her chest as she stood near the edge of the kitchen, hesitating. Should she answer the door? Who was it? Churchill wouldn't do that; he knew she lived alone and disapproved of the fact that she didn't have security cameras.

Nigel was thousands of miles away.

Her father was in Laguna Beach.

Mike was dead.

A thought occurred to her as she edged over to the door, peering out the glass portion and saw the person had edged closer and looked like they were going to knock again. Before she could worry even more about who was standing outside her door, she opened it, and immediately recognized the lanky man in the dark windbreaker and jeans was Zac Field, her former boyfriend.

"Hey Zac, come in. What's going on?" She wanted to keep talking to calm her nerves as he walked in and shut the door behind him. She switched on the kitchen light.

"Hey Yo, I wanted to tell you how great that bakery show was. I'm so proud of you for getting on TV like that and being the best – wow, that's just amazing."

She nodded. "Thanks, Zac. So, what brings you here tonight?"

"I heard about Mike's death."

"Yeah, who hasn't? Mike showed up here the night before he died. He gave me a suitcase to store in my closet but didn't tell me why or what was really in it."

"What was in it?"

"Meth. A lot of it."

"That's just so wrong of him to do that to you."

"Well, the main thing is figuring out who killed him."

"Yolanda, maybe the person who killed Mike will try to kill you – did you ever think of that? And why did you let him keep a suitcase full of meth in your home?"

"Well, dummy, he didn't tell me what was in it. He said it had important papers and he'd be back for it in a couple of days. But then he winds up dead in a dumpster behind the yummery."

"I know, I saw it on the news. Tabby Flynn thinks you did it."

"Why would I kill Mike? That makes no sense."

"I know that. You know that. Tabby probably knows it but wants to get good ratings and her own news show or something."

"I know. She strikes me as the highly ambitious type," Yolanda said. "So, what have you been up to, Zac?"

"I'm in the running for that TV show I auditioned for, you know, the one called *Start Me UP!* Mike was supposed to be associate producer on it. Starliner Productions has a ton of reality shows on both cable and network TV. It's not a fly-by-night company and this show will probably start filming next month."

"That's great, Zac!"

"So, where's Nigel?"

"In London on family business."

"Didn't he hate Mike?"

"I think hate's kind of a strong word. But he definitely didn't like him."

"And now he's in London – on the run maybe?"

"Zac, are you suggesting that Nigel killed Mike?"

"I don't think so. I mean, he's not that stupid."

"Zac, Nigel's my boyfriend and I know you don't really like him but could you at least be civilized?"

"I am being civilized, Yo. It's just odd that he's suddenly in London on family business."

"No, it's not. Nigel travels a lot."

"Yeah, well are you going to be playing junior detective trying to find Mike's killer?"

"Detective Churchill is on the case. I have a lot of confidence that he'll solve it. It's what he does."

"I'm glad you said that. Try to remember it when you start sneaking out of the yummery and driving all over the place searching for clues."

"If I had any clues I'd hand them over to Detective Churchill. But I don't."

"Okay, okay. I just wanted to make sure you're okay because of what's happened to you in the past. I know you went out with Mike and I know that it was just friendly. I want to help you if I can. Because the one thing it's not good for is your business."

"That's the understatement of the year."

"I'm your friend and I want to help you. Maybe I should switch careers and be a detective." Zac paused, looking at the kitchen cupboards, and then back at her. "Nah, who am I kidding? I love golf and I'm still obsessed with the BioDome Mini Golf Course idea. If I win the *Start Me Up!* show – or even place in the top ten – there's a big chance of having my dream come true."

Yolanda smiled upon hearing the enthusiasm in his voice. "That's great, Zac." She stifled a yawn. "Oh, would you like some coffee or hot chocolate or something?"

He smiled. "Thanks, coffee would be great."

She hesitated and stepped over to the counter and plugged in the coffee maker.

"I was just joking, Yo. I can't have any caffeine because I need to get up early tomorrow. But thanks."

She nodded, unplugging the machine. "Okay, that's fine. I hope it goes well for you and that you win the show. It'd be awesome."

"I know. So, gotta go now." He gave her a quick wave and hurried out of the kitchen.

"That was weird," she said as Miss Chef walked up to the door and began sniffing it, and then pawed at the doorframe. "Miss Chef, is there a bug there?"

The cat continued sniffing and pawing, sharp claws audible on the tile surface.

"Stop that," she said absently, noticing the headlights of Zac's BMW vanish down the street. She double-checked the door's lock and headed down the hallway to her bedroom.

Miss Chef stopped her tirade and followed Yolanda into her room. She was about to close the door when her phone rang, and she saw it was the good detective. "Did you find out who killed Mike?" she asked as a way of greeting.

"And good evening to you, Yolanda. No, this isn't an episode of *CSI*. I wish I could say I have but it never works that way. So, what are you doing?"

"I'm exhausted. And I get to do the same thing tomorrow. Now the TV show and the case is getting some mixed publicity. I'm starting to have more haters – really obvious haters. Like I got dozens of bad reviews on StinkyBiz.com and other sites."

He sighed. "I know, I heard about it. I even saw a couple of them. I don't know what to tell you about that. And some of them aren't even anonymous. I recognized the name of one washed up actress."

"Listen to you – you sound like a Hollywood insider!" Yolanda went over to the closet and yanked open the door.

"I have a cousin who acted for a few years, mostly straight to DVD movies. A few times the parts weren't even seen due to ending up on the cutting room floor." He chuckled. "I signed up for Central Casting just before starting college. The day they called me for an assignment, I was in my abnormal psychology class and I didn't get the message until afterwards – like about ten minutes too late. So, they never contacted me again."

She reached into her closet and grabbed the first polo shirt she saw and dropped it onto her overstuffed chair. Returning to the closet, she found the tiered hanger with her five favorite pairs of jeans and pulled off the bottom pair. "I guess you've learned more than you've wanted about abnormal psychology on the job."

"You're right. I'm always learning something about abnormal psych. Rarely normal psych if such a thing exists."

"You are so cynical!"

"I'm a detective in the second biggest city in America. What do you expect? And well, I know that I can trust you with this, but I found a silencer in that suitcase."

She frowned. "What does that mean?"

"It's not good. I'm guessing that Mike was going to kill someone up close and personal. He was in the kill or be killed world. He wasn't even a movie producer, not a real one. Just a pretender. Hanging out with the Hollywood crowd. Fake Texas accent. We're looking into his family, and he's not related to Eugene O'Neill, the playwright. A sister in Colorado and an uncle and cousin in Texas and Rhode Island along with a cousin in Canada, I think."

"Fake Texas accent is right. I remember how strong it was when we first met. Then it started to fade."

"And he faded out. The drugs did it. Dealing and using is the worst combo."

"I guess it is." She sat down on the floor and pulled out a pair of mint green ballet flats, turning them over to see how worn the soles were.

"You sound kinda tired," the detective said.

"I am. I don't mean to be rude, but I must get up super early again." She picked up the shoes and carried them over to the chair. A yawn escaped. "I wish I could sleep in but I can't."

He chuckled. "So do I."

After the call ended, she looked down at the tiny cupcake, gently touching the miniature jewels. It seemed so young and girlish. She removed the necklace and earrings, holding the dainty set in her hand. Walking over to her dresser, she opened the white jewel box her mother had given her for her tenth birthday. Lifting the lid, a tinny rendition of *Somewhere My Love* played, and she carefully placed the new additions in a red velvet compartment that contained a golden charm bracelet she used to wear in high school.

Back before people wrote bad reviews about the yummery. Back when Mike O'Neill was in his early twenties. What had he been like? Where was he living? What had happened to his family?

CHAPTER 5

Yolanda was surprised the next morning when more than two dozen of L.A.'s finest trooped into the yummery. Detective Churchill led the group of uniformed and plainclothes officers, along with some office workers. The muscular Officer Aikens was near the head of the line that quickly formed, and Nick was the one who doled out samples of brownies and cookies to the eager appreciated guests. "Where's Teagan?" Yolanda asked Jeannie. The older woman was busily bagging brownies and other goodies. The pasted-on grin didn't hide her clenched teeth as she nodded her answer, too immersed in gathering the sweets and ringing them up. BB rushed in with a tray of chocolate chip Yolanda's yummy 6-pack cookie stacks. "I have more cookie stacks," she said as she hurried back into the kitchen. Yolanda stood near the edge of the fabric divider and called, "BB, please send Rusty come out to help bag the orders."

Rusty's gaunt face was pale beneath the bright lighting. Jeannie pointed out a fancy vanilla buttercream Magical Cake of Love and he bent down to retrieve a box, almost falling over. Nick glanced his way, and then returned to the cash wrap area and took the order of a young office worker wearing a snug sweater.

Suzie minced out holding a sample tray filled with chocolate and raspberry macarons and offered them around. She beamed at the handsome officer who stood near the brownie display. "Have you tried our French macarons, officer?" She cocked her narrow hip as she hoisted the tray closer to the large man.

"No ma'am can't say I have. I can say I want to very much!" He grabbed a chocolate one and bit it in half, chewing it slowly, savoring the rich delicacy. His eyes were half closed and his mustache had collected a few brown crumbs.

"You're sampling the double chocolate ganache with Grand Cru Valrhona that..."

His eyes snapped open, and he finished the cookie. He stared at the woman in front of him. He swallowed the last bit, and when he smiled, his face glowed. "I have no words to describe what I just ate!" He reached into his pocket and retrieved his billfold. "I want to order a dozen more. And if you're single," he bent down to peer beneath the tray to see her left hand. "I want to take you out for a night on the town that you'll never forget."

Suzie swooned; the tray slid a few inches, and the officer had the reflexes to catch it. A raspberry macaron skidded to the edge and his hand almost touched it. Suzie laughed. "You're a quick one, aren't you?"

He nodded. "It's my middle name."

"I didn't catch your first name, Officer Aikens."

"Tyler. And what's your name, pretty lady?"

"Suzie Palmer." She didn't hesitate and her smile was dazzling.

Yolanda observed the scene as she strode over to the end table where Detective Churchill had seated himself, so he was facing the yummery. She stood near the navy-suited man. "I've never seen her looking that happy before."

"It's the macarons—people love them."

"You really think so?"

He nodded. "But I think poor Rusty's having a tough time."

"NO! RUSTY!" Jeannie shouted.

Yolanda rushed over to the cash wrap unit, almost knocking Nick over as Rusty lurched backwards, falling on the floor, legs spread out and kicking the side of the counter. The heavily frosted cake flew and plopped face down on the man's shoulder and chest. For an instant, there was silence as everyone in the yummery stared at the unusual spectacle. Rusty awkwardly rolled onto his side, got up, covered in buttercream frosting and crumbled yellow vanilla cake pieces. "I'll get the mop," he said. Rusty hastily fled to the kitchen, sliding in the mess, stumbling into the curtain, and leaving behind a blob of frosting on the fabric.

Jeannie stood at the cash register, staring at the closed fabric divider. Nick tapped her on the shoulder. "Don't worry, Jeannie, I'll help clean up the mess."

Yolanda approached the next appreciated guest in line, a smiling young detective in a beige suit. "Welcome to Yolanda's Yummery. Would you like to try one of our macaron samples?" She looked over at Suzie and Officer Aikens who were wordlessly staring at each other. Behind her, Rusty had returned with the mop and Quinn walked into the yummery, wearing his blue and brown apron.

"Sorry I'm late, Yolanda, I got stuck on the 405 and...wow, what a crowd!"

"I don't think I could ever eat another doughnut again," Officer Aikens said to Suzie. "I'm a macaron-loving cop. I've just been upgraded!"

She laughed. "Yes, you have. And I must make some more. I'll see you here at five?"

"Yes, you will, Suzie. I'll be here at five. And I need to order a dozen of these to get me through the day because it's going to be a very long day without you."

****

Later that afternoon, Yolanda received a text from Zac. "Meet me at Teagan's place ASAP."

Yolanda went into the kitchen to see who was working on what. Rusty wore a fresh polo shirt and matching green apron and was in the process of loading the van up for a delivery. She wanted to tell him to be careful and not drop anything, but she said nothing to avoid embarrassing the man. How would she feel if she'd spent two decades locked up only to encounter so many cops at once?

Suzie was humming as she was piping pale blue vanilla macaron shells in perfect circles. The woman was transformed into a cheerful employee all because of one brief meeting with a bachelor cop.

Or was he?

Yolanda stopped herself with that line of thought. She'd only seen the man a few times and the time Churchill had mentioned him was in passing. She could've sworn he said something about a wife. Or an ex-wife? Curiosity overtook her and she pulled out her iPad and quickly typed his name into a search engine. There were a few others with that name, but more scrolling turned up his Farcebook page and a quick look at his status indicated that he was single. She sighed with relief and put her iPad away just as the woman slammed a tray of just-piped shells on the counter several times. Yolanda had gotten used to the sudden banging noises and knew that it was done to remove any air bubbles. The first time she'd heard the noise when she was in her office with the door open, she thought that temperamental Suzie was throwing a fit.

Zac and ASAP could mean anything, Yolanda thought as she went to her office to retrieve her jacket. BB knocked on the doorframe just as the jacketed young woman carrying her purse approached. "Hey BB, I'm on my way out. Is it important?"

BB shook her head. "No, Yolanda, it can wait. Will you be back soon?"

"Sure will. But if you need to tell me now, that's fine."

BB looked down at the floor. "No, that's okay. I'll tell you when you get back." BB was about to say something else, but she turned and hurried back to the counter where she resumed rolling out the pie dough.

Yolanda glanced at the younger woman and quietly muttered an "okay" as she strode out of the kitchen and toward the back door. BB was usually more up front about things. As she reached her car on the chilly and gloomy day, the urgency of Zac's message was emphasized as he was in the process of sending her another text. It only said one word: HURRY.

Ten minutes later, Yolanda sat down on an oversized grey plush chair in the living room of Teagan's apartment. Several aromatic candles were burning and the large room smelled like a field of summer flowers and meadowgrass with accents of ocean breeze. Teagan was lying on the sofa; her uncombed hair was loose and she was bundled up in a blanket. On the other end of the sofa sat Zac, looking stiff and formal.

"I want to run this by you before I contact the police."

Yolanda tried not to sneak a glance at her watch. "Teagan, we've known each other far too long for this. Why couldn't you stop by the yummery?"

"I'm being careful. Between a killer and a stalker..." Teagan said. "It's just that I think I might know who killed Mike O'Neill."

Yolanda looked at her friend closely, noting the red face and bloodshot, swollen eyes.

"Who killed him?"

"I think it was Rocky Montoya—my ex-boss."

"Rocky? You mean that creep who ran the Wicked Fun Gentlemen's Club?"

"Which is about to go out of business, thanks in part to you."

"Me?"

"Well, he blames it on you because he lost the competition. And then he was found out about the dog shelter that he pretended to donate money to but was really using to help remodel his house. Not that it was a lot of money for such an expensive place, but enough to get him in trouble. And he never got all his business back and he's mad that your yummery is doing so good."

"We think he's the guy who's been writing all those bad reviews about the yummery. Or his friends." Zac chimed in. "Last night and today you got about fifty of 'em on HelpReview.com and lots on StinkyBiz.com. They all basically said that you put drugs in your cakes and that's why they're magical."

Yolanda's eyes widened. "Oh my gosh, what a stupid thing to say! Why would I put drugs..."

"And the reviews stated that your cakes and cookies and everything else need to be tested for drugs."

"That's ridiculous! I've been getting more bad reviews since being on *America's Best Bakeries*. But that's to be expected. I've only seen a couple about adding drugs to my goodies. Though I didn't read all of them."

"We haven't read them all either. But if they suspect drugs in food, they'd have to close you down while they test all your products and all your ingredients. You'd also have to pay for it and the yummery wouldn't be earning any money for the time it would be closed."

"How do you know this, Zac?"

"Because I looked it up online. I found a link between Mike and Rocky."

Teagan cleared her throat. "I talked to Catelynn who still works at the club. She said she overheard Rocky and Mike talking in the club last year."

"Yeah, Rocky was determined to get you out of business and that's why he used Mike to set you up. He hired Mike to play the millionaire Texan and be a pretend producer. The most he could do was get him an associate producer job because Mike was such an idiot."

"Mike wasn't that much of an idiot. Because of him, Knick and Knack got engaged at the yummery. That helped boost sales even more for us."

Teagan said, "No, that was Rocky. Rocky met them at the taste-off, remember?"

"I wasn't there. I was at the mini golf tournament," Zac said. "Winning it," he added.

"I was at the taste-off and Knick and Knack were there and afterwards Rocky found out who they were and that's how they all met," Teagan said.

Yolanda shook her head. "This makes no sense for him to have Knick and Knack promote the yummery. He's part owner of my competitor, Freeze N Bake. Wouldn't he want them to promote his brand?"

"I don't know, Yo," Zac said. "I guess you're right about him having nothing to do with Knick and Knack at the yummery. But I know you can't trust him, and Teagan's told me enough about him to know that he's not a nice guy."

There was a loud knock on the door. Teagan jumped. Zac sidled closer to her. "Don't worry, Teagan, I'm here."

Teagan's face was white and drawn. "Yo, could you look through the peephole and see who it is? Like, if it's Sean, I'm not answering." She burrowed deeper under the blanket and her widened eyes made her look even younger than her years.

Yolanda quietly walked over to the door and paused, looking out. She saw a large red gift box. "Teagan, can I open the door to see who left you a box?"

Teagan sniffed. "No, don't do that. Wait for a few minutes and then pick it up. Is it gift wrapped?"

Yolanda nodded. "Red wrapping paper with a sparkly pink bow. Very pretty."

"Must be another post-Valentine's Day gift. It can sit there."

"What if it's something you want? Like chocolate?" Zac said.

Yolanda chuckled. "If there's chocolate in there, it's enough to feed everyone on this block."

She stretched and yawned. "I'm curious now. Bring it in," Teagan said.

Yolanda opened the door and reached for the package. She walked over and plopped it down on the couch next to her friends. "It's not heavy," she said.

Teagan sat up, yanked off the bow, and peeled off the wrapping paper. Opening the box, she saw lots of crumpled red tissue paper. She picked up a large wad and smoothed it out. Reaching in the box, she pulled out another wad of tissue. She saw a metallic flash of white and royal blue plastic. Puzzled, she yanked it out and saw it was a cheerleading pom pom. Looking in the box, there was a second one. She laughed. "What the hell am I supposed to do with these?" She picked them up and waved them over her head. Zac and Yolanda laughed along with her. "Yo, see if there's anything else as stupid in that box!" She continued waving the pom poms, the metallic colors catching the light from the floor lamp.

Yolanda tentatively reached down into the box and found a blue and white sequined hair bow, which she handed to her friend. "Here you go—he's into color coordination at least!"

"Yeah, like blue, white, yay team fight!" Teagan put down the pom poms and looked at the bow with the attached ponytail holder. She giggled and put it in her long hair. "Do I look like a cheerleader now?"

Zac was looking at her and laughing. "Yeah, you look like a cheerleader."

Yolanda pulled out another bunch of tissue and her laughter was louder than before. Her friends stared at her. "Okay, Yo, how bad is it?" Teagan asked, removing the bow and dropping it on a pom pom.

"It's so bad it's good!" She lifted a blue and white sleeveless croptop with metallic silver trimming. Next was a tiny skirt in the same color scheme. She tossed the two items over to her friend.

"Try it on!" Zac said.

Yolanda looked at him. "Really, Zac? I think Teagan was more covered when she worked at that strip club."

"No, it's about the same," Teagan said.

"What a perv." Yolanda shook her head and stood up. "I'm assuming this is Sean's way of..."

"Trying to win me back." Teagan picked up the skirt and was about to throw it back into the box, when she noticed a hanging thread. She flipped the skirt inside out and examined the seam, "What horrible stitching," she said, "I could do better than that. Much better."

"I'm sure you can. You always could sew. I can't even sew on a button," Yolanda remarked. "My mom can sew but that gene wasn't passed on to me."

"I made my prom gown," Teagan said. "It fit me just right. Column-style in canary yellow silk with an asymmetrical hem. I even did the beading. My parents were impressed!"

Yolanda nodded. "I know I was. You showed me the picture. It looked so professional. I don't know why you don't sew more."

Teagan threw the skirt back into the box. "You're right. Maybe I should do more sewing. I know I could design kickass cheerleading outfits and prom gowns. I've still got my sewing machine." She got up and went over to the box. "Let's see if there's anything else..." She found more tissue paper and smoothed out each piece, placing the squares on the floor in a pile. A tiny box wrapped in royal blue and white gift-wrap fell to the floor. Teagan shook it, hearing a muffled sound. She hesitated before opening the box. "I hope it's not a..." the ripped paper fell to the floor. A white box with a lid. Another pause: she lifted it up. She laughed, holding up the box. Inside was an old penny. "He always was a cheapskate."

"Look on the bright side, maybe he's gone for good," Yolanda said as she headed for the door. "I really must get back. But thanks for the info about Rocky. Haven't heard anything about him or his company in a long time. Then again, I don't really care if I ever do."

Teagan had finished dumping the gifts and tissue paper and gift wrap into the large box. "I'll drop this off at a thrift store next time I go out. I think some high school kid might like this," she said.

"Can't you try it on just once?" Zac asked.

She kicked the box across the room. "Grow up, dude."

Yolanda waved and left, annoyed at the unnecessary drama of Teagan and Zac. They were good friends but why had she gone to them? Teagan had missed work because of bad online reviews and conjecturing.

"Well, at least I didn't have to drive across town for that nonsense," she muttered as she reached her car parked near Teagan's apartment building.

An old gray pickup truck drove slowly by, unnoticed by Yolanda.

When Yolanda returned to the yummery, BB tentatively approached her. "Um, Yolanda, is it okay if I leave a little bit early this afternoon?"

Yolanda nodded. "Sure, of course. What time?"

"Um, would like five or five-thirty be okay? Well, maybe five forty-five?"

She smiled at the younger woman who was twisting a clean piping bag. "BB, why don't you leave at five? That's fine."

"Gee, that's great! Thanks! Um, the reason's because last week I met Allen downstairs in the laundry room and he works at Universal and he's got free tickets so we can go see a movie at CityWalk."

Yolanda laughed and hugged BB. "I'm so happy for you. Leave at five and have a great time. You deserve it!"

CHAPTER 6

Just as Yolanda and Quinn were about to close the yummery that Saturday evening, a man rushed inside. "I have to get a dozen macarons for my wife or I'm a dead man," he said. "I'm glad I got here before you closed."

Yolanda nodded. "Well, we're about to close and I'll have to go to the kitchen to get them. What flavor or flavors would you like?"

His eyes were studying the floor. "Whatever you have on hand, miss. I know she just loves anything sugary."

"Quinn, you can go if you like, I've got this."

Quinn stood near the door and stared at the man. "No, I'm in no rush tonight. I've got all the time in the world." He pointedly stared at the man wearing a hooded Forest Mountain jacket, camouflage pants and hiking boots. "I also recommend the chocolate macarons."

The stranger nodded. "Okay, I'll take the chocolate macarons."

Yolanda disappeared behind the curtain and Quinn had edged over a little closer to the man, still maintaining his observant stance and looking outside. "Your wife ever tried any of the coffee cakes?"

The man shook his head. "Um, no, can't say if she has or not. She saw this place on that Best Bakeries show and you know how it is with women – always wanting the best."

Quinn smiled. "Most of them are like that. Your wife is right, she'll be getting the best when she bites into a macaron from our yummery. The pastry chef we hired was trained in Paris. And of course, Yolanda also makes them."

Yolanda hurried out holding a pink box with the signature pink, green and yellow ribbon. "We have a half dozen chocolate and the other six are raspberry chocolate." She set the box gently on the counter next to the cash register.

"I'm sure the wife'll love 'em. It's our anniversary tonight, you know." He reached into his jacket to pull out his wallet. There was a pause. He pulled his hand out, removing a glove. His brow wrinkled. "I thought..." The man reached into his left side pocket. Yolanda and Quinn watched the man yank out a large flashlight from his jacket. He lunged for Quinn, the beam highlighting the Beverage Bar manager's startled face. As Quinn saw the shorter man coming towards him, he stepped away, barely avoiding being hit with the heavy object. He almost fell but steadied himself.

Yolanda screamed and rushed back behind the cloth barrier, wishing it was a locked steel door. The man clattered over the glass countertop, knocking an empty lidded sample tray off the counter. The glass tray shattered into thousands of pieces and the clean display cases were smeared with mud.

Yolanda shrieked and locked herself in her office. Her heart was racing and she reached for her desk phone to call 911. Just as she picked up the receiver there was a very loud banging noise on the door. She hit the speakerphone button and scrambled to the other side of the office, grabbing the guest chair, shoving it beneath the doorknob. More pounding on the door. The phone was answered. "Help me I'm at Yolanda's Yummery and…"

Outside she heard scuffling feet and a fight ensued as she overheard the noise of a body slamming against the door, causing it to shake. Another harder slam against the door and wall. The operator was asking Yolanda for her address.

"Help! There's a big fight…" Suddenly her desk phone rang loudly, startling her.

The phone stopped ringing and there was no noise other than running footsteps. Yolanda went over to the door and paused. *Is Quinn okay?* The front door banged shut. She grasped the doorknob and tentatively opened the door, stepping out. Quinn was leaning against the wall across from her. His hand was holding the side of his head. "Quinn, are you okay?"

"Yeah, I've got a thick skull."

****

Detective Churchill was sitting in Yolanda's office with her and Quinn.

"Yolanda, I'm so sorry this happened to you and Quinn."

She nodded. "Thank you. It's so strange. It just happened so quickly."

Quinn was seated next to the desk. "That guy had someone waiting for him."

Churchill flipped his notebook back a page and studied his scribbling.

"You said that the suspect was very fast and that there was a waiting pickup truck in front of the dancewear store."

"That's right."

"And he was wearing a hoodie or a hooded jacket?"

"A hooded jacket like the kind worn when it's very cold out."

"Jeans? Boots?"

"Camouflage pants and boots."

"He appeared to be military?"

She nodded. "Yeah but he didn't pull out a gun or knife. It was a flashlight."

"Could it have been a police baton?"

She shook her head. "No, because it was on. That's why I knew it was a flashlight."

Churchill nodded. "Could've been both. No idea who he was?"

"No. I don't."

"Was this individual tall or short? Was he small of build? What race was he? Did he speak American English, or did he have an accent?"

Quinn piped up. "He shone a flashlight in my eyes but afterwards I saw that he was probably about average height. He was in good physical shape because he jumped over the counter. He claimed he wanted to buy macarons 'for the wife.' He used that term. He also said she liked chocolate macarons. I don't really think that's a lot of information."

Churchill looked at his notes. "You never know. I also want to have the mud that he left on the display case sampled."

"Great. I want to clean it up ASAP."

The detective smiled. "I understand, Yolanda. We'll get the sample taken tonight and it'll be ready for those Magical Cakes of Love tomorrow morning."

"The guy wore a Forest Mountain jacket," Quinn stated. "I recognized the brand when he was hopping over the counter. It has that distinctive triangle mountain label on the back." He pointed to the small part of his back. "I know they cost a lot and there's a waiting list for 'em. Unless it was a knockoff made in Tijuana."

"Right, I've heard of that brand and maybe we can come up with something.

Meanwhile, I'm going to have the bootprints analyzed along with the mud for a soil analysis. He left enough of that behind."

"Yeah, tell me about it. When you're done I'm going to have to clean those cases very thoroughly. And I'll have to replace the broken sample tray." She sighed. "I think I have an extra one at home. Whenever I get home tonight I'll look for it." Yolanda glanced at the clock above the door and saw it was seven-thirty.

"I'm sorry, Yolanda. I'm sure you've had a long day," Detective Churchill said.

She sighed. "I don't want to complain, and I know you work even longer hours than I do."

"I think Dr. Franklin will be able to do this very quickly," the detective pulled out his cell phone. "Plus, he knows Dr. Greely, the forensic geologist that'll help us." He flipped through his phone's address book. "I'll stay here with you until we're done so you can close. I'm very concerned about what's happened to you today. I really think you should invest in a complete surveillance system."

"I guess I should. But for now, I'll be fine, Win."

CHAPTER 7

Yolanda felt as though she was sleepwalking that Sunday as she'd been at the yummery until almost eleven o'clock the night before. She realized that ever since January, she'd been working every weekend again. It was because of Valentine's Day and the upcoming one-year anniversary. In March, she vowed to return to a six or even five-day workweek. Churchill texted her just as she pulled into her parking spot. "Dr. Franklin will have the results back tonight or tomorrow." She thanked him. "Dr. Greely the forensic geologist is backlogged. It might take a week or two for the soil analysis."

She quickly typed in her thanks and put her iPhone back in her purse. It was still dark out and a shadowy figure was coming towards her. She automatically checked to make sure her car door was locked.

The figure was clearly seen when he walked in front of the shining headlights. Rusty waved at her, his eyes squinting in the sudden brightness. Relieved, she flipped off the engine and stepped out. "Good morning, Rusty."

"'Morning, Miss Yolanda." He was hunched over, holding his arms, as his thin windbreaker wasn't doing much to keep him warm on such a cold morning. He forced a grin and stepped forward. "Need anything unloaded from your car, Miss Yolanda?"

She looked at the fancy glass sample tray edged with white scalloping and sporting a heavier dome lid with an ornate handle. It was one of her father's earlier works and she was looking forward to displaying it on the countertop and filling it with macaron samples.

She got out and reached behind her to grab her tote bag and purse and unlocked the passenger's side door for him. "If you don't mind, Rusty, I have a new sample tray."

"Yes ma'am!" he brightened as he walked in front of her car to retrieve the tray. Once he reached in and lifted it up, a grimace of pain flickered across his pale face. He hid it as he lifted the heavy glass tray. "Mighty fine piece of craftsmanship, Miss. Did your father make this?"

She nodded as she went behind the car and over to the other side to close the door behind the man. "Yes he did, Rusty. About ten years ago. That was during his Ornate Period. His designs have changed over the years. They've gotten simpler."

Yolanda rushed over to unlock the back door.

The man checked his balance to keep from staggering beneath its weight.

Yolanda nervously watched the man's face redden with exertion and his breathing grew more labored as he made his way up to the front counter. She reached his side just in time to help him carefully place the tray on the countertop. He leaned against it to catch his breath and looked over to his right where he saw the muddy case. "What happened?"

"We had a majorly unappreciated guest last night," she said.

"I'd say so," he replied. "Want me to clean that up for you?"

"I was going to do it but since you're here..." she glanced up at the clock. "You're very early this morning."

"Yes ma'am, I've been hanging 'round waiting for...well, now lemme get changed and clock in and I'll clean up this mess."

"What do you mean by hanging around? How long have you been out there?"

"Well, ma'am," he was looking at the cushioned mat in front of the cash register. "I was just, um, stretching from walkin' here."

"Rusty, you walked here from Monrovia?"

"Um, well, yeah, I mean..."

She pulled out her iPhone and pressed an app. A few seconds later, she looked up at him. "Rusty, Monrovia is twenty-five miles from here."

He nodded. "My bike and cash were stolen. That damn halfway house is full of thieves, I just can't stay there no more. Much as I liked it, I can't afford to stay at Miss Heather's it being in that nice Hancock Park area 'n all."

"Rusty, you can't be walking around like this all night. You need to find a place to live that's safe. I'm going to call Heather and get this straightened out." She looked at the clock. "Well, I'm going to text her because she doesn't answer her phone before seven."

Rusty made his van delivery soon after the yummery opened and she noticed that while his shirt and apron were clean, his posture was more slouched than usual, and his face was pale. As soon as he left, she went into her office and called Heather. To her surprise, Heather answered the phone. "Hey Heather, I was wondering about that apartment that Rusty looked at."

"You mean the one he said he can't afford on his salary?"

"Yeah. His situation's gotten worse. He's way out in Monrovia and the place he lives in is awful. His bike was stolen. He spent all night walking to get here on time. I thought you were going to give him a reduced rate due to his situation?"

Heather sighed. "I guess I will. BB's going to rent the suite upstairs and she's moving in on March 1. So, I'll see what I can do for Rusty."

"That's great. I feel so bad for him, I can see how strained he is."

"Since Rusty has no transportation, I can technically charge him less but he won't have access to the garage. I'm still a little hesitant to rent an apartment to an ex-con."

"I know how you feel. So far he's been great."

"Working with someone and living with someone are two different things. Of course, he won't have access to the house and my car's in a locked garage..."

"I understand, Heather, I really do. Especially since Barry's moved out and you have a mortgage."

"And a shop that's opening up at the Beverly Center this summer."

"Yikes, I can see why you don't want to cut back on rent with all you have going on," Yolanda said. "But I can't have him stay with me."

"Why not? You have an extra room."

"I know that, but I don't think Nigel would stand for it for a second. Which reminds me, I still haven't heard from him."

"Not again. What's his excuse this time?"

"He says his father's having open heart surgery."

"That's very serious."

"Yeah. But the guy's in great condition. He runs marathons and eats vegan food and drinks the best kind of green tea that he can find."

"If you say so. Okay, if Rusty really needs a place, I can go down a few hundred."

"Thanks, Heather. You have no idea how much I appreciate this. I'm in enough trouble right now with Mike's dead body. If the news ever got out that I also have a homeless ex-con employee---well, that wouldn't be great for business."

There was a gentle knock on the door and Yolanda looked up at the closed door. "Well, I've got to get back to work, Heather. Talk to you later."

The call ended and Yolanda got up to open the door. She giggled upon seeing her father standing there holding a large sample tray. "Great to see you, Dad!"

He walked into her office and set the tray down on her desk. "You mentioned something about a broken tray when you called last night...and I just happen to have an extra one."

She got up and hugged him before going over to the tray and admiring it. Then she lifted the lid. "Hey, it doesn't seem to be as heavy as the other one."

He laughed. "That old thing you're using now. Nah, I've streamlined my art since then."

"I know, dad." She went back around her desk and sat down. Frederick slid the guest chair closer to the desk and seated himself.

"You haven't said much about the um…" he cleared his throat, "the incident out back."

"That's a very diplomatic way of saying it." Yolanda looked at the stack of file folders in her in box and picked the top one up, sliding it in front of her. "I have no idea who killed Mike, why, nothing. At least I'm not a suspect."

"I know that. Churchill knows that."

"But we're no closer to solving it than we were when it first happened." She shook her head.

"We? Are you and Churchill a couple?" Frederick raised his eyebrow and cocked his head to one side.

"No, not a couple. Nigel's jetted off to the UK again as his father's in the hospital having open heart surgery."

"That's awful. I'm so sorry to hear that. I thought he was only a few years older than me."

"I don't believe Nigel. His dad's as healthy as you. I think it's an excuse. I hate to say it, but maybe he knows more about Mike's murder than he's letting on. He couldn't stand Mike. He didn't trust me around him."

"You don't think he killed Mike?"

Yolanda shook her head. "No, I don't think he killed him. But maybe he knows who did. I mean, I didn't tell you this, but when he came over on Valentine's Day for dinner he had a piece of black duct tape on his coat. The same duct tape that was wrapped around Mike's suitcase."

Frederick was staring at his daughter. "Are you sure it was the same duct tape or..."

"Well, it was black, and Winston hasn't gotten back to me about it yet. Forensics is working on a lot of the clues including the muddy bootprints and Churchill's trying to find Mike's family and all sorts of stuff."

"Yolanda, black duct tape is the most common color. Still, it seems odd."

"Dad, I wish I could go to London and check up on Nigel. I really could. I've always wanted to go there but I just can't leave the yummery. And I have to be here to work. The one-year anniversary is in ten days."

Frederick pulled out his cell phone and looked at it blankly, then fished around in his jacket pocket.

"They're on top of your head," she remarked.

He chuckled as he reached for them and put them on. "Thanks. I hate it when that happens. Anyway, I'm caught up on most of my orders and I've been to London."

"Yeah, back in like 1985!"

"Actually, it was – well, doesn't matter, just that I've been to London and Brighton and Cornwall and a few other cities."

"Cornwall's a city?" Yolanda was on her computer and had found a map of the UK.

"I'll have you know that I was in Truro, which is the biggest city in Cornwall."

"Like 18,000 is even a city?" Yolanda laughed.

"Well, I guess they define city a little differently over there," he said. "But I wouldn't mind going to the UK for a few days and checking up on Nigel. I can wear my shades and part my hair differently. Or wear a hat. He won't recognize me. I can even wear conservative clothing, so I'll blend in more."

"Dad it sounds like you've been watching some movies. But if you're thinking that being a detective is another career, first you need to be able to find your own glasses!"

Frederick laughed. "You're right. You've learned a lot about this field, lately." He sighed. "You know, I'd love to take your mom, but she just won't stop working lately. She says Pilates is making her feel better all the time and she loves her students. Her batik work is taking a back burner to her Pilates. Now that Cynthia's working part time doing some batik work for Mom, she's even happier."

"I'm just glad Mom is feeling so well again. I was worried about her when she got sick last year." She paused. "How could I have forgotten to give you some macarons? I completely forgot!" She pushed her chair back and rushed out of the office. "Just a sec..."

"Now who's the forgetful one?" Frederick asked as she disappeared into the kitchen.

She returned a minute later holding her signature gift box and presented it to him.

He admired the pastel striped box with the pink satin ribbon. "I'm officially an appreciated guest. This's quite an honor. I'm sure your mother will put these in the freezer, so she doesn't pig out on them."

Yolanda giggled. "Are you going to open it or are you just going to pass it on to Mom?"

He smiled. "If I open it, I wouldn't be able to stop at just one. Besides, I really have to get going. I want to relax and enjoy your goodies, not eat and dash." Frederick stood up, tucking the box under his arm. "And I think I may be making some London-bound flight reservations though I want to sleep on it and make sure." He gave her a quick kiss on the cheek and left.

****

Just before closing, she sat back down at her desk and looked at her calendar. The first anniversary of the yummery was less than two weeks away! What if her father did go to the U.K.? What if Nigel wasn't going to be back in time? The press releases had gone out last month, she was going to have a big party at the yummery and have many freebies and a unique surprise guest.

173

Naturally, there would be free samples galore.

All that swirled through her mind as she walked back to her car behind the yummery. Yolanda clutched her iPhone, in case she had to make an emergency call. Nestled in her coat pocket was the container of pepper spray. She looked around her, glad the back lights were on as well as an overhead parking light. Stepping into her car, she quickly made sure the doors were locked and switched on the engine. The radio came on and she heard an old 80s song as she was driving down the street to the intersection of San Vicente. She cranked up the heat and turned on a news channel. The radio announcer said, "The body of Hollywood producer Mike O'Neill found on Valentine's Day in a dumpster behind Yolanda's Yummery in Brentwood."

CHAPTER 8

"Turn that garbage off!" shouted a voice from the backseat. She slammed on her brakes, the car skidding up onto the curb and back down to the street. Behind her, the sound of squealing brakes drowned out the radio. Her teeth chattered in fear as she pulled over and was about to turn around when the cold metallic feel of a gun was shoved against the side of her head.

"Don't turn!" The voice was muffled, as though the person had covered his mouth with his hand. "Now turn it off!"

She obeyed, and the only sound was her labored breathing and the sudden chiming noise her phone made. The gun was jammed harder against her head. "Don't answer it," the muffled voice said.

"Why?"

"Shut up and drive."

"Where?"

"Home, you stupid girl. But I want you to go a different way. And make sure that no one's following you."

Yolanda's phone continued to chime.

"Turn that damn thing off," the man said. "It's against the law to drive and talk on the phone anyway."

Yolanda reached over and grabbed the phone. *It's against the law to carjack someone*, she thought.

"Don't try anything..." the voice said and the gun slid down to her neck. "I mean it."

"Okay," she said, flinching even more as the cold surface pressed against her neck. She picked up the phone and for a second was ready to enter the three numbers that would summon help. Or speed dial Winston's private number. It was number nine and she was relieved it was just one digit. Turning the phone away from him as she pretended to fumble for the off switch, she pressed it and suddenly coughed. The riskiness of what she was doing didn't register immediately; the gun could have been triggered or the man could have reached over and stopped her from summoning help by grabbing the phone and crushing it or tossing it out a window. She quickly entered the code that she and Churchill had worked out in case there was ever an emergency. If ever a time to enter those three digits, it was now. As she coughed again, she shakily pressed the numbers 623 and switched off the phone.

"Gimme that phone," the voice demanded. The voice wasn't as muffled.

She said nothing. Who was that man in the backseat? Why was he threatening to kill her? Why was he kidnapping her?

She cringed when she heard the window roll down and the gust of cold air she felt, as she knew her phone was tossed outside. The window remained open. "Go left on Grandview," he shouted almost in her ear, the frigid steel of the gun pressing against her ear.

That pepper spray, if only she could reach for it without getting her head blown off. She began fumbling for it, but the gun was pressing harder against her.

Yolanda missed the turn, deliberately staying on San Vicente. She wanted to cut over to Wilshire and it didn't matter what side street they took, as long as it was an apartment and condo-lined avenue.

Suddenly, a big Mercedes station wagon shot out of a driveway and almost rammed into her car. Instinctively, she slammed on her brakes and her hands twisted the steering wheel to the left. The force of the gun was absent but she concentrated on avoiding the car and protecting herself and the vehicle.

Ignoring the yells from the station wagon, she pressed down on the accelerator and drove, almost knocking over a motor scooter. *Why don't those college students keep their scooters on campus?*

At the corner of Wilshire Boulevard, she stopped at the red light. There was no gun pointing at her. No sound coming from the back other than street noises due to the open window. She looked around, puzzled, and saw the man was lying down on the seat. There was no sign of a gun, just a person wearing a black jacket.

Grabbing her purse, she yanked open the door and ran out of her car.

In the windy night, she rushed to a brightly lit convenience store across the street. There was an old pay phone in front of the store and the corded phone was off the hook. She grabbed it, punching in the emergency number. There wasn't any answer. She clicked the flap at the top of the phone a few times and heard a dial tone. Relieved, she pressed the three digits. An operator responded.

"My name's Yolanda Carter and I've just been kidnapped, I mean carjacked..."

After she explained what happened, she hung up the phone, hurried back across Wilshire Boulevard to her illegally parked car, and flipped on the emergency lights. It didn't stop the horns from annoyed drivers who were temporarily inconvenienced by the unmoving white Honda.

The car jacker was immobile in the backseat, and she couldn't see his face as he wore a black hooded jacket. Was it the man from last night who stormed into her yummery? Yolanda wanted to look but knew enough about the law to leave everything alone until the police arrived. "I wish I could remember Churchie's number," she said quietly to herself. The adrenalin coursing through her from being carjacked and careening down dark streets as a gun was held to her head kept replaying in her mind. A stranger was passed out—or dead—in the backseat of her car. Where was her phone thrown out? That was several blocks away. She looked around, not seeing a police car or anything other than a homeless man shuffling down the street with a duffel bag slung over his shoulder.

A glance at her watch and she thought about her two cats at home with empty food bowls. "I've got to get my phone," she muttered, as three guys got out of a new red pickup truck. The tallest man looked over at her car and then at her. "Miss, are you broken down?"

Do I look like that big of a wreck? She just smiled, not letting her fear get the best of her. "No, thanks, I'm fine. Just waiting for a tow truck."

The man nodded and continued down the street towards Wilshire, followed by his buddies. One of them turned and looked at her. She noticed a blue and white Georgia Gamecocks jacket. She froze. Clearly, the man wasn't Sean Weller as he was stocky and had ginger hair. The man turned and hurried off with his group. Before she could ponder the coincidence of seeing a Georgia Gamecocks jacket in West L.A., Churchill's car rounded the corner, tires squealing. The car parked in the alley behind the office building. She ran over to his car and he quickly got out. "That GPS tracker I installed on your car works!" He smiled. "Oops, I wasn't going to let you know."

"Churchill! Have you been spying on me?"

"Just since this morning. I'm concerned about you and this open murder case." He looked at her car. "You're parked in a tow away zone."

"I know. I'm sorry, but I couldn't find a parking spot."

"It's okay, I'll make sure you don't get a ticket."

They walked over to her car and his expression grew serious when he saw the figure in the back seat. "CSI should be here any minute. But let me check..." Churchill pulled on a pair of latex gloves and opened the coupe's door. The overhead light illuminated the figure in the back seat and her iPhone fell out, clattering to the curb. Yolanda stepped over to the curb, but he blocked her just before she reached for it. "Sorry, it's now evidence. I'll get it back to you ASAP." He leaned inside and checked the pulse. He paused, then leaned closer and checked the neck and wrist. "There's a faint pulse. Must've hit his head on the side." He leaned back and pointed at the opposite wall. "He needs to get medical attention first. Then we need your statement."

****

An hour later, Yolanda finished writing out her statement and fingerprints were removed from her iPhone and it was returned to her. It was easily determined that the last call made was to Churchill.

"The man has no ID on him whatsoever," Churchill said. "He's at Santa Monica Memorial Hospital and is a person of interest. He'll be kept under guard overnight so if you could go in tomorrow morning and see if he looks familiar, that'd be great."

She nodded, looking at her watch. "I've really got to get back home and feed the kitties. And maybe get some sleep."

****

Yolanda returned home. She carefully looked around. Nothing unusual was occurring. The security lights were working. Her next-door neighbor's lights were on. It seemed as if every room was lit up. The living room window was covered with a haphazardly hung bed sheet. She saw three people moving a large piece of furniture.

"Neighbors, as in plural," she said softly, unlocking her kitchen door. "I should make a welcome to the neighborhood gift basket

181

for them. I still have plenty of macarons and cookie stacks. I hope they keep the rosebushes nice...Mrs. Steele always took such good care of them."

She stepped inside her kitchen, flipping on the light, looking around, ever cautious. From her bedroom ran the meowing cats. A quick glance to her left and she saw a pair of empty food bowls. "I'm so sorry, kitties," she said as she headed over to the counter and opened the cupboard, grabbing a can of cat food and popping it open. She scooped the food into the bowls as Miss Chef and Mr. Whisker went to their respective bowls and began chowing down. "Now I have to look around..."

Yolanda's pepper spray was in her left hand and her iPhone in her right hand as she walked around her house checking to make sure the doors and windows were closed and locked and that no one was hiding anywhere.

Returning to the kitchen, she found the container of treats and doled out a handful to each still hungry feline. There were intermittent meows and purrs and Miss Chef nuzzled her leg before finishing her treat.

She checked her texts. Churchill said he'd be sending a patrol car to check out the area every hour or two. She smiled in relief and sent him a thank you and he replied that the mysterious man in room 304 at Santa Monica Memorial Hospital had an identity: Emerson Northman of Tacoma, Washington. She sent her last text, put the phone back in her purse, and headed down the hall to her bedroom. The cats followed her. "You know, I haven't even had dinner tonight. I got carjacked. Needles to say, it's been a heckuva fun night!" She lay down on her bed and didn't bother removing her clothing or sliding beneath the covers. She fell asleep and slept through the night.

CHAPTER 9

Sunlight streamed through the bedroom window and Yolanda sat up, puzzled about being fully dressed and lying on her bed without having removed her shoes. Her iPhone was beeping, and she knew there were probably several messages and the fact that it was 8:00.

Eight o'clock in the morning! What day was it?

Yolanda pulled off her jacket and ran into the bathroom. "Wait, I need a new shirt," she muttered. "I'll take a bird bath and then call in." Two hungry cats had followed her inside and were staring at her intently as they meowed in their breakfast order. "Um, I'll feed you guys, call in, and wash up."

****

The day was bright and sunny, and the temperature was in the mid-60s. Yolanda parked her car behind the yummery and she dashed inside past Rusty who was returning from his morning smoke break across from the dancewear store. "Hey Miss Yolanda, good to see you," he said.

"Good to be here, Rusty." She nodded and ran into the shop. "I'm so grateful to you, BB, Quinn, Crystal and Jeannie. I don't know how I could run this place without you guys."

He followed her inside. "Yeah and Nick and Teagan showed up around an hour ago. Jeannie called 'em. She's really worried…"

Jeannie met Yolanda just as the young woman reached her office. Yolanda was about to unlock the door when Jeannie stepped over and gave her a hug. "I'm so sorry, Yolanda. That nice Detective Churchill came by and inquired about you. He said you had a rough night."

Yolanda nodded as she pulled away from the motherly employee. "Um, yeah, that's one way of putting it. Did he…"

"You can ask him yourself." Jeannie stepped aside as the detective pushed aside the fabric covering and greeted her. "I hope you're doing better today, Yolanda," he said.

"Thanks, I am. I completely crashed when I got home. Didn't even take off my shoes. I can't remember the last time that happened."

"I understand only too well. Now do you want to come to the hospital with me or do you want to drive? It should only take about an hour – maybe less."

"Hospital? Who's sick?" Jeannie asked, a worried look crossing her features.

"We may have a suspect," the detective replied. "Yolanda, are you ready?"

She nodded and followed him out the back way. "You drive, detective. I have a lot of work to do when I get back and maybe you can put the light on and return even faster than I could." She grinned at the man.

****

They stood next to a handsome young police officer with a name tag that read Fernandez. "Detective Churchill! Emerson Northman just had breakfast."

"Good. Okay, Yolanda, let's hear what he has to say."

"Thank you, Fernandez." He nodded at the slender police officer.

Inside the small room, the suspect was sitting up in bed with a bandage covering the right side of his head, tufts of curly dark hair sticking out. He was about the same age as Yolanda and had a broad forehead and high cheekbones. She stopped as she entered the room and focused on the man's face. There was something familiar about him. She had seen him before in the yummery? Or was it somewhere else? The light reflecting from the open shades flooded the room, emphasizing his features.

"Are you on TV, Mr. Northman?"

He shook his head, eyes and lips narrowing. His posture straightened and he seemed very tense when he looked at her.

He's in police custody and he's just been injured, she thought. *It's not like I'm meeting him at a party.*

"You look familiar. What's your favorite dessert?"

He glanced at the detective, then back at Yolanda. "Huh?"

"Are you an appreciated guest at the yummery? Do you like the cookies or brownies or..."

There was a ghost of a smile on his lips. "Appreciated guest? Yummery? You're weird. I don't like sugary foods. They're not healthy."

"Yolanda makes some of the best energy bars in the world," Churchill interjected. "Especially the lemon coconut energy bars. They're very healthy."

"I wouldn't know about a...a yummery?" The man's smile revealed his natural handsomeness.

"Dude, you carjacked me outside of my yummery last night."

The man shook his head. "I don't know what the hell you're talking about. All I know is that I was hit on the head, and I can't remember a thing." He gently touched the bandage but the IV pulled on his arm and he let it fall to his side.

Churchill rolled his eyes and shook his head. "That's what they all say. I've seen this scenario play out a hundred and one times. Of course, once you're in the courtroom, you'll suddenly remember a few things so you can plea bargain. But I know about your record, Mr. Northman, I know about what happened in Seattle last July and how you had to skip town."

"It was never proven!" the young man shouted.

'Yes it was. You just got lucky. But carjacking is a very serious crime. Under California Penal Code section 215, carjacking is a felony carrying a prison sentence of up to nine years."

The man's eyes widened, and he looked down at the bed. "So?"

"So? Carjacking is a 'strike' under the three strikes law. That means you have to serve at least eighty-five percent of your sentence before you're eligible for parole. So, it's a very serious crime. And you should be grateful that Yolanda wasn't injured."

"Yeah, but I am. Look at my head. It got banged up pretty bad."

"It wouldn't have happened if you hadn't gotten into my car and carjacked me. And how did you get into it?"

He shrugged his broad shoulders. "Me no speaka English."

"Yolanda, do you recognize this jerk?" Churchill's face was reddening and he clenched his fists.

Yolanda stared at the man. "I wish I could place him. I know I've seen him and I know I've seen him on this side of town, if that helps."

"A restaurant? A bar? A coffee shop?"

"No, but it had something to do with food. It wasn't a bar, though I did go to that party in Marina del Rey for the restaurant opening. What was the name? Oh, the Fish and the Hook. Maybe that's where I saw him."

Northman just grinned at her.

She looked at the man and then down at her watch. "Detective, I have so much work to do today. Look, I'm not sure, I want to help, you know I do. But ..." she reached into her purse and fished out her iPad. "This takes better pictures." She adjusted the device and aimed it at the bedridden young man. Two clicks later, a brief pause and she moved to another area of the room with the sunlight behind her. She took some more photos. "Thanks, dude," she remarked as she tapped the button a final time and returned the iPad to her purse. "I'll edit these and send them to you, detective. I'll figure out who he is and where I've seen him."

"Good luck, babe," the man in the hospital bed smiled at her and began licking his lips.

"Same to you." She looked at Churchill and smiled. "I'll see you later, detective." She started to walk to the door.

"How are you planning to get back to work? Take the bus?"

****

Yolanda gulped down a strawberry energy bar, yanked on the oven mitt and pulled a tray of oatmeal raisin cookies from the oven and onto the rack. "Where on earth is Suzie?" she asked. "Wasn't she hired to make macarons?" Rusty finished boxing up some macarons. "Wait a minute..." She dashed into her office, yanking off the mitt and leaving it on the counter. Sitting in front of her computer, she hastily typed out a few lines on her Word program. Printing it out, she returned to the kitchen. "I mean, why couldn't she have called up and said she wasn't coming in?"

"Maybe she forgot," Rusty replied.

Yolanda shrugged. "Well, I've either got to replace her or...let me check with Jeannie and BB to see if she called the main line. I know there's nothing on my private voicemail."

She strode out to the cash wrap and watched as Jeannie waved at a silver-haired businessman carrying a large bag. "Now don't forget to wish Edna a happy anniversary," the older woman said.

The man gave her a big grin and before he could answer, his cell phone went off, filling the area around him with a loud polka ringtone.

Yolanda smiled, "Jeannie, you just have the best way with all the appreciated guests."

"Yolanda, I enjoy being here."

"Well, it certainly shows. By the way, I was wondering if either you or BB heard from Suzie today. Did she call the main line?"

BB put the last of the raspberry chocolate cupcakes in the display case.

"Nope. She didn't call but she showed up for about two hours and made some macarons. She left before you got here, and she was really upset about something."

"She was?" The yummery owner shook her head. "I know I was late opening the store and I didn't want to announce it to everyone why I was late. Um, let's just say I had a kinda unbelievable evening and when I got home I completely crashed. I hope to tell you the story one day but until Mike's case is solved I just can't."

"Oh hon, there's no need to apologize," Jeannie said, patting Yolanda on the shoulder. She saw a pair of middle-aged women sitting at a nearby table and knew that was the reason that her boss wasn't saying anything revealing. Both were gaunt, and like so many Angelenos, their hair wasn't the natural color they were born with. One had bright red locks that contrasted nicely with her green turtleneck dress. The platinum blonde in a fuzzy white sweater was listening as she stared at her tablet and the red velvet cupcake was held in her hand, unmoving. Jeannie had learned all about body language as a forty-year veteran of working in offices filled with a variety of personality types. The redhead was also more involved in her tablet than her decadent chocolate cupcake.

Yolanda nodded and went over to the shelves displaying the boxed macarons and cookie stacks. "I have some new neighbors...I'll be making them a welcome gift basket. But I better see how many baskets we have first because I don't want to run out."

"Did your neighbor pass?" Jeannie asked.

"No, her family sent her to an assisted living center, so she'd get 'round the clock care." Yolanda sighed. "She'd moved into her house around the same time my grandparents moved into theirs." She paused on the way back to the kitchen. "I haven't met the new neighbors yet." She glanced at the white sweatered woman at the table and wondered how much was overheard. The front door opened and in walked her father. She beamed upon seeing him and appreciated his impeccable timing. "Dad!" She went around the counter and as soon as she reached her father, they hugged each other. "So good of you to show up."

He was still smiling as he pulled away, and then a look of surprise crossed his features. "You're not wearing an apron!"

She looked down at her pink polo shirt and black jeans. "New dress code," she said. Leaning closer she whispered, "Um, can we talk outside?"

He nodded. "I'll get that box from my car."

"Okay. Let me help you with it." She followed him out of the yummery. The pair swiftly walked over to his blue Prius parked in the middle of the parking lot. They got into his car, and he peered over at her. "Shoot straight with me, kiddo, what's up?"

"Are you going to England?"

He grinned. "That's what I was on my way in to tell you. I've got a flight that leaves tonight at six-thirty."

A look at the car's clock made her shake her head. "How will you get there in time?"

"I'll make it. If not, there's another flight at seven. So, tell me what's going on? I've never seen you not wear your apron at work."

"Dad, I can't go into detail right now. I hope Nigel's not a suspect. Maybe we found one today, I don't know ... you can never tell."

"You sound as cynical as me." He chuckled. "I'm hoping that detective friend of yours is keeping you in his sights."

"Yes, as a matter of fact, he is. He's even sending around a patrol car every hour or two."

"Good, I'm glad he's watching out for my little girl. Even if she's getting to be cynical."

"Well, I've also discovered I have new neighbors. They moved in last night."

"You don't say!" he shook his head. "She only went into the assisted living care place last month was it? I thought the housing market was soft..."

"Well, I don't know the whole story or even much of it. I just know that her daughter's in Pasadena and that's where the assisted living place is. I know nothing about these people. Other than the fact that they hung a bedsheet up in the living room window."

Frederick chuckled. "Now that's classy!"

"So, you really are going to London and check up on Nigel for me?"

The man nodded. "That I am. I have a return ticket scheduled for the twenty-fifth as I don't know how long I'll be there or what will happen. Maybe I'll be back sooner. I know it's imperative I'm back in time for your anniversary celebration."

"You know, ever since the yummery's opened my life's gotten really weird. I mean, I've been kidnapped, stalked, carjacked..."

"Carjacked? When?"

"Um, last night. The carjacker's in the hospital. It's okay, Dad."

"Yolanda! Being carjacked is NOT okay! I thought that detective friend of yours was looking out for you."

"He is, Dad!"

"Whatever next? Well, I'm going to do my best to make sure that Nigel is or isn't the killer. I certainly hope he isn't. I also hope that he's being completely honest with you."

Yolanda stared at the windshield and nodded. "I know. It's sad that it's come to this, but I really need to know. I never would've thought that my dad would be a p.i.!"

"I'm a glass blower first, my dear. No wait, I'm a glass artisan. That's my title according to the *Laguna Beach News*."

She smiled, turned, and looked at her father. "I just can't thank you enough for doing this. And I wish I could go with you – under better circumstances. He invited me to spend Christmas with him. But I couldn't."

"I know that, dear. I also have this crazy idea in the back of my mind about a yummery in London! Didn't he say he wanted to open a chain of Beverage Bars?"

"I think he meant in America, but it'd make sense to have some in London as that's where his company is, right?"

In her mind, she saw Mr. Whisker frantically shaking his head.

"Ever since 1901. Nigel has a nice office here. A yummery in London? Wow, that'd be ... well, if I wanted to build another one

I'd want it to be in Beverly Hills or Santa Monica or Sherman Oaks. I have enough on my plate keeping the small section in the Santa Monica Beverage Bar stocked, I can't really think about a second full size shop."

"I know, you're only one person. But it's all about hiring the right people and so far you've done that, Yolanda."

She shook her head. "I'm not so sure about Suzie. She left early and didn't even tell me about it."

"That's a strange woman from what you've told me about her," he said.

"Yeah, the temperamental artist type."

"Thanks, kiddo, I'm an artist."

"You're not that temperamental. And it's not like she's a teenager like Nick or even BB. Heck, they have a better work ethic than she does. Nick's called in sick once and BB hasn't ever…so I don't know what's wrong with Suzie other than the fact that she must've been really sick to leave without warning."

"Keep in mind that some people don't work well with others. You said she was co-owner of a patisserie in San Francisco that went under? Then a show online and she's been making those cookies for several years?"

Yolanda nodded.

"Right, so she's used to being in charge. And now she's suddenly not. Plus, her boss is someone young enough to be her daughter. If you look at it from her point of view, well, it's hard for someone her age to accept that. It'd be like if my business went bust and I had to work for a glass artisan that was in their late twenties. It'd be hard for an old fart like me."

She giggled. "Dad, you're not an old fart!"

"Easy for you to say. I have another reason I want to go to London, especially by myself...well, I was there once before I met your mother. It was in the eighties. Things were different back then. Maybe part of me wants to go there to get in touch with my past, remember what it was like to spend six months there, just bumming around and meeting people. Sleeping in youth hostels, heck, I had the student card and could ride BritRail for half off. Being a student meant big discounts. And back then I really needed 'em." He reached over and hugged her. "I'll miss you, daughter. Make sure you call your mom every day and stop by and see her at least once while I'm gone. Well, unless I get all my answers right away and am back in a day or two!"

****

Just as she was returning to the yummery, her cell phone rang. She saw who it was and smiled.

"Hey Win."

"Hey Yo., I need to warn you that Emerson Northman was released from the hospital and as soon as he got to jail he was bailed out. There will be a unit in the area again. I don't have to tell you to be super careful."

"Win, thanks for the warning. I really appreciate that." The call ended and Yolanda went into the walk-in fridge, gathering up strawberry and chocolate cupcakes along with an apple pie. Back in her office, she set the big basket on her desk and rummaged in the bottom drawer for a bag of multi-colored crinkle shred. Finding one in the yummery's pastel shades, she tore it open and spread it on the bottom. Suddenly, she flipped on her iPad's audio feature and cleared her throat. "Ideas for yummery – gift wrapping/boxing, gift baskets and shipping. Also need to update the website to have this feature. It'll increase business and visibility. Will have to hire people just for the mail order side. This can also work with the Beverage Bar, especially the coffee cakes and any additional coffee beans or ground coffee, etc. Will consult with Nigel about this."

She flipped off the switch and soon the festive basket was filled with macarons, oatmeal raisin cookies and a six-pack of cupcakes. She added clear cellophane and tied the top with a grosgrain ribbon. "This needs a card." She opened the center desk drawer and found a box of note cards in the yummery's colors and quickly added a welcome message and signed her name.

Yolanda attached the card, then stepped back, admiring her handiwork.

She picked up the basket and walked into the kitchen just as Rusty was returning from a late afternoon delivery. He was wreathed in the stench of cigarette smoke and had she not been carrying the basket; she would have fanned the stinky air in front of her. She merely grinned at him, breathing through her mouth.

"Hey Miss Yolanda, want me to help you with that?"

"Thanks, Rusty, that'd be great. Please take it out to my car and put it on the floor in the back. I'll get my keys."

She hurried back to her office and pulled her keys out of her purse, which was stashed in the bottom desk drawer. "Here you go and thanks again," she said, rushing out to the counter area to help close for the day.

****

It was well after nightfall when Yolanda returned home. Again, the house next door was showing off all its inside lights and the lower-level picture windows were now covered with white-lined draperies.

She eagerly stepped out of her car. The sight of a black and white cruiser driving by was further reassurance. She reached into the backseat, lifting the gift basket. Shutting the door with her foot, she made certain the alarm was set and closed the garage door behind her, heading into the house.

There was enough food in the bowls but a quick glance inside the cupboard revealed that the treats were almost gone. "Okay, kitties, tonight I'm going to make you a fresh batch of chicken treats." The meows of her two cats were louder than usual and she knew they understood what she just said. "But first, I'm going to meet the new neighbors. I hope they like cats!"

She retrieved the basket and her keys, locking the kitchen door behind her. The patrol car cruised down the other side of the street and she smiled in the direction of the officers in the car. *Good old Winston,* she thought, heading up the walkway toward the former Steele residence.

Mrs. Steele had maintained the large Cape Cod-style house nicely on the outside, especially taking care of the numerous rose bushes and other flowers that flourished under her care. It had been a couple of years since Yolanda had been inside the home and she recalled the well varnished hardwood flooring and the knickknack filled living room. In her younger years, Mrs. Steele enjoyed crocheting doll clothing and the shelves along the wall boasted dozens of Barbie dolls in colorful frilly dresses with matching floppy hats.

Yolanda paused before ringing the doorbell. *Suppose they don't want to meet anyone just after moving in?* The basket was growing heavier in her arms and she thought about just setting it on the front porch and leaving. There was a card inside so it wouldn't be anonymous.

She tentatively rang the doorbell, shifting the weight of the basket so it rested against her hip. She heard muffled footsteps on the floor—the person was wearing shoes or there were rugs on the floor. The light above the door illuminated the large cement porch with the railing separating a deep pink cabbage rose bush.

"Hello?" A tall sandy-haired man wearing a soiled T-shirt and cargo pants flung the door open. His face changed as he smiled upon seeing Yolanda and the gift basket. "I'm speechless," he declared.

The sound of heavy footwear grew closer and Yolanda was expecting to see a man due to the noise. Instead, a middle-aged woman wearing high-top sneakers, almost shoved her husband aside to see the unexpected visitor. "My goodness, is that for us?" The woman's eyes widened upon seeing the large basket filled with the prettily packaged sweets. "You must be Yolanda Yummery!"

"Well, I'm Yolanda Carter of Yolanda's Yummery...but close enough! I live right next door."

"Please excuse my husband's manners and come into our disorganized home! My name's Bunnie Davenport and this is Big Jake Davenport."

Yolanda stepped inside and handed the basket to the man who carried it over to a modular naked wood table at the edge of the foyer. The couple stood in front of the basket for a moment, admiring it. Bunnie gently picked up the envelope, lifted the flap and removed the colorful card. She smiled upon reading the short message.

"I love the colors of the yummery," Bunny said, noting the pink, yellow and mint striped box. She handed it to her husband.

"Thanks, I really like pastels," Yolanda noted, watching as the woman's rough looking reddened hands opened the basket. *I wish I'd added a bottle of lotion*, Yolanda thought.

Bunnie impatiently ripped through the cellophane and reached for the striped box with the grosgrain ribbon, quickly untying it. She paused for an instant before lifting the lid, noting the dozen macarons inside. "I love macarons, don't you honey?" She pulled out a chocolate one and bit into it, chewing it quickly, and jamming the whole thing into her mouth. She closed her eyes as she enjoyed the macaron.

"You likin' it dear?" The man looked at the remaining eleven macarons and selected a pale blue with dark specks of vanilla beans. Before she could answer, he bit into half the macaron and shook his head. "Wowsers!" Another bite and it was gone, and the couple stared at the box of remaining macarons.

"Dear, I think we'll have to ration these!" Bunnie said as she put the lid back on them. "Plus, Yolanda gave us a package of cookies and another box....and I spy a box of cupcakes!"

"Yolanda, you sure know how to throw a welcome party in a basket," Big Jake commented.

She giggled. "It's no big deal I'm happy to have neighbors. Mrs. Steele was really nice and friendly but the past few months I hadn't seen much of her."

Bunnie picked up the six-pack of cupcakes. "I need to put these in the fridge, so I don't eat them all tonight. Along with everything else."

Big Jake reached inside and picked up the pink box, opening the lid. The chocolate mint brownies caught his attention and he stared at it as he bent over to inhale the aroma. "I can't think of a better flavor than chocolate mint," he said.

Yolanda giggled. "I guess I got lucky and picked the right flavor. I only had that or chocolate peanut butter."

Bunnie returned to the foyer. "Did I hear chocolate peanut butter?"

Yolanda asked, "Do you like chocolate peanut butter?"

"Is the sky blue?"

"Well, actually not in the Valley it can be tinged with brown," Yolanda said. "Sorry, hope I didn't disillusion you. Are you from around here?"

Bunnie shook her head. "No, we're from Flagstaff and before that a tiny town in New Hampshire by the name of Endicott. But that's where I learned how to make and refurbish bar and serving carts, which is why I'm the owner of Bunnie's Bar & Serving Carts."

"That's right. I restore cars from the 1960s through the 80s."

"That's cool. My dad used to have a Camaro when I was a kid."

"The Z/28 Camaro was born on June 28, 1966, and the best Camaros..."

"Big Jake, I think Yolanda's trying to stay awake and probably doesn't want to hear about the birth of the Camaro," Bunnie remarked.

Yes! Thank you so much! Yolanda thought, as she smiled with relief. "But I didn't want to interrupt you as I imagine you have a lot of unpacking to do and..."

"Oh, we got a big chunk of it done today," Bunnie said.

"I want you to know that I do most of my car and engine rebuilding at a warehouse in Van Nuys. But I'll be storing some of my cars and parts here. I'm setting up a small tent in the backyard tomorrow, but you'll never even know it's there. Plus, we have a three-car garage. Well, your kind former neighbor had the foresight to have room for three cars, but I really have three cars – and then some!"

There was an old-fashioned ringing sound of a phone and Big Jake turned and rushed out of the room, his heavy footsteps thudding on the floor.

Yolanda kept her grin on as she played the part of the good neighbor. As she turned to the front door, a turquoise cart near a side window caught her attention. The lines were sleek, and the chic cart had two large wheels with shiny antique gold spokes. Two mirrored trays looked like they'd just been cleaned and she imagined how they'd look holding her father's glass cake stands filled with her goodies.

"Could you make this in pink or yellow with three glass trays?"

"Yes, I could. That would look so beautiful. I have a new part time helper who only works with bamboo and other hardwoods. He's a real craftsman. He'll be here tomorrow and will work from two to eight or nine. Actually, if you can stop by tomorrow evening I'll have all my samples unpacked along with my catalogue. Right now, I'm trying to get my paperwork organized for my new office. I'm so looking forward to being able to work out of my house."

Yolanda nodded. "Cool. That's a huge advantage. The only thing I can bake out of my house is my own food and my cat treats. Speaking of which, I have two cats that are looking forward to me baking more as they've just run out."

"My Percy would probably love them. He's asleep upstairs. He has his own special bed that I made for him. Percy's a real sweetie and I hope you and your two kitty cats all get to meet soon!"

"I do too," Yolanda said as she edged over to the front door. "It was so great meeting you, Bunnie, and make sure you tell that to your husband. I mean that I'm happy to meet him."

"I will, dearie," the woman said as she waved at Yolanda. "And I'll drop off a catalogue in your mailbox tomorrow or as soon as I find one!"

****

Yolanda returned home and closed the door behind her, making sure it was locked. Removing her coat, she hung it up on a wooden hanger in the closet along with hanging her purse on a peg on the back wall where it was out of sight. "Okay, kitties, I'm making your treats now. Our new neighbors have unique names – Bunnie and Big Jake. They also have a cat named Percy but I didn't meet him."

Both cats stared at her. Mr. Whisker broke eye contact and looked at his empty bowl, nudging it with his right paw. He softly meowed as he sat on her foot, flicking his tail against her ankle.

"Meow to you. Right, I'll get you guys some regular hard food and then I'll make your treats. I think tuna and chicken combo this time?"

Miss Chef's chirpier response made her giggle. "I get the hint, little girl!" After filling their bowls, Yolanda went over to the cabinet and pulled out the einkorn flour and a small bag of organic brown rice. She reached inside the cabinet and removed a can, glancing at the label. "Pork? How did this get here? I know I bought tuna." Yolanda opened the other cabinet and looked around. Then she hoisted herself up on the counter and checked the shelves, moving cans and bottles, searching for the canned tuna. She jumped down and shut the doors. "Well, looks like I gotta go to the store. But I better make sure I have enough eggs." Yolanda opened the fridge and saw the transparent plastic egg container was almost full of brown and pale green eggs.

Yolanda went over to the closet and yanked her coat off the hanger, flipping it onto the floor with a clatter. Sighing, she bent down to retrieve it and put it back on the rod. She grabbed her purse and pulled on her coat, not bothering to button it. "My day never ends," she grumbled. "I'll be back

ASAP. With tuna and a baked chicken because I don't have time to bake a whole chicken for us now."

Ten minutes later, Yolanda pulled her car beneath a light pole near the supermarket. Aware of her surroundings, she looked around just after closing her car door and making sure it was locked with an extra click of her remote keyless entry fob. As she was about to step up to the curb outside the supermarket, a car sped by, almost hitting her. She leaned forward and a uniformed security guard emerged from the shopping cart storage area. He stood next to her as she shakily watched the car making a sharp turn out of the parking lot.

"Miss are you okay?" the older man asked.

She nodded, still staring in the direction the car had just taken. "Um, yeah..." she felt for her purse and her keys. The key ring had fallen to the asphalt.

The security guard noticed and retrieved them for her. "Thanks, thank you very much," she sighed with relief as she clutched the ring of keys in her hand. Keys that kept the places she loved safe: her home and her yummery. A key to her parents' front door in their Laguna Beach home. She wondered what her father was doing in London. She smiled at the uniformed man and went inside the large store, grabbing a shopping basket for the few items that she was going to purchase.

A man in a quilted jacket brushed past as she strode by the beer-filled end cap near the paper product aisle. Was he out to get her? She shook her head, marveling at how paranoid she was behaving in the big, overly bright store.

"Excuse me, miss are you the one who was on *America's Best Bakeries*?" A polo shirt-wearing stock clerk in his late teens was staring at her with wide eyes.

She nodded, feeling a rush of pleasure at being recognized in a positive way. "Yes, I work at Yolanda's Yummery," she said. It wasn't admitting she owned the place, but his reaction was only focused on the yummery and not the murder.

"Cool. I need to go there sometime. I wish there was one in the Valley."

"Maybe there will be," she said. After all, she lived in the Valley. The idea of one in London seemed inconceivable—especially since she'd never even been to the U.K.

She smiled as she went down the canned foods aisle and found that there was a sale on albacore tuna along with the standard tuna. She grabbed several cans, and the basket was a lot heavier.

The next aisle contained pet food. Her backup plan was to also stock up on some organic salmon goodies and a small bag of catnip which would either be added to the treats she made or sprinkled on their standard food occasionally.

On her way to pay for her cats' food items, she suddenly stopped in front of the almost empty heated display case housing a lone rotisserie chicken. *I wonder how long this's been sitting out here.* Reluctantly, she picked it up and put it into the hand basket.

A man in a brown bomber jacket cut in front of her at the only open lane. He carried a shopping basket that contained a bunch of green bananas and a jar of peanut butter. He was chattering on his Bluetooth in a language she didn't recognize and was intent on his conversation, ignoring both her and the cashier. After he paid for his items, he quickly departed, and she watched him stride out of the store.

Yolanda unloaded her items on the conveyor belt and smiled at the cashier with gray hair and round black eyeglasses. "No one even knows I'm here anymore; this might as well be one of those self-checkout stands," the cashier said.

Yolanda looked at the older woman with the gnarled hands and the hunched posture. She nodded. "I know what you mean. I work in retail and see it a lot."

"I've worked in this store for thirty-two years. Never used to be like this with people looking like space aliens with antennas sticking out of their ears. Or those little cell phones that they talk on constantly. I feel like I'm invisible." The older woman scanned the items and told Yolanda the total.

Yolanda handed the woman the correct amount of money in cash.

"And I'm seeing less and less of this too," the cashier droned on. "Nowadays it's debit or credit. And it used to only be paper bags but now it's more and more plastic and customers have to pay for them, too."

She felt the sadness of the cashier and wondered how much longer the woman would work there. As she reached forward to help bag her items, a young bagger sauntered up and finished the job in about as much time as it would have taken the cashier. He shoved the bag in her direction, not even bothering to pick it up. Yolanda took it and walked out of the store.

Once next to her car, she looked around and didn't see anyone nearby, only a couple getting out of a truck near a fast-food restaurant at the other end of the parking lot. She put her bag on the front seat and looked inside first, not wanting a repeat performance of last night's craziness.

Inside her locked car, she started the engine when her cell phone gave off its mom-coded signal: a lively calypso tune.

"Hey Mom," she said.

Silence.

"Mom? You there?" She was looking around her, brow furrowed. "Mom?"

A beeping noise, like buttons being pushed on a cell phone.

"Yolanda?" Abby whispered.

"Mom? I can barely hear you!"

"Yolanda, call 911. There's..." the call was disconnected. A frantic beeping noise pulsated in her ear and she slammed the phone down on the seat. She was about to drive out of the parking lot, when she retrieved the phone and hit the speed dial number for her mother. It rang five times and went to voicemail. "Mom, let me know you're okay. Call me back ASAP. Meanwhile, I'll call 911 and then I'll call Dad." She disconnected and dialed the three digits.

After the greeting, the male 911 operator asked for her location. "It's not me, it's Abby Carter, my mom on 223 Sunny Glen Drive in Laguna Beach. She didn't state her emergency but told me to call because she's in trouble. I know I'm not giving you a lot of info but that's all she told me. It's not a joke, if she called she's in serious trouble."

She operator assured her that he'd have a police officer there ASAP.

Yolanda exited the parking lot and drove west on Ventura. Ahead of her was a long drive down to Orange County, one she'd made countless times, but never under such terrifying circumstances. Ignoring the law by using her cell phone when driving, she dialed Churchill's number. She got his voicemail.

"Churchie, I've just called 911 but I'm calling you in case this has something to do with Mike's murder. My mom called me like five minutes ago and told me to call 911. I could barely hear her because she was talking so softly. There's something seriously wrong. Her address is 223 Sunny Glen Drive. Laguna Beach. I'm on Ventura about a mile from Sepulveda and I'm on my way there. Let me know when you get this. Bye."

Running a yellow light, she continued west on the busy street. She punched in her father's number. "C'mon Dad, I know it's early in the morning for you but please...." It rang three times and her father picked up, his voice jolly.

"Darling, good to hear from you! It's almost six a.m. but I've been up for an hour and I..."

"Dad, did you hear from Mom?"

"Of course I did. We talked last night. She's doing fine. In fact, she was discussing the line of stoneware that..."

"Dad, she just called and was whispering. Jeez, I can't remember the last time she whispered. But she told me to call 911 and then we were disconnected and when I called back it went right to voicemail."

"You called 911?"

"Of course. I told them what I told you because that's all I know. They're sending the police there ASAP. I also left Churchie a message and told him I'm on my way."

"Yolanda, with all the problems you're having lately I want you to be extra careful."

"Yes, Dad, I am."

"I mean it, kiddo. I may be 6,000 miles away, but I am going to be back tonight. I mean tomorrow. As soon as I hang up I'm booking a ticket on the next westward bound flight."

"Okay, Dad. Good thing you've got your car at the airport. I hope to heck that Mom's okay..." the signal disappeared for a few seconds, and she had to slow the car down as an SUV in front of her suddenly was flashing red taillights. "Okay, Dad..."

"You still there?"

"Yeah, but traffic's getting heavy as I'm about to get on the 405. Love ya Dad."

"Love you, Yolanda."

The call was disconnected and not five minutes after merging onto the 405, she heard Celtic music. She shook her head. Why was Nigel calling now? What happened between her father and Nigel? She was tempted to answer the phone, but her priority was to get to her mom's house fast.

****

As soon as she drove down Sunny Glen Drive and saw the darkened house on the right, her chest tightened, and her mouth was drier than if it was stuffed with cotton balls. Something was wrong. Instead of parking in the driveway, she backed her car up and parked on Vista del Mar, the small cross street that curved its way into a dead-end overlooking the ocean. The name literally translated as sea view.

Closing the door, she pocketed her cell phone and buttoned her coat against the bracing night air. Yolanda wished she were there for a friendly visit along with a cup of herbal tea that her mother made. Tea was usually served in one of her batik-themed mugs that showed off Abby's design skills. Her latest project was batik-themed stoneware dish sets that would be launched in the spring. She was also going to make soap dishes and lotion dispensers for Heather's new shop for display and sales purposes.

Sunny Glen Drive was very quiet that night. Too quiet.

The house next door had a pair of outside security lights shining—it looked like Dr. Martinson and her husband were either not there or asleep for the night.

Yolanda noted the cottage across the street that was owned by Clark Riley, a widower. He was a retired travel agent. The septuagenarian took advantage of heavily discounted airline and hotel rates in various European and Asian countries. Some lights shone from inside the house so it was likely that he was at home. Or a house sitter was doing their job.

Yolanda approached her parents' house, looking around for any sign of activity. No sign of the local police. A glance at her watch made her wonder where Churchill was when she called him. Or what he was doing? *He's a detective, dummy. He has other cases...the detective even took time off sometimes.*

Approaching the front door, she paused, inhaling sharply, nervous about what was or wasn't behind that door. She was gripping her key ring and was searching for the door key when a loud noise made her jump. She didn't know what it was or if it was coming from inside the house or in the back. Rushing down the sidewalk and near the garage area, she saw it was empty. Usually, one of the cars was parked in the driveway to show that someone was home. As the Prius was at a Long-Term parking lot near LAX, that left the VW Bug in the garage. Well, her mother drove it occasionally, but when there was hauling of equipment or products then the Prius was used. To the right was the small backyard with the standard kidney-shaped pool that was popular back in the 1980s when the house was built. Her mother used it a few times a week to swim laps. The sliding back door opened to reveal the ceramic tile patio and the pool. She didn't recognize the black van parked in front of the sliding door. The door was open, allowing the cool night air inside the house. That sight frightened her. Abby was cold-blooded and kept the windows and doors shut at night.

"Mom!" Yolanda rushed inside the house, noting Carson, the orange tabby, streaking past her, heading for a hiding place beneath a couch. She knew it was futile yet was unable to help herself as she looked in each silent room. Past the kitchen, was the U-shaped breakfast nook. The floor to ceiling French doors revealed a spectacular sea view. The doors were also open. *What on earth's going on?* Yolanda wondered. Turning around, dashing past the Viking six-burner range, noting a kettle on the front burner, she tested it for warmth. It hadn't been used in a while.

The house was dark—too dark. Going to the edge of the kitchen, she flicked on the light. Nothing happened. Power outage.

Was it just her parents' house or the whole neighborhood? She went back to the kitchen and over to the island where she fumbled through one of the drawers and pulled out a flashlight. She switched it on.

Another loud noise was heard, and it sounded like it was coming from upstairs. Yolanda raced through the foyer and up the curved staircase, her sneakers pounding on the hardwood steps and then on the hallway. A tufted wool rug muffled the noise for a second and then she stopped, realizing she was making too much noise in the cold and dark house, the only light being the shaky beam from the flashlight. She focused the light on the open door to her left—her parents' bedroom. Fumbling for the light switch, she flicked it on. Nothing happened. The yellow light picked up a few potted plants and the lingering aroma of an herbal candle that had recently been extinguished. Yolanda rushed into the room to check the walk-in closet and saw nothing unusual.

In the bathroom, she almost tripped over a bathmat on the tile floor. The beam played on the wrinkled bathmat, and she bent down to touch it, feeling the wetness. She must've just taken a bath...the light shone in the whirlpool tub and the cluster of candles near the corner gave off a primeval forest like aroma. Another clue was the lumpy looking bath towel – her mother always took the few extra seconds to hang up a towel on the wall-mounted towel bar. Why was it bulging out? She wanted to reach out and straighten it but that thought fled from her mind when she again heard that sharp, cracking sound. What was it and where was it coming from?

The guest room across the hall was empty due to the plan to remodel it. She stepped inside and looked in the closet stuffed with an array of batik garments. Running her hand across the dresses, T-shirts, and other items, everything appeared to be in order.

Yolanda left the room and went to the end of the hallway to her former bedroom. The door was closed. She opened it and flipped on the light switch as she had done countless times in the past. The overhead light remained dark. She shone the flashlight directly ahead of her where the twin size canopy bed stood. A heavily pillowed bed still loaded with stuffed animals and a few dolls. Her childhood greeted her. The floor was thickly carpeted, and the vanity was beneath a highset curtained window. To her left was a spacious cushioned window seat where she had read her books with the ocean as a backdrop. Going over to it, she looked outside the window, noting that the outside lights were on as well as the streetlight. *I guess it's just us*, she thought. There was no sign of her mother or anyone else in her room.

Another sharp, cracking sound was heard, and she looked around, the light dancing on the heavily pictured walls. Before she thought it was coming from upstairs but now it sounded like it was outside.

Yolanda hurried back downstairs, holding onto the railing and shining the light in front of her. There was only one more place to look for her mother inside the house – the basement/studio. Frederick Carter's studio was a block away in a small shop near the beach. He worked there and sold many of his creations there. He oftentimes would craft his glassware as the public watched him make the cake stands, glass sculptures, trays, cookie jars and even jewelry and beads. He adored his work and it showed. "There's no secret to changing the shape of glass...only patience," he often said.

The basement was warm and inviting as the batik and Pilates vibes emanated from the large subterranean room. Blond hardwood flooring had been installed and there were some thickly padded mats that were used by her mother for practice. A pair of oversized folding tables held stacks of fabrics; shelves and cubbyholes contained supplies. The newest shelving unit was stocked with assorted sizes of ceramic mugs, stoneware dishes, and coffee cups and saucers.

Abby Carter practiced and taught Pilates as well as made batik and tie-dye bags and clothing. Her business had expanded to include pillowcases, linen sheets, placemats, tablecloths, scarves, handbags, totes and clutches. A smaller workstation had been added for Cynthia, her part-time employee.

No sign of her mother in a place where she was known to spend up to fourteen hours a day. She raced back upstairs and decided to go out the front door. No one had used that entrance as the deadbolt was locked. She unlocked it, opened the door, stepping out of the dark house. A Laguna Beach Police Department [L.B.P.D.] SUV with flashing red and blue lights had arrived. A lone investigator was emerging from the vehicle, straightening his jacket.

"Ma'am, please excuse the delay in response time. Our system was down and I only just got the..."

She went over to him and stopped a few feet away, staring at the officer in dismay.

The husky man had partially zipped up his jacket and nodded at her as he smirked. "Well, if it isn't Yolanda Carter! We used to be in science class together."

"Alfred..." she leaned forward noting his name tag. "Alfred Drummond. Yeah, I remember. We had um, environmental science. Anyway, how are you?"

He ran his tongue over his lips and smiled showing off his straight but yellowing teeth. "Yolanda, I was good but seeing you has me feeling a lot better. I heard about you being on that bakery show. I hope they repeat it 'cause I was working when it was on."

"Um, yeah. I can get you a DVD of it. But right now, I'm really worried about my mom being missing. She called me and told me..."

Detective Winston Churchill's vehicle turned into the driveway and parked. The young man got out of his car and rushed over to her. She almost hugged him and realized she was still clutching the flashlight. "I'm so glad to see you. I checked the whole house but my mom's not there.

She was recently because the bathroom towel's wet."

"Yolanda, did you check the house? I mean the whole house like the attic, basement, and garage. Any back rooms or sheds on the property?"

"I checked the basement but not the attic or garage."

Officer Drummond nodded. "The house is dark. How'd you check?"

She held out the flashlight. "I used this."

"Yolanda, did you check the circuit breaker box?" Officer Drummond asked.

She shook her head and stared at the men. "Um, no, is that the fuse box that has all the electrical stuff?" Her face reddened.

"It's okay. I don't expect you to know that kinda stuff," the officer said, hiding his sneer. "It's the circuit breaker box and it might be in your garage or the basement or a hallway. It's a large rectangular metal box."

"Yeah, it's in the garage on the right. Near the bicycles."

"Okay, I'll check it," Drummond said as he walked up to the front door.

"Fine. It's to your right when you go inside."

"Thanks, I got this," he pulled out his flashlight and went into the Carter residence.

The detective smiled. "Good, he's getting the ball rolling. Let's visit the neighbors."

He looked at the house on the right. "Who are they?"

"Dr. Martinson and her husband Cole. I don't know if they're home or not."

"We'll find out soon enough."

A flagstone walkway was lined on both sides with desert plants and the amount of grass they had was minimal due to the serene rock garden that made up the front yard. Churchill rang the doorbell and there was nothing but silence.

"Guess that explains the lack of light," she said.

There was a shuffling noise followed by a thump. A few expletives were heard.

"I think Mr. Martinson's home," Yolanda remarked. "I think he's..."

The door was yanked open by a slender gray-haired man holding a half-full bottle of scotch. "What'd'ya want?"

"Excuse me sir, are you Mr. Martinson?"

The man was standing there holding his bottle behind him and weaving slightly. "Who're you?"

"My name is Detective Churchill from the L.A.P.D."

"I didn't do it!"

The detective raised an eyebrow. "You didn't do what, Mr. Martinson?"

The older man shook his head. "Nope. Not me. I didn't do it." He hiccupped and shakily brought the bottle up to his mouth, taking a large swig.

"Yessir, we're here to..."

Mr. Martinson squinted at Yolanda. "You look familiar."

"My name's Yolanda Carter and I'm the daughter of Abby Carter, your next-door neighbor. She's missing. We wanted to know if you've seen her."

The man leaned forward and squinted at her. "Carters—I know them!" He looked over his shoulder and extended the bottle to his right. "Neighbors. Good neighbors. Good people."

"Have you seen them—my mother or my father? Anyone next door?"

The drunken man closed his eyes and leaned backwards. His posture was shaky enough for the detective to rush forward and stand next to the man. Mr. Martinson leaned over, placing the bottle gently down on the slate floor of the foyer. Then he sat down on the floor and looked up at the pair. He grinned.

"Yeah, matter a fact I have."

"My mother or anyone else?"

His bloodshot eyes were wide open for a second, but he closed them and lay down. "I saw Abby and a van." He waved his arm above his head, but gravity pulled it back to the floor. "Night." Mr. Martinson's head rolled to one side, and he was still.

"I think he's passed out," the detective commented.

"There was a black van parked on the patio," she said.

"Why didn't you tell me that?" He yanked out his gun. "I'm gonna check it out. You stay here."

"No, this is my mother we're talking about. Let's go."

Detective Churchill shut the door behind them, and they hurried across the rock garden to the Carters' house. They approached the rear of the house from the other side, so they saw the front of the van. "Can I borrow your flashlight?" he whispered.

She handed it to him and watched as he shone it on the front of the van.

"It's old—late 90s," he noted as he memorized the plate number. "Just follow behind while we look."

He reached for the driver's side door and tried to open it, but the door was locked. Then he went around the other side and found out the passenger's side was also locked. He glanced at her and went to the back of the van to check the door, which he swung open. The flashlight played over the dark interior, highlighting its emptiness.

The detective shut the door and kneeled on the patio, then shone the light beam beneath the van as he peered down to have a look. A few seconds later, he stood up, shaking his head.

"Okay, let's check the house across the street. What's the owner's name?"

"Clark Riley. He's a retired travel agent who's never really retired. He's not there a lot."

"Great. I guess he leaves lights on when he's not here?" The detective led the way across the street to the neat little ranch house. There were two high wattage motion detector lights and a brightly shining picture window that either meant someone was home or pretending to be.

"Yeah, he usually has a house sitter, so he doesn't worry about security." She looked around. "I don't see an extra car. But it could be in the garage."

The detective approached the door with a faux Douglas fir wreath sporting a puffy red bow on the bottom. "Guess he doesn't bother to take down his Christmas decorations." Churchill rang the doorbell, and they heard the first few notes of *Jingle Bells*.

"Nope. Never," she said.

They waited long enough to hear the familiar tune comprised of various types of ringing bells. Yolanda was too concerned about her missing mother to appreciate the Christmas music.

The sound of breaking glass caused him to raise his gun as he crouched, assuming the ultra cautious posture of a seasoned detective searching for a potential kidnapping victim. He passed the bushes alongside the house, shining the flashlight in them as he made his way toward the origin of the noise.

It was a backyard patio only this was paved with red bricks and the yard was surrounded by a rustic wooden fence. A large Monterey cypress tree decorated with soft amber lights took up a portion of the yard along with native plants and shrubbery.

Shards of broken glass had fallen to the brick surface from a small window. The light beam picked up a lone golf ball that had rolled to a stop near the sliding glass door. He glanced at the green and white ball while she noticed the broken kitchen window. Then she saw the ball with the ABC logo and a palm tree motif. "It's Mom's!"

"Stay here, I'm going in," he whispered in her ear.

"I wanna go. This is MY mom."

"You're not paid by the L.A.P.D.. Now be a good girl and wait here."

After glaring at her, he walked over to the sliding glass door and tried pulling it open, but it was locked. His expression was tense as he stepped around the corner and looked for a side door but found nothing. As he stepped past the small bamboo grove, a figure leapt out and attacked him, knocking him onto the ground. His gun fell with him, landing an arm's length away in the middle of the greenery. He felt around for it but the attacker reached it first, grabbing it and pointing it at the detective.

Yolanda peered around the corner, seeing the man towering over Churchill as they were within the range of a security light. She noticed his Forest Mountain jacket, camouflage pants and hiking boots. *That's the man who attacked Quinn in the yummery.* Seeing Churchill in a position of weakness frightened her. The detective suddenly grabbed the man's knees and knocked him over, causing the gun to fire. She jumped back, startled by the earsplitting noise of gunfire, heart racing as she feared he'd been shot.

Just as she was approaching the men, Drummond raced over, his gun drawn. "Get back NOW!"

Startled, she stepped out of the way, unable to see the men.

Shouts rang out in the backyard. Yolanda froze, hiding behind a hedge, and she jumped in fright when the sliding glass door unexpectedly opened. Her mother was removing a piece of duct tape from her wrist. The woman slunk over, putting her finger to her lips. "Dear, let's go back home."

"Mom, are you okay?"

"I wouldn't want a repeat performance." She ran her fingers through her damp and messy hair. She glanced down at her mud splattered lime green pants. "Nor would I paint a design like this."

"It's natural, though," Yolanda said as Churchill rounded the corner.

"Are you ladies up to making a statement tonight? We had to hogtie him but...wait a sec..." Churchill ran back to the side of the house.

Drummond rushed over. "You can't go back to your house tonight, Mrs. Carter. That idiot tried to destroy your electrical panel by yanking out wires and pouring water on the floor right beneath it. It's a good thing Yolanda didn't go in there to check it out. I'll send my uncle over first thing in the morning to fix it. He's an electrician."

"Thank you very much. But I have to make sure my cat has enough food and water till morning."

****

Upon entering the West L.A. police station around midnight, Yolanda was glad her black coat hid her yummery attire, as she had no treats to dispense to the officers and staff members. She also had her mother with her, and the woman was shaken and exhausted from her kidnapping ordeal. "I just need to sleep," she declared more than once. Churchill gently informed her that it was just a written report, and her memory was at its strongest. As soon as she was done, she could go to Yolanda's house.

After writing their statements, Churchill hugged them. "You know we'll be doing our best to get this man convicted for a few decades, at least." He winked. "And I know Yolanda agrees with me. So, I'll be booking the interview room tomorrow at noon—think you can show up? Maybe bring one of your brownies with California walnuts? It might even speed up a confession of guilt!"

Yolanda chuckled. "I think I can manage that. But do you think the employees can handle some macarons, too?"

"*Oui, mademoiselle!*"

Churchill pointed to the file he was holding. "We've gotten some evidence on him already. Look at these."

Several monochromatic photos featured the man in the Forest Mountain jacket. They were prints from a video surveillance camera in the Brentwood Grove Shoppes parking lot focused on the storefronts. The clearest picture showed him entering the yummery. Inside the old gray pickup truck sat a woman wearing a black hoodie and large sunglasses. She was either very short or slumped down in the seat.

"We've tried zooming in to ID the driver but that's as good as it gets. She wasn't interested in being onscreen. The plates are from a stolen car," Churchill said.

"That figures," she remarked.

"That's how it goes sometimes, my cynical friend!"

Yolanda looked at the clock on the wall. "Maybe I'm a little tired due to being up since dawn. And I've got another big day ahead of me. My dad's supposed to be back but mostly, I want my mom to be able to rest."

Churchill nodded, his greenish gray eyes staring intently into hers for a few seconds. She felt his genuine concern and smiled. "I didn't mean to complain, it's just..."

"You're exhausted. Your mother was kidnapped. I get it."

"Thank you, Churchie."

CHAPTER 10

At sunrise, Abby Carter walked into Yolanda's kitchen and turned the stove on to warm up the teakettle. The woman had changed into a roomy velour warm-up suit and wore plush slippers that her daughter had provided. The room was silent as the cats were still asleep with Yolanda. Abby pulled out two tea bags and put them in the mugs.

Just as the water boiled, the door opened, and Yolanda and her cats walked down the hallway.

"Good morning, Mom. It's so nice to see you here. What's for breakfast?" she laughed. "Just kidding."

"Not just kidding we need to eat especially after that ordeal. Did you want me to get breakfast at Du-par's? Or I can make a spinach and cheese omelet?"

"Mom, I can make an omelet. But I don't know if I have any spinach. Let me feed these guys first."

Yolanda went to the cabinet to pull out the cat food. "Darn, I still have to make cat treats. Well, at least I have some store-bought ones but I think these fussy cats won't like 'em as much."

"They'll appreciate yours even more when you make them."

"I suppose." She poured the food into the bowls. Mr. Whisker and Miss Chef quickly began eating.

"I've got to get back so the electrician can fix the fuse box. Then I'll see how much food will have to be replaced, hopefully not much. Of course, Carson will need more food and I'll put the heat on because it's cold again today. Oh, and your dad should be back by eleven."

"Yeah, I won't see him till this afternoon. I want to be there when he interviews the suspect. Hopefully, he'll confess and then he'll be locked up for so long he won't be kidnapping and doing whatever else he's done to make him such a moron."

"He's very angry and confused," Abby said as the water began to boil.

"Mom, you're so calm about it. I'd be really freaked out."

"Well, it's something that took me years to learn. When I was your age, I would've freaked out, too. Doing Pilates helps tremendously, as does thinking and believing that all people have an inner goodness. Though it can seem invisible, it's still there."

"If you say so," Yolanda said.

"By living in the moment, focusing on my breathing and letting things just naturally unfold, I found that box of golf balls and threw them to get your attention. Being calm helped me more than if I was in a state of panic. Or maybe it was God telling me to do that."

Yolanda stepped over to the stove and took care of pouring the tea. "Maybe you're right about that. Now, let's sit in the dining room. Then I'll make the omelets."

"No, it's okay, I'll eat later."

"Mom, you really need to eat. I can wait till I get to work and have some energy bars."

"Dear, you can't live on energy bars. You need a real breakfast like I taught you."

Yolanda laughed. "Okay, I'll make an omelet for us, but I'll have to pour more tea because it'll be cold by the time it's done."

Abby sighed. "I've got so much to do today from making sure there's electricity to getting out some orders that are now late thanks to that, um, rude interruption last night."

Yolanda opened the fridge and pulled out the eggs and a package of shredded cheddar cheese. "I hope you're okay with non-organic cheese though the eggs are. I found a new place that sells organic free roaming chicken eggs. The chickens all live on a big farm and have indoor and outdoor access."

"That's good, dear. Those kinds of eggs always taste so much better. Here, why don't I just scramble mine? It'll take less time and I think we both have to be places by seven, right?" Abby got up from her chair and walked into the kitchen. "Plus, I need to find out when that electrician's coming so I can be there for him." She stopped. "Wait a minute, he can get inside through the garage door as there's no power."

"Right, but I'll take you back there as soon as we're done with breakfast. I hope BB's okay with opening again. I don't know what I'd do without her. I better call her and make sure."

****

Yolanda went to the police station at noon armed with four yummery tote bags filled with boxes of macarons and other yummery creations for the officers and the staff of the West L.A. division. In the fourth bag were some apple pies, which BB had made the day before and hadn't sold.

The break room was lined with vending machines on one side and a few tables and chairs on the other. She put the tote bags on a table and began unloading them.

"I wish you stocked our vending machines," Officer Springer said, stepping over to her and watching each movement she made.

235

"No, you don't. They wouldn't be fresh," Yolanda replied. "Stale baked goods taste awful."

"That's all we know," the young officer said.

"They wouldn't stay in there more than five minutes," observed a goateed office clerk.

"Please let me know if you'd like some help unloading those," Springer was leering at her, and she noticed his intense dark eyes.

"Thanks, I'm good. I've done this before!"

Several of L.A.'s finest stood nearby and watched as the bags and boxes were placed on the table. She emptied out the last tote bag as quickly as possible, adding a stack of napkins, paper plates, and forks.

"Okay, now this time I've labeled all the boxes and bags of cookies," Yolanda said as she backed away. "But if you have any questions, let me know."

There were some mumbled thanks and a few nods, as the hordes swooped down upon the tempting sugar feast.

An administrative assistant approached Yolanda, handing her a slip of paper. She left as quickly as she arrived. A glance at the paper caused her to smile.

Nervousness about being so close to her mother's kidnapper. Behind her, the door closed, and the bang made her jump, almost dropping the sweets resting on the napkins.

"Hello Detective Churchill," she winced at how shaky her voice seemed. "Here're your chocolate walnut brownies." extending the yellow napkin, she did it quickly so no one would see her shaking hand.

"Thank you, Yolanda. Yolanda, this is our suspect, Emerson Northman. You may have caught a glimpse of him last night or some other time?"

Yolanda stared at the man in his late twenties wearing inmate attire of dark blue scrubs. She noticed his muscular physique. "I have chocolate walnut brownies and oatmeal raisin cookies," she said to the man.

He grinned. "Oatmeal raisin, thanks." Emerson held out his hand and she gave him the cookie and tried not to dash away. She noticed his blue eyes were almost as dark as his uniform.

"Okay, so this is the best yummery in the city of L.A. The only one. And it was featured on *America's Best Bakeries*," Winston said.

"I know," replied the man just after finishing the cookie. "Got another one of these, miss?"

He's the one who was in the yummery who roughed up Quinn, she thought. *The one in that expensive jacket. And he knows about the yummery.*

"So, you like my cookies?"

The man nodded. "Yes miss, you make excellent cookies." He was staring at her intently. "I can't recall eating better cookies in my life."

"Jailhouse cookies aren't made from the finest ingredients," Churchill said.

"Yep. The sugar high's kicking in right now."

"I'm glad you like them."

Emerson leered at her, admiring her tight shirt. "Sure do, miss. Mike told me about you."

Churchill was staring at them. Neither paid attention to the camera recording everything they said and did.

Yolanda leaned a bit closer and was using her dazzling smile to encourage him.

"What did he say?"

"He said you were such a nice person. Loved animals, especially cats. Close to your parents. Didn't have a boyfriend. He was really attracted to you but knew you were a good girl."

She nodded. "So?"

"He thought you were old fashioned. Mike knew if you found out about him, about the truth, well, that wouldn't work out."

"What truth?"

"About the lies, the drugs. The fact that his parents are dead, but his uncle and cousin aren't. How they used him..."

"You mean his uncle and cousin?"

"Yep. That they did. His uncle's meaner than a rattlesnake and Mike's cousin's just the same. They were all workin' a con.

Rented a big ol' Malibu house, a fancy Italian car I never even heard of it--was even better than a Ferrari. They was gonna make it big in the movie biz. Real big."

"What was their plan?" Churchill asked.

"Shoot, what they wanted was what most folks want." He stared at Yolanda. "Got any more cookies? I've got me a big cookie craving."

Yolanda looked in her purse where she'd stashed additional sweets. The man needed more than samples if he was going to talk. She couldn't say no to his simple demand, especially if he told them even more details. "I've got an energy bar."

"Miss, I can always use some energy." He licked his lips.

There went her lunch. She handed it to him, watching as he peeled off the wrapper and bit into the chewy energy bar, his expression softening, his mouth working the healthy snack. His blissful look made her smile. Even Churchill managed a slight grin.

"Emerson, could you tell me more about their plan...um, what are their names?"

"Murray. Grady's the uncle and his son's Craig. They look alike."

Churchill was on his tablet accessing the database. "Go on, Emerson."

"They weren't really much to look at. Kinda all 'round average, y'know...I mean, I'm a guy...I don't pay much attention to other guys." He shrugged.

"Got it," Churchill said upon seeing the photos. "We have a match on Grady R. Murray, 52, born in Austin, Texas and residing in Hawthorne, California. Last released from Chino four years ago for aggravated assault. Nothing since then." He checked the information on the son. "Craig J. Murray has nothing. He'll be 29 in March and has one paid parking ticket from two years ago."

"Yes, but how did they get the money for the house in Malibu and the car and everything else?" she wondered aloud.

"You're kinda dumb, miss. They manufactured meth in an abandoned warehouse on Prairie Avenue. The warehouse owner was involved too."

"What's his name?"

"Can't remember. Common name like Jim or Jack or John."

"Last name of Smith?"

The suspect smiled. "Could be."

Yolanda looked in her purse and pulled out a small box of macarons. "I may be kinda dumb but when it comes to macarons..." She set the box down just out of reach of the man and slowly pulled off the pastel striped lid. "...I have a *Le Cordon Bleu* trained pastry chef working at the yummery who knows how to bake these delicious chocolate and raspberry macarons." The lid was gently placed on the table and revealed three chocolate macarons and a trio of bright pink ones.

The sight made everyone stop and stare at their beauty and the fragrance of rich chocolate ganache and fruity raspberry mingling together. The man leaned forward and sniffed harder but Churchill grabbed the box from him and held it.

"Thanks, Yolanda, I think I could go for a chocolate one," Churchill said, picking one up and slowly biting into it, making a show of enjoying the macaron, chewing it slowly and with gusto, even closing his eyes and opening them up only to notice the ceiling.

"Hey man, I really could go with one of those things," Emerson said, captivated by the sight of them. "What do they taste like? I mean they smell even better than that granola bar."

"Energy bar," she said. "French macarons are like sandwich cookies only they have a very light and delicate shell that's made with finely sifted almond flour, egg whites and sugar. The filling is chocolate ganache made with French chocolate and heavy cream. Or a raspberry buttercream that's made with butter and cream from cows who are free to roam around and graze and aren't penned up. Same goes for the eggs. The fresh organic raspberries are lightly cooked and strained and added to the buttercream."

"Miss, you sure know your baking. And I don't mind trying one and I don't even care which flavor 'cause they both smell so gooood." He was grinning as he alternated between looking at her and the box of macarons that the detective was still holding.

Yolanda picked up the yellow napkin and reached into the box, pulling out a raspberry macaron, placing it on the napkin and sliding it over to the man.

He stared at it, and then picked it up and smelled it before tasting the small delicacy. Emerson popped it into his mouth, eating it in a single bite, grinning as he did so. He shook his head. "Best dessert ever!"

"Thank you. Who killed Mike O'Neill?"

Churchill's grip on the box tightened and he stared at her, surprised that she was being so direct. That she was doing his job. He did nothing, as he didn't want to ruin a potential answer to Mike O'Neill case.

"Those Murray guys. They got into a big fight about money. Mike had stolen a lot of their meth and money and guns. But they didn't know where he hid it. Then they found your business card which he dropped, and after the fight, they dumped his body in the dumpster behind your place."

"So they killed Mike?"

"Yeah, they killed Mike."

"But why did you kidnap my mother?"

"Because I couldn't kidnap you. I tried to but the cops were watching you."

"Why kidnap me or my mother?"

"Were you born yesterday? I wanted the ransom money."

"Were you trying to kidnap me in the yummery when you came in late that night? And then carjacking me?"

He shook his head. "I never carjacked you. That was Craig. He couldn't even do that right."

"Where're Craig and Grady now?"

The man shrugged. "No idea. And even if I knew, why would I tell you?" He looked at the box of macarons. "Can I have another one?"

"You want to try the chocolate?"

"Sure."

"Then tell us where we can find the Murrays."

"Mike said he took you to his house in Malibu."

"I thought they live in Hawthorne." Churchill commented.

"They have more than one house. The one on Torres Road overlooking the ocean is also their place. They were just letting Mike pretend it was his. Like the Bugatti."

"You can go back to Central jail now." Churchill closed the box and returned it to Yolanda.

"Hey man, where's my macaron?"

****

An hour later, Churchill's car pulled to the side of a road near the exclusive home on Torres Road. He pulled out a pair of binoculars and handed them to Yolanda. "Is this the place?"

She looked through them, adjusting the lenses until the modern ocean-view home was clearly seen. For several seconds she stared, noting the glare of the glass in the noonday light. "Those windows are immaculate," she said.

"I don't care about that." Churchill sounded more impatient than usual. "Can you see anyone? Any activity?"

"Not inside, no," she replied. "Hang on." Focusing the lenses, she shifted the position a few degrees to the east. "I see movement." She focused and paused for a few seconds. "There, just to the right of the pool..." Yolanda stepped over to the edge of the car and saw a woman in a sheer cover-up with a plunging neckline emerge from the cabana holding a towel in one hand and a wineglass in the other. "You'll want to see this, Churchie." She handed him the binoculars.

As soon as he focused on the woman, she saw his grin. "She looks familiar."

"Like an actress?"

"Mmmmm, that's possible. Or a model."

"That's not a surprise considering the way she looks and the, um, neighborhood," Yolanda said. "She kinda looks like Dani Kramer only Dani lives in Marina del Rey."

He shrugged. "I wonder how much she knows about the Murrays. 411 says he's been divorced for years, but he could be living with someone."

"Someone who makes meth lives in the Broad Beach area of Malibu?" She shook her head. "That's so sad."

"I agree. But we'll get him. We'll get them." He looked through the binoculars. "Hey, there's a car backing out of the garage."

He focused on a new black Toyota Corolla and a quick swipe at the plates indicated it was a rental. "There's Craig Murray." He put the binoculars down. "Get back in the car; I'm going to follow him."

They got into Churchill's sedan, and he waited until the black car headed south on Pacific Coast Highway. "Looks like this guy's in a hurry. Hang on, Yo, this might get rough."

****

Teagan Mishkin rushed into the yummery and looked around for her friend. Only Jeannie was behind the counter taking care of the appreciated guests, including a couple of college students who weren't feeling too appreciated as they were at the end of the line. "I'll be right there, Jeannie," the younger woman said, rounding the corner and going behind the counter.

"Where's Yolanda?"

Jeannie shook her head, and shrugged, too busy to respond as she swiped a credit card. BB carried in a tray of decadent chocolate cupcakes and quickly refilled the tray in the display case. "Rusty's helping make pies," BB said to Jeannie and Teagan. They should be ready in about an hour." She returned to the kitchen.

****

Churchill followed the rental vehicle by a few car lengths in the heavy eastbound traffic of Sunset Boulevard. They continued to travel along the winding road until they reached the western edge of Beverly Hills and the car turned right on Green Palm Drive.

"Go on, I think he's heading for Wilshire," Yolanda said.

"Are you sure?"

"I'm not sure, I have a hunch he's...." the rental car's brake lights flickered and then it sped up.

Churchill tailed the vehicle, knowing when to give it space, and when to follow almost directly behind it. The sun had disappeared behind the scudding storm clouds. To their left, the Hollywood sign was hidden.

The car drove past the open wrought iron gate. A tall white brick wall surrounded Hollyview Cemetery, hiding it from the residential and commercial buildings. Yolanda almost snickered at the irony of the name, but she knew it was filled with celebrities who wanted their privacy in the afterlife—along with that of their family, friends, and fans. When the sun was out, the Hollywood sign loomed over the manicured lawns, rows of tombstones and the marble mausoleums found at the back and both sides of the cemetery.

Obeying the single digit speed limit, the black car drove to the rear of the cemetery. At the very back stood a green tent with a peaked top and no sides. The closed casket had a huge spray of flowers covering it. Three rows of folding chairs faced the casket.

The rental car pulled over to the side of the road and the driver stepped out. He wore a black shirt and jeans. Yolanda noticed sweat stains on the back of his shirt. The temperature was a cool fifty-two degrees. *He must be warm-blooded, or very nervous*, she thought.

It was almost two o'clock and several people and their vehicles were in the graveyard. Churchill backed the car up and pulled onto another road that had fewer parked cars. "Yolanda, I'm going to hang out over there," he pointed to a level evergreen hedgerow. "I want you to observe what you can since you know Mike O'Neill."

"Knew him," she said. "The Mike O'Neill I used to know wasn't the guy I remember seeing at my doorstep last week." She eyed the small cluster of mourners congregating near and beneath the tent. "I still say that both Craig Murray and Emerson Northman look familiar, and I wish I could place them."

"I'm sure you will, Yo."

She stared at the young man. "Craig looks even more familiar to me than Emerson did."

A Channel 55 Live news van drove up from the other side of the road.

"I wonder if that's Tabby Flynn," she said.

"I think we'll find out in three, two, one..." he remarked as the door opened and a black clad young woman stepped out looking a little too chipper for such a somber occasion. She scraped her hair back into a ponytail, fastening it with a barrette she pulled out of her coat pocket.

"Her hair looks better loose," Yolanda commented as she slunk behind the hedge near Churchill. "I don't want her interviewing me."

"I doubt if you can avoid that," Churchill said as his eyes widened slightly.

Yolanda sighed as the younger woman spotted her and strode over to the area, causing Churchill to duck and move further away.

The cameraman was trotting after her, along with another man, one wearing a green yummery polo shirt beneath an unzipped jacket.

Yolanda stepped from behind the hedge and headed in the direction of the green-shirted man. "Nick? What are you doing here?"

He smiled at her with all his boyish charm. "I'm helping Tabby out. Isn't that great?"

"How did you..?" She stood there and stared at the college student and part-time yummery employee. He was supposedly in class. Was he taking investigative journalism?

They looked at the tent and the people milling about beneath it. "It's highly possible that all the suspects are standing beneath the tent," Churchill said.

Nick and Yolanda nodded. "You're right, but only one is the killer," she remarked.

Churchill scanned the group of mourners. "One – maybe more than one. Maybe none of them. Each case is different. You know that."

Tabby approached them. "Do you think the suspect's here?" She looked at them, and her gaze swept the interior of the tent. A couple walked beneath the canopy, the woman holding a compact folding umbrella. Following them was a tall platinum blonde woman in a designer coat and high heeled boots. She adjusted her oversized sunglasses as she walked to the second row of chairs. She dabbed her nose with a tissue.

Yolanda noticed the camera was pointed at her and the mic was a few inches away.

A black-robed man hurried over, covering the camera lens with his hand.

"Please, no filming or questions now. Afterwards yes, but not now." He pressed his hands together for an instant, bowed, and dashed off to the front of the tent next to the casket.

Tabby and the cameraman went back to the van and returned a few minutes later minus the camera. They stood at the back, watching the mourners.

Yolanda also studied the people around her and spotted the sweaty black shirt-wearing Craig Murray. He turned and noticed her, his face reddened, and his eyes widened in surprise. Opening his mouth to speak, he froze. No words or sounds were heard.

Churchill approached and stood next to Yolanda. It was like in the hospital room but with the uncomfortable man standing there instead of lying in a bed.

"How's it going?" Churchill asked.

"I'm attending a funeral," he looked down at his feet.

The Reverend strode up to the casket. "Good afternoon, everyone. Thank you for being here on this sad and poignant occasion. I'm Reverend Sterling and we're here to honor and remember Michael Paul O'Neill, a young man whose life ended too tragically and too soon..."

A man at the other side of the tent inadvertently coughed, covering his mouth, wanting to erase the noise.

Yolanda noticed the middle-aged man had rigid posture. When he turned in her direction, she noticed the broad forehead and high cheekbones. He resembled Craig and Emerson—like an older version of them. *I've seen that man before*, she thought, studying him as unobtrusively as she could.

****

Reverend Sterling read a couple of Bible verses and then encouraged family and friends to share their memories. A flutter of exchanged glances at one another and at the casket. The silence was uncomfortable and grew stronger with each passing second.

Finally, the man with the excellent posture stepped forward and stood next to the casket. He pulled a piece of paper from his shirt pocket and unfolded it, hands shaking. He loudly cleared his throat. "This is a very sad day for us. We have lost such a great person. I'm sure that my nephew has meant something to all of you. To me, he will always..."

Yolanda watched as the man tonelessly read from the paper. He looked so darn familiar. As she stared at him, she suddenly recalled that evening in Mike's Malibu home. How they'd driven there in his Bugatti. The admiring glances from everyone who saw the costly sports car as they drove through West L.A. and Santa Monica. In the Malibu home, they sat on the patio admiring the exquisite ocean view and had a specially prepared dinner...that was it! She had to cover her mouth to keep from crying out. That chef with the perfect posture was Mike's uncle! And the guy in the black shirt was his cousin Craig as they looked so much alike. She wanted to tell Churchill the news but couldn't. Nor could she whip out her iPad and send him the information at that moment.

She watched him and listened to his lengthy speech that told of how funny Mike was and how he was a movie and TV show producer. Yolanda recalled the bedraggled-looking man showing up at her doorstep at two in the morning. Hadn't he mentioned something about parking on Ventura? Hadn't he seemed nervous about being followed?

A disco ringtone emanating from inside her purse jarred her. The older couple in front of them turned around in unison, their furrowed brows and downturned mouths silently accusing. She reached for her phone to turn it off, muttering a quiet apology as she headed outside the tent and into the windy afternoon. It was her father; he was probably back from his London journey. Yolanda returned to the side of the tent, watching as an elegant petite woman in a formfitting pantsuit said a few words about Mike. Mostly Bible and Shakespearean quotations. Yolanda tried not to roll her eyes when she heard the last one, "He that dies pays all debts."

The reverend said a prayer and touched the wooden casket. The mourners filed past for the last look at Mike O'Neill's final resting place. Yolanda felt the solemnity of the occasion and reflected on how the man would never show up at the yummery again.

****

Back at the yummery, the number of appreciated guests had dwindled to a manageable level. BB and Suzie were back in the kitchen mixing up a batch of macarons.

"Good gravy does Yolanda ever show up?" she muttered. Even Suzie looked surprised to hear BB complaining. Just as she was about to comment, her phone rang, and she stepped into the break room to accept the call. She lapsed into French, and her voice was overheard throughout the yummery. A door slammed and BB hurried over to see Suzie heading down the back hallway. BB asked, "Where are you going?"

The woman turned around and stared at the young baker. "Pierre Larouche told me our macarons are stale! I told him they're barely 24 hours old. He's stale. I must get some cigarettes." Suzie pivoted and took the last few steps, kicking the back door open. The door slid shut and a few seconds later, it opened again. "I need my purse. Smokes aren't free. But I could get a package or two with my good looks."

BB cupped her hands over her mouth to hide her sudden fit of giggling.

****

As Yolanda and Churchill were returning to their car, Tabby Flynn and her cameraman stood in front of the tent trying to interview the mourners. Nick was in the background watching the young woman. He smiled and waved at Yolanda. She strolled over to him, walking him away from the camera and the newscaster. "Nick, you're on the schedule tomorrow morning, you know that?"

He nodded. "Sure, I do, Yolanda. But I think I'm changing my major to communications so I can be a newscaster like Tabby. It seems even more awesome than playing video games."

"Yeah, that's true but it's a lot more work and you have to be able to..."

Churchill was eyeing the Murrays. Craig suddenly dashed away to his car.

"Yolanda, I must do this alone. It's too dangerous. Call for someone to take you back to the yummery."

Yolanda was about to protest when the camera swung in her direction and Tabby was heading over to her. *I'd rather take a bus than be interviewed right now.*

Churchill had already gotten into his vehicle and Yolanda dashed over to it, jumped into the passenger's side, and locked the door. "I'm going with you. Mike's body was tossed in a dumpster about fifty feet from the yummery. Then Quinn was attacked. I've been carjacked, and my mom..."

"Fasten your seatbelt, it's the law." He revved the engine and hit the road at a speed that was well above the posted limit. "I'm following the black Lexus with tinted windows driven by Grady. I suspect him the most. I'll call in Craig's plates and get someone to check him out."

He paused, watching the black Toyota. "Craig just turned right and is headed east."

Yolanda gripped the door handle. He was close to the Lexus, but the driver suspected nothing as Churchill slowed down and drove the speed limit.

"We're heading west, so maybe he's going to his beach house."

Yolanda pulled out her phone and checked the messages. "Okay, but if..." she trailed off. Reading the text from her father, she typed in a quick response and put her phone away, staring into the dirty windshield. "How do you see out of this?"

"Just fine." He paused as he concentrated on driving and made a right hand turn on a side street headed toward the Hollywood sign.

****

On a winding narrow road north of Sunset Boulevard, the Lexus stopped in front of a two-story sandstone brick home on Larkspur Drive. All three garage doors were closed but the one on the right suddenly rolled upwards. Grady got out of the car, looking around him. As he scanned the vicinity, he noticed Churchill's car for an instant. Yolanda held her breath as she observed the laser like focus of his dark eyes, much darker than Mike's were, and she exhaled as soon as he looked at a delivery van further down the road.

"He's going inside," Churchill commented as they saw the black-clad man disappear inside the now open garage with a silver Range Rover parked inside. "It has a Colorado license plate," he mused, pulling out his tablet. After a couple of quick taps on the screen, he called up the information. "I knew it!"

"Knew what, Churchie?"

"Mike's sister Ruth lives in Vail, Colorado. Married to political consultant Bill Shrampton. She's also a third-degree black belt in judo."

"That's pretty high, right?"

"Not the highest which is eleven, but yeah, I'd say that's almost Olympic level."

"Are you thinking what I'm thinking?"

"I don't know, I'm not psychic."

"Motivation. Does she have the motivation to kill her brother? If she's strong then she could've hit him over the head and dumped the body. It wouldn't be that hard for her to lift him up and put him in a dumpster."

"No, especially since he lost weight due to the meth," Churchill replied. "Wait, I see..."

The platinum-haired woman dressed in a skintight jumpsuit walked into the garage carrying a knapsack. She was talking to Grady in a soft voice that neither of them could hear. Winston held up his tablet and focused on the pair, recording them. He whispered two words in her ear: "lip reader."

She nodded, knowing that an expert lip reader would later interpret what they were discussing. And it was intense as she hoisted the plaid knapsack on her back and began walking out of the garage, directly toward them. *How did she change clothes and get here so fast?* Yolanda thought.

Churchill ducked but kept the tablet up so he could record the events going on in the garage. He didn't have to stay down in the seat for long as she got into the Range Rover.

"Are we going to have to follow her?"

He nodded. "I think you should take a cab back to the yummery. This could get ugly."

"No, I want to help."

"You can't anymore, not if I have to..."

The Range Rover backed out of the garage, swerved past the Lexus, and sped right for Churchill's sedan. He shifted his car into gear and stepped on the accelerator, barely avoiding a collision with the SUV. Seconds later, the SUV slammed into drive and was driven into the center garage, the door closing behind it.

Churchill shook his head. "That's a crazy driver." He picked up his cell phone, pushing one of his top speed dial numbers. "Assaulting a police officer. Right, now I can go after her." He got out of the car and ran across the street. Yolanda cautiously followed him, staying out of sight behind a large yucca bush.

The detective's knocks on the front door were ignored and he pulled out his gun but tested the door handle. He turned the doorknob and pushed the door open. Yolanda stepped forward, finding herself pressed against two lemon trees. The fragrance of them reminded her that 'Lots of Lemon' would soon be a flavor of the week. She saw no sign of the detective or heard any noise from Grady or his niece, Ruth. Worried, Yolanda stepped up to the front door and looked inside the house.

The furnishings were so sparse it didn't look like anyone lived there. The floor was covered with loopy wool carpeting. Cautiously entering the living room, Yolanda saw the knapsack sitting on the floor.

There was a creaking noise from the back of the house. Beneath the arched doorway in front of her, the detective tiptoed past, glancing in her direction. The expression on his face was a mixture of surprise and anger. She knew he wouldn't say anything to her. He frantically gestured with his gun, and she stepped behind a faux Chinese screen, hiding from his sight – for the moment.

To her right she heard a whining noise, like an engine starting up. It was familiar, and she couldn't think of what it was. Not a refrigerator recycling or a disposal, and the sound was getting closer. The detective ran up to her and whispered in her ear. "Backup will be here in five, I'm going up."

He turned and rushed for the spiral staircase near the kitchen. Yolanda knew she should stay hidden from sight but her curiosity was on high alert so she couldn't help following him. He was halfway up the carpeted steps. The noise in the wall stopped and there was another noise, like something heavy sliding. Suddenly, Churchill was bearing down on her as he'd reversed his chase and Yolanda had to turn around and go back down the slippery steps, feeling the heat of the man as he was following her so closely.

"Yo, be careful," his breathing was heavy as he ran out to the garage in time to see a pair of young men wearing designer tracksuits and sneakers frantically trying to open the door. The smaller man with the floppy hair jabbed the button on the wall, and the chubbier guy bent down, searching for a way to lift the automatic garage door. In the dimly lit garage, the sense of desperation and fear was palpable, and it was magnified when a shot rang out, hitting a hole in the upper part of the metal door, allowing a tiny shaft of daylight to filter in. Churchill turned toward the connecting door and saw Grady and the woman standing there, both pointing their guns in his direction.

Yolanda had hidden next to an armoire wardrobe and a matching desk, hoping to avoid being seen. She had wanted to stow away inside the armoire but one of the doors was missing and the other side contained drawers.

The beefy young man near the bullet hole stood with his back to the door, looking at the four adults. "I didn't do nothing wrong," he shouted.

"Shut up!" Grady said. "We know that. And they'll learn," he nodded at Churchill and made a gesture at the woman. "We were on the way out, before we were so rudely interrupted by these two...intruders."

"I'm Detective W. E. Churchill, L.A.P.D."

Since when is he going by his initials? Yolanda thought.

Police sirens blared in the distance. This noise alarmed the teens, who charged for the connecting door along with Grady and Ruth. The woman ran to the front door. "Grady, lock the door! They can't come in if we hide."

After trying a few more times to open the garage door, the teenage boys left the garage's confines and raced toward the kitchen. Churchill placed his foot in their way and one stumbled while the other fell to the carpeting with a thud. The loud sirens were outside the home, the brakes squealed, and car doors opened. Inside, the frenzied movement of the older adults was almost comical. As the six-foot-plus woman in stilettos turned to leave, her heel caught a loop in the carpeting. She fell to the floor, twisting her ankle and crying out in pain. Yanking off her shoes, she limped up the spiral staircase, followed by Grady.

The door burst open; two middle-aged police officers dominated the room as they gripped their pistols. The one with the name tag reading Krupa introduced himself.

"Okay, guys 'n gals, you know me, and my partner Officer Price are with the L.A.P.D. Let's get this sorted out."

No one budged. It was as though the police officer had said something completely out of the ordinary.

Grady and Ruth were upstairs at the far end of the room with the small balcony overlooking the living room below. Yolanda thought that the aerial view showed off the bald patches in the old carpeting. *Would the woman jump down?* Yolanda wondered. Krupa went over to the far side of the living room, pointing his weapon up at the pair. "Hey, the two of you deaf or something? Get down here 'cause you don't want me and Price coming up for you."

The chubby guy in the tracksuit lifted his hands. "I'm DEA. I didn't bring my ID with me today but I've been making drugs for those two and I've worked seven days a week since Christmas. No days off."

Officer Price with the handlebar mustache and the narrow green-blue eyes looked at the tracksuited fellow. "Then maybe you can tell us your badge number and the case number."

Krupa asked, "Who's your supervisor?"

"Um, it's 8769921-00U and the case number is 1407. My supervisor is ASAC Hank Schrader."

Krupa smiled, still looking around the room at everyone else. "Wrong, wrong and wrong. Nice try though. Especially that name. I get it!"

"Yeah, me too," Price said as he hid a smile.

Gunfire erupted from upstairs, and the high-pitched motorized noise was heard as Yolanda stood in the corner of the room watching the craziness unfold.

Churchill was trying to capture the tracksuited men as they headed for the front door. Between him and Price, they caught and cuffed the young men, putting them on the one modern sofa near the stairs.

Just before the humming noise stopped, a clapping sound was heard. Krupa ran across the room and around the corner. "Price, over here!"

Price had just taped the hands of the suspects behind their backs and ran over to where Krupa stood. The cab of an elevator was empty but a pair of black high heels remained on the wood floor.

"She's in the area," Price said, looking around. "Try the other garage."

"I think they have three garages," Krupa commented as he headed for the first one, which had the bullet hole in the door. They entered, noticing the armoire. "Check in it and behind it," Krupa said to Price.

Opening the door with the drawers showed nothing other than rolls of garbage bags and cleaning supplies. He reached over, shoved the armoire, and saw the small doorway cut into the drywall. On the other side was the large garage with the Range Rover that was about to back out as the door finished rolling upwards.

Four shots burst the tires and the officers swooped in to make the arrest as Churchill joined them.

Yolanda tentatively stood in the smaller garage and watched the proceedings unfold. Her phone rang and she reached inside her purse to retrieve it. Her father was calling. She smiled as she saw it. "Dad? Can I call you back in a few minutes? I think a major problem's being solved!"

****

That afternoon, Larkspur Drive was lined with news vans including Channel 55 and Tabby Flynn, and the Other Patrick Stewart of Channel 10 NewsTeam. Pulling up after the others was Vern Hess of Channel 12 Action Street News. They and other news teams interviewed the detective and officers, but the suspects had already been taken into custody. Yolanda was exonerated and a neighbor talked about "more traffic than usual since they bought the place last year."

When she returned to the yummery, she took care of appreciated guests and getting caught up on the paperwork. Nick had left a funny saying yesterday:

IF YOU'RE AFRAID OF CHANGE,
LEAVE IT HERE.

Yolanda laughed. "Nick's a clever guy."

That afternoon, she baked a couple of batches of cookies, feeling a sense of relief as she mixed the batter and scooped the dough onto the parchment paper-covered cookie sheets.

BB remarked on Yolanda's good mood. "I had a great time hanging out with Allen on Saturday night. He wants to go out again next Saturday."

"I'm so happy to hear that, BB."

Suzie banged a sheet of vibrant yellow macarons on the table. "Lemon macarons are one of my favorites." She hit the sheet a few more times and then slid it in the oven. "By the way, never go by someone's Farcebook profile. Tyler said he was single. Hah! But I'd rather know upfront."

"I'm so sorry," BB said. "Don't worry, you'll find someone." She glanced at the oven. "I love lemon, too. I can't wait to try those macs."

"Me too," Yolanda said. "Those will be great for the anniversary celebration and as a flavor of the week in March or April."

Several times, she glanced at the clock or her watch or checked her phone. Jeannie noticed and commented on it. "Yolanda, what is going on? Do you have an important date?"

She nodded. "Yes...and no. I'll know it when it happens! I'm sure I'll be able to explain more tomorrow. Make sure you watch the news tonight. I can say that I'm no longer a suspect in the Mike O'Neill case."

"I never thought you were!" exclaimed Jeannie. "But I'm sure as relieved as you are that they've cleaned that scum off the streets."

****

Near the yummery was Jimmy Janga's a Tex-Mex restaurant that had an outdoor patio setup in the back with tall latticework fencing interwoven with ivy. The name was a play on the word *chimichanga*, which was a deep-fried burrito.

The detective and Yolanda were the only ones outside on such a chilly night. A heater was next to their table, keeping them warm. After waiting for only a few moments, the red frilly dressed server returned with the food. The plate containing the *Mucho Grande Jimmy Janga's Carne Burrito* was given to the detective. She opted for the *Camarones Rancheros*. All the necessary condiments were placed on a wood lazy Susan at the table's center.

Churchill had dumped enough chili sauce on his main course to keep him warm enough in case the heater stopped functioning. He nodded his head once, acknowledging the tastiness of dinner. She had a smaller amount with only a dab of chili sauce. And even that was too hot.

He swallowed his water and cleared his throat. "Let's start from the beginning. Last year Grady and Ruth rented that house just outside of Beverly Hills. They didn't want to be in the BH Zip code due to the police being so quick to respond. At first, the house on Larkspur Drive was an investment. It was empty. At first. I haven't pieced it all together yet, but it was Grady and his son Craig, remember he always referred to him as a nephew, who met Emerson Northman up in Washington. Since Emerson and Craig could pass for brothers, even fraternal twins, they decided he was a huge asset. They were planning to move up there to set up shop in the Tacoma area. Meanwhile, they were making the meth in a warehouse in Hawthorne and selling it all over the place. They had that Malibu house, and they never did anything illegal there. It was all at the warehouse in Hawthorne. Mike also had a small house in Hawthorne about two miles from the lab."

"In the Malibu beach house is where they played waiter and chef at their own house, letting Mike pretend it was his."

"Right. Mike told me his wine cost like $10,000 and that the meat was flown in from Japan. I bet he just picked it up at a supermarket."

The detective chuckled. "They were on a roll once they started the LightningEnergy Company. Each pill looked like a normal capsule, but it had powdered meth mixed with potent herbs and caffeine. They were supposed to give you energy and burn fat, but they did way more than that. You saw what Mike looked like when he showed up at your door. We're getting reports of girls as young as twelve taking them. They paid twenty bucks for one capsule. They lost weight and some have brain damage, in some cases joint pain, severe acne, sleep deprivation and severe depression." He shook his head. "Joint pain and depression in kids, you know that's some nasty stuff. Anyway, they used the house on Larkspur Drive as a packaging facility. They added the powdered mixture to the capsules and sold them online and to various clinics and doctors. Even to school kids. They used convincing packaging as it cited FDA approval. Our local representatives from the FDA aren't happy about this mess."

"How'd they get stuff up and down the spiral staircase?"

"They didn't. You heard it. The elevators, the one that was in the garage. Easy access."

"Did you say elevators?"

Churchill nodded. "Plural. If you drove by that house, you'd never know they had one elevator, let alone two. That's how they got up and down and there aren't any fumes like when it's being made. The house has two upper floors, not just one. The second elevator was near the kitchen. They had a clever system."

"It seems like it. But what about Ruth, Mike's sister?"

"Ruth didn't live out here but she visited him from time to time. Apparently, she had a dispute with Mike about the amount of product he was using and how it was affecting him and his work. She's a third-degree black belt in judo. She's strong, obviously. Too strong for her little brother who was deteriorating mentally and physically."

"How'd she kill him?"

"A few blows to the throat. Then she used her handgun to make sure he was dead, or it was a hit. In Colorado, it's legal to carry a handgun. She has a clean record, a few parking tickets, and a speeding ticket. Now she's committed second degree murder. She'll be a guest in our state for the foreseeable future."

"But why dump his body behind the yummery?"

"She wanted you to get blamed for it."

"Me? Why? She didn't even know me."

"She was always in Mike's business, and she didn't like you at all."

"What? Like how would she know me?"

"Ruth used to visit him. She was in the yummery once or twice so she could see what was so great about it. Said it was nothing special and that Mike should be concentrating on his producing and get that reality show up and running. She wanted him to be successful at something legit."

"It doesn't make much sense. Did she kill him because he was using and selling meth?" She winced as she heard the disco ringtone, which meant her dad had left a message. Or more than one, she realized, as she hadn't checked in a while.

He shrugged. "Who knows? A few years ago, there was a case where a teenage girl was beaten to death with a gaming console. Her ex-boyfriend said he had to kill her because she was the wrong astrological sign according to his new girlfriend."

"That's even weirder than Ruth killing Mike and dumping his body behind the yummery."

"She wasn't his sister; she was his stepsister. She'd always loved him. That's why he never married or settled down.

She only married her husband because he was wealthy. People can do all sorts of selfish and mindless things. I deal with the results all the time. I also try not to discuss them with you. But in this case, since it directly affects you, then I will."

After taking a sip of her mineral water, she replied. "I know and I really appreciate it, Churchie." She glanced at her watch. "I still haven't seen my dad since he got back from London. At least I know that Nigel's not a suspect. By the way...what about that duct tape I found on Nigel's coat?"

Churchill laughed. "No match. Nigel was never a suspect. But it's so cool that your dad took the time to investigate it for you."

She laughed. "I know. I'm biased. It's also the first time he's been out of the country in like four or five years."

Neither of them ordered dessert and Yolanda returned her dad's text and he agreed to meet Yolanda at her home and spend the night there.

As they were walking back to their cars, they chatted about the case and Yolanda said she and her father would be watching the newscasts that night.

****

Her father had fed the cats and was sitting on the living room floor tossing a plush catnip-filled toy at them. Mr. Whisker was closer, so he pounced on it and held the blue fish in his paws as he tried chewing its tail. Miss Chef swatted at the toy, but he clutched it closer to his chest.

Yolanda and her father stood there and watched the cats until Miss Chef managed to wrestle the toy away from her brother. She held it in her mouth as she ran down the hallway and into Yolanda's room.

She hugged her dad and asked if he'd had dinner yet. "No, but I had a late lunch if that counts."

"Dad you can't be starving yourself. I've got some..." she watched as her father opened her fridge.

He checked out the freezer. He smiled when he saw a box of pasta primavera and grabbed it, handing it to her. "If you want to cook, just put this in the microwave for the allotted time and I'll be one happy camper."

Yolanda opened the box and put it into the microwave, punching in the amount of time and watching as the numbers began counting down. She grabbed a bowl from the dishwasher along with a fork and set it down on the counter. "Dad, please sit down, you must be so tired."

"I sat on a plane for twelve hours. I'm a little tired of sitting down."

"I want to hear all about your trip, Dad."

He smiled. "I know you do, kiddo. But I also know you want to hear about Nigel."

She glanced at him and then looked down at the floor. "You know me."

"Yes, and for more than twenty years. So, I'll cut to the chase. As you know he's not a murder suspect and we both aren't surprised about that."

Frederick pulled out his phone and set it on the center island. "I edited this on the way back so you can see the highlights. But I also have the raw footage in case you need to see all of it."

She nodded, hesitant about pushing the button so she could see what Nigel was up to. Her finger hovered over the camera icon.

"You don't have to, you know. I can tell you both versions, long and short," he said.

"No, I need to see for myself." She tapped the icon and placed her palms on the cool quartz surface for a few seconds, staring at the tablet. An image filled the screen. A brightly lit ice rink. The camera phone rested against a skate bag that was set atop the perimeter surrounding the large indoor rink. Only a few people were skating, and they glided past the camera. She noticed the tall lean man dressed entirely in black from well-fitting T-shirt to custom-made figure skates with gold blades. His partner was more than a foot shorter, and her white rhinestone-studded dress sparkled beneath the lights. They spun in unison. She did intricate edge moves on one foot. He skated by himself, and his speed picked up with each silent stroke of his blades. He launched into a jump, which she recognized as the triple axel, his nemesis jump, the one that caused him to fracture his ankle and stop skating for several months. Only now, he was clearly back in the skating groove. Nigel launched into a high flying camel spin and the girl imitated him on the opposite side of the rink.

Yolanda pushed a button and stopped the skating video just as the microwave dinged to let her father know that his dinner was ready. She was glad to have the excuse of transferring the steaming hot dinner into a bowl and hand it to her father who was sitting at the dining room table. He began eating as she stared into space. "Oh, what would you like to drink?"

He shrugged. "I'm easy to please."

She went back into the kitchen, retrieved a cold bottle of root beer, and hurried back to the table, setting it down in front of him. "How long were you there?"

"At the rink?"

She nodded.

"Long enough. Long enough to see that he'd rather skate than run his family business."

"That's the impression I got. I'm not good enough for him. Geez, even his cousin Emily's not good enough anymore apparently."

"After he skated we talked. His new partner, Indigo Weaver, is a phenom. She's almost nineteen and has won British

Nationals twice and medaled at Europeans last year. Her mother was a skater in the 80's and she never knew her father. She only knows skating, couldn't even finish the equivalent of a high school diploma over there. When Indigo and Nigel met they just clicked—but it's only about skating with them."

"I don't know they looked pretty happy together."

"Dear, they must look that way if they want to make nationals and the Olympics. And with her as his partner, it might happen."

"Yeah, and he's so busy skating he hasn't bothered to let me or his staff know when he'll be back? And what about his father's open-heart surgery? How did that go?"

"It turned out to be not as serious as that although Mr. Garvey does have a mild heart condition. As far as you and Nigel, I hope you two talk things out soon. You've got to work together though I suspect you won't be seeing him as much if he's serious about his skating goals."

"Well, he left a message but after all that's gone on today I haven't had time to return his call. I still must watch the news, you know, all the reporters showed up at that house where Mike's sister was caught." She stretched her arms and yawned. "But I really want to hear more about your trip to

England and what you did and where you went—aside from a skating rink."

"After I finish my meal, dear."

She sighed, looking out the window. "You know what's weird...I've never forgotten to call Nigel back. Maybe this means I need to give the relationship a rest."

"That's possible," her father said, then began eating his pasta.

She went into the kitchen to retrieve a box of macarons from the refrigerator. "It's still busy at the yummery and next week's the first anniversary celebration so that'll keep me and the staff occupied. Will you and Mom be there to help?"

"Wouldn't miss it, Yolanda. I remember being there on opening day and how proud of you we were. And that hasn't changed one iota!"

"Thanks Dad, you and Mom are the best!" She placed the box of macarons on the table right in front of him. "I made sure it has all your favorite flavors."

"Whatever flavor of macaron you make is my favorite, dear daughter."

CHAPTER 11

The following evening, she carried several bags of groceries she'd picked up on her way home from the yummery. It was almost eight o'clock and she was so hungry that the idea of opening a bag of organic potato chips and diving into it as she walked to her house seemed like the best supper imaginable. The bag with its salty and crinkly contents was the perfect balance to the sweets she'd snacked on that day. Why not? The cats wouldn't mind. Mr. Whisker wasn't adverse to licking the salt off one or two. As she lugged her groceries over to the kitchen door beneath the security light, she noticed that the Davenports' house had lights blazing from every window. Most of the curtains they'd installed were open and she noticed a man walking past the living room window.

"I bet they'll have a big electric bill," she muttered as she set down most of her bags to unlock the door.

She heard the Celtic ringtone -- Nigel was calling. They had a lot of talking to do and it wouldn't be done when she was tired and hungry. As much as she loved him, she knew that whatever they talked about could wait until tomorrow.

"Yoo hoo! Yoo hoo Yolanda!" called her new neighbor as she strode up the driveway.

"Hey, Mrs. Davenport," Yolanda replied as she forced herself to smile.

The older woman wore a bulky sweater and matching lilac leggings. She laughed at the greeting. "Please, just call me Bunnie!" The woman said and laughed.

"Bunnie, right," Yolanda hid a smile as she pushed open the door.

Bunnie reached over and picked up two of the bags. "Please, allow me to help you."

The neighbor followed Yolanda inside the kitchen. "Thank you so much, Bunnie."

"Anytime, Yolanda. That's what neighbors are for! I'm so happy that you're my neighbor. Your desserts are just so wonderful!"

The woman set the bags on the island in the center of the room and looked around. "What a lovely kitchen you have. It's so modern for such a historical little cottage."

"Yes it is." Yolanda wondered how long the woman was going to stay.

"I'm so sorry about all the trouble you had although I'm glad that they caught the killer," Bunnie said.

"That makes two of us," Yolanda replied, removing her coat, and hanging it up. She only wore her pink polo shirt and matching jeans and felt the chill of the minimally heated house. All she wanted to do was crank up the heat and have dinner—even if it was only potato chips and a root beer or a container of organic mango juice. Maybe a cup of noodles or a microwaved dinner. She had no interest in cooking.

Yolanda politely nodded and made sure all the grocery bags were lined up on the island, grabbing one of them and putting it on the counter next to the refrigerator. Her empty stomach emitted a low growl, which she hoped wasn't overheard by her new neighbor.

"I can see you want to unload your groceries so I was wondering if you'd like to stop by later this evening so I can give you a cart?"

Yolanda was about to lift another bag when she stopped. "A cart?"

"Yes, I happen to have a handcrafted bamboo bar cart."

The cuckoo clock began chiming. Bunnie jumped, her hand covering her chest as she let out an "eeek!" She watched the cuckoo announcing the hour along with accompanying gong sounds. The little cuckoo returned behind the door, and two pairs of dancers wearing dirndls and lederhosen spun around to a tinny rendition of "Edelweiss."

"Wow, that's a cool clock you have," Bunnie said, still looking at the over-the-door spectacle.

"Thanks. It was my grandparents. They used to live here."

"I see. But I also can see you need to put away your groceries. So, if you'd like to stop by around nine, that way my assistant, Liam, can help you out."

"Okay, sounds great. I'll be there." Yolanda followed the woman to the door and waved good-bye, relieved to go back to her kitchen and transfer the groceries to the fridge and the cupboards.

After a light dinner of salad and potato chips, she changed into a heavy sweater and old jeans. Yolanda went over to the Davenports' house. A multicolored WELCOME mat was placed in front of the red door. Bunnie quickly opened the door, beckoning her inside. "It's so cold at night this month," she noted, as Yolanda didn't waste any time entering the house.

The yummery owner was impressed with the tidiness of the place and observed that the walls were hung with paintings of mountain and forest landscapes. The living room had black accent tables and a dove grey sectional sofa and matching chairs. A massive teal rug provided the needed color.

"I'll show you the library slash cart room!" Bunnie led the way to the back of the house in what was once the home office of Mr. Steele, a retiree who had a huge collection of antiquarian books. Floor to ceiling fluted cherry bookcases lined the walls. A built-in window seat with fluffy tan and turquoise cushions invited the reader to lounge there.

The rest of the room was filled with assorted sizes and colors of wheeled bar carts. It looked like a cart parking lot, and the one that Yolanda noticed first was the closest one: a pastel pink painted two-level bamboo wood with two glass shelves. She knew it had just been painted and the way it shone beneath the lights made it look so inviting. Magical Cakes of Love, macarons, pies, brownies--any of her products would look even more tempting displayed on that work of art. She walked over to it and ran her finger along the handle, feeling the satin smooth combination of polished and expertly painted wood.

From the hallway, she heard light footsteps. A man entered the room, and she didn't recognize him as Big Jake because the newcomer was shorter and slighter. She smiled at him, as there was a natural friendliness about the man who she hadn't yet been introduced to. *Maybe he's a relative or friend*, she thought.

"Oh, Yolanda, this is Liam, Liam Atwood of AtWOOD Custom Designs. He's built and painted this beautiful bar cart just for your yummery."

"He did? I mean, you did?" Yolanda looked at the man standing next to her, a man slightly taller than her and probably older as he smiled, and the laugh lines showed on his golden skin. He had almost black hair and his eyes were golden amber – a similar color to Mike's. For an instant, she felt the sadness of losing someone she knew who'd died too soon.

"Wow, that's awesome. I mean, thank you. Thank you so much. This cart will look so sweet in the Gift Corner."

"Thank you, I'm glad you like it. I can deliver it to your store tomorrow. Bunnie and I just wanted to make sure you'd like it, and you'd have a place for it."

Yolanda tested the cart with a gentle push. "Yes, this will be perfect for samples. I'll still have the sample trays, but I think this will work even better. And for the Beverage Bar." She turned to look at the man. "Can I order one for the Beverage Bar in turquoise and brown? I'll give you the exact colors to match the logo, but one of these would be perfect in there, too."

"You're an excellent businesswoman, Yolanda," Liam said, grinning, his eyes focused on her. "And from the cookies Bunnie gave me, an outstanding baker."

"It's what I love to do." She glanced down at the cart. "Probably as much as you love making these carts."

He nodded. "You're right. I love any kind of carpentry work. I also love working in this library as the person who crafted these shelves did so impeccably. A true craftsman."

She looked around, noting the arched upper shelves and the warm tones of the wooden bookcases. Nothing like the ones that were sold in a box and later assembled. No wood veneers or plywood. "I've only been in this room a few times. I know Mrs. Steele used to read but she seemed to spend more time on the phone."

"Yolanda, let me know when a good time to deliver this would be. Then we can discuss what you'd like for the Beverage Bar," Liam said.

"Sounds great. How about eleven?"

"Eleven it is." He reached over and shook her hand. "I look forward to seeing how the cart looks in your yummery. And in seeing you again." His grin lit up his face with the naturally high cheekbones.

"Same here, Liam!" she waved and turned to leave. "Thanks again for your kindness. And thank you, Bunnie!"

Yolanda didn't want to leave the warm library with the friendly woodcrafter.

Once she was back home and the doors were locked, she decided to go to bed so she could rise early and do some cat treat baking and then work on lining up the goodies for the anniversary party for the last day of the month.

Entering the dark kitchen, she switched on the light and noticed her cell on the kitchen counter, and she wanted to switch it off and not have to talk or text anyone that night.

Two pairs of light footsteps were heard on the floor and Mr. Whisker jumped up on the counter. He purred and rubbed his head against her arm. Miss Chef softly meowed and began circling her legs. "Snacks, anyone?"

A chorus of meows showed her detective skills were as good as ever.

CHAPTER 12

*I*t's *been a whole year since the yummery's been open,* Yolanda thought as she parked behind the shop that last day of February. Traffic was unusually light that dark Sunday morning and she arrived just before five o'clock.

Entering the yummery alone in the dark. There was silence and stillness in the air. Peace and quiet. Solitude. It wouldn't last long. And there was so much to do. "I hope Suzie shows up on time," she whispered, not wanting to make any noise in the unprecedented silence. Just as she removed her coat and hung it up on the coatrack in the break room, there was a loud banging on the back door. Looking at the clock on the timecard machine she knew who it was. Rushing to the back door, she looked through the peephole to make sure. That was one lesson she'd learned since becoming the owner of the yummery.

The red Yolanda's Yummery hat was a leftover from Valentine's Day, but it was now Rusty's preferred headgear as he wore it all the time.

Quinn's car was pulling into a parking space, and Suzie's Volvo was driving down the alley.

"Look at all the early birds," she said, opening the door for her employees. And then the realization hit her. None of the three had been here last year for the grand opening.

Going into her office, she put away her purse and hung up her jacket. Her phone rang and she answered it.

"Dahling!" Nigel greeted her.

"Hello, darling! What time are you arriving to help celebrate the anniversary?"

There was a catching of breath. "Well, dear one, I just wanted to congratulate you but there's been a major event here."

Yolanda glanced at her watch and the realization struck her even before he said the words. Too many thoughts were flooding her mind for any intelligent language to form. Her silence gave him the chance to explain.

"I'm in London training. Indigo landed her quad toe and I'm working on mine too. This means one thing: the Olympics. There's a chance we can beat the Russians. The quad is the weapon we need."

"Nigel, I have ten toes. And they're right here in the yummery."

"Dear one, you're not happy for me? For us?"

"For you and your skating partner? Yeah, great. But I was expecting you'd be here today for the anniversary. Is that too much to ask? Never mind, gotta go. Got too much work to do."

She slammed down the phone and muttered to herself, "I don't have time for this. We need all hands on deck today of all days." She picked up her phone and hit the speed dial button. After two rings, a sleepy voice answered. "Yes daughter, we'll be there around eight. See you then."

"Thanks Dad, you're a lifesaver."

****

The yummery had been decorated with colorful ribbons and balloons. The sparkling silver First Anniversary banner had been hung up by Rusty just before the store opened at eight o'clock. BB, Teagan, Nick and Jeannie had all showed up just after sunrise. Music played in the background and the glass sample trays were brimming with sweets.

Nick proudly taped a new sign on the tips jar.

THANKS TO ALL OUR APPRECIATED
GUESTS
FOR MAKING THIS POSSIBLE!

Right after the yummery opened, Frederick and Abby, wearing matching green yummery T-shirts, hurried inside. Frederick was carrying a large box and he rushed behind the counter and into the kitchen. "Daughter, I have a couple of new sample trays just in case." Yolanda smiled and waited until he placed the box on the floor next to the walk-in fridge to give him and her mother big hugs. "So glad you could make it today, Mom and Dad!"

"We wouldn't miss this for the world. It reminds me of your first birthday, Yolanda."

She rolled her eyes. "I know, you've told me all about my first birthday cake."

Jeannie walked by, fixing her sparkly pink and silver headband. "I bet she was a sweet baby."

"Yes, she was. And she loved sweets," Abby said. "Now, do you need extra help making the brownies or what?"

"Cashier and packaging duty, for now," Yolanda replied. "Wait, Dad can you also check the stock of packaging, especially the mini cupcake liners for the samples? And probably more baking in about an hour so we don't run out of anything too early."

Abby smiled. "You've learned well, Yolanda. Preparation and preparedness." She gave her daughter a quick hug and went into the yummery.

****

Vern Hess was standing in front of the display case later that Sunday morning as the sun was streaming into the busy yummery. He was holding a large brown and turquoise coffee mug from the Beverage Bar and on the counter next to him was a Crazy 4 Coconut Magical Cake of Love in a transparent glass cake stand. Artie was standing near the corner of the store, making use of the sunlight as he filmed the reporter.

"Friends, viewers of channel 12 Action Street News, stop by Yolanda's Yummery today for the amazing first anniversary celebration! Lots of free samples and lots of brownies, macarons, and those romantic and special Magical Cakes of Love."

Yolanda had just finished adding miniature cupcake liners containing cookie quarters that she slid on the lower glass shelf of the new pastel pink bar cart. It was laden with samples of macarons, miniature cupcakes, cookies, pie slices and assorted flavors of brownie bites.

When the newscaster approached the now-seasoned interviewee, she made sure to gently push the cart in the direction of the camera and was happy to promote her yummery. "It's our one-year anniversary today! We're giving away tons of samples, of course. Everyone who purchases a Magical Cake of Love gets two free brownies of their choosing. Make sure you stop by this afternoon to hear the heavenly harp player,

Bettina Werner, who'll be the featured entertainer from three until five o'clock closing time. She's internationally known, studied at Julliard and in Austria, and is super talented."

Vern grinned. "There you are, Angelenos. Visit Yolanda's Yummery at the Brentwood Grove Shoppes, the shopping center here on the west side of L.A. just of San Vicente Boulevard. Yolanda and her dedicated crew of bakers puts the yum in yummery. Stop by to celebrate their first anniversary. You can sample the Magical Cakes of Love, try some French macarons, and the brownies are literally to die for. And don't forget the Beverage Bar next door where you can enjoy a variety of coffees, teas, and hot chocolate from all around the world."

Teagan was walking around with a glass serving tray containing a variety of macaron flavors, most of them in the yummery's colors. A silver-haired woman wearing a knitted dress took a green one. "Is this pistachio?"

Teagan smiled, "Yes. The yellow is lemon curd, the pink is strawberry, and brown is chocolate."

The older woman took a bite, paused and then finished the delicacy. After swallowing, she nodded. "Oh, my goodness! It's outstanding! I'd like to place an order for my reading club. We're reading about French desserts next month."

"Cool! Let me hook you up with Yolanda, she's the owner."

By the early afternoon, the crowds of appreciated guests were feasting on samples and sitting at the few available tables. Most of the people were milling around, and a few were perusing the Gift Corner.

Not long after Vern and his team left, Yolanda had another newsperson showing up, the young, ambitious reporter and blogger who used to be known as the Other Patrick Stewart. His polished appearance had also been transformed recently, but today he didn't wear a necktie, only a pale-yellow shirt beneath his classic brown suit.

"This is Patrick J. Stewart, Channel 10 NewsTeam. I'm here at Yolanda's Yummery bakery in Brentwood, and it's the first anniversary of the yummery today. I was here last year reporting on it when I was an independent blogger, but now that I'm an anchorman and journalist, I wanted to make sure all the channel 10 news viewers are aware of this special happy occasion. I can vouch for the brownies—I was at the Taste-off when Yolanda was trying to save the cat shelter. And now, here she is, the one and only Yolanda Carter!"

"What does the J stand for?" Yolanda asked.

Captain Angus, wearing soiled captain's duds, walked by, holding a paper bag-covered bottle. "J stands for Jerkface if ya ask me."

"You weren't asked, sir," Patrick replied, turning his back on the older man.

The stocky young cameraman wearing a backwards baseball cap turned off the camera. "Pat, let's redo this intro."

"You bet, Lyle."

Frederick was close enough to observe the situation. He quickly picked up a box of brownies and rushed over to the captain. "Hello Captain Angus, I thought you might want to try some of our German chocolate brownies."

Captain Angus smiled and immediately grabbed the box. He set his bottle on the counter and tore open the lid, chuckling at the sight. Picking up a brownie, he jammed half of it into his mouth before running out of room. He mumbled something as Frederick patted him on the back and turned to leave.

Reaching for his bottle, it slid to the edge of the counter before being retrieved by the captain who swallowed the brownie and headed for the front door. Yolanda and Patrick were watching as he almost crashed into the door but when it opened from outside, he did a big step to the side and gallantly gestured for a young woman to enter.

"Whew, glad he's okay," Yolanda quietly said.

"Glad he's gone," Patrick muttered, fanning his hand in front of his nose. "Showering isn't optional, dude. Now, Lyle, let's finish this. Gotta get to that Beverly Hills party."

The exchange was much shorter than in the past, and the tasting of a large slice of the Crazy 4 Coconut Magical Cake of Love didn't muster up the enthusiastic reaction that he'd shown in the past.

After he left, Yolanda commented to her mother. "I guess he's not much of a fan of coconut."

"I wouldn't worry about it, dear. Vern made a big fuss and you're super busy on a Sunday."

"I'm always busy on Sundays, Mom." She sighed. "Nigel's in London training and I wanted to try to bake some of Mildred's pie recipes this month so I can start writing that dessert cookbook."

"Dear, you have plenty of time to do that. Nigel's doing what he wants because it is a once-in-a-lifetime opportunity. Just concentrate on enjoying your first anniversary." She hugged her daughter and was about to leave when a commotion at the front door made them look in that direction. An enormous, padded object was being wheeled on a dolly by a bearded man in a dark hoodie. He was looking around for a place to set the musical instrument down.

Abby rushed over to him. "Yoo hoo, Mr. Werner, please go to the eastside corner," she pointed to the area where the Valentine's Day tree had stood. It was a sunny section in front of the main window.

"Hello, Abby," the man said, carefully setting the instrument down at the corner. "Bettina will be along in a minute. I'm just going to the van to get her seat."

He rushed out of the yummery. When he returned, he was carrying an elegant purple and gold padded stool. He deftly unpacked the majestic concert grand harp with a red velvet column cover that revealed the lovely wooden harp with the tall column carved with golden embellishments, flourishes, and flowers.

Minutes later, the harpist arrived who smiled lovingly at both her husband and her musical instrument. Her hip-length champagne blonde hair was tied back with a lavender ribbon, and her matching chiffon dress was long and flowing. Teagan stopped to stare at the woman, then extended the sample tray with the macarons. "Would you like to try some macarons?"

"I'd love to," said the man who stepped over and grabbed one. "Bettina can't eat before a performance, but she sure can afterwards!"

There was laughter and he had to pause before eating a chocolate macaron. He licked his lips and shook his head. "Mighty fine macarons, miss. Just as good as the ones in France and Italy where Bettina's performed."

Teagan nodded. "Thanks, our pastry chef trained at *Le Cordon Bleu*." She continued to stare at the harpist. "I just want to say that your dress is so gorgeous. The color and style are so perfect."

"Thank you," the harpist said as she went over to her harp.

Abby and Frederick rushed over, staring in admiration at the impressive musical instrument before addressing the musician. "You are so kind to be able to come to our daughter's yummery on such short notice," Frederick began.

"I wouldn't miss it. I've never played in a yummery before."

Her husband moved the chair back so she could sit down. "Abby said that she was open to anything Bettina would like to play. I'll get you the list of suggestions that we printed out, but my wife and I certainly understand improvisation."

Within a few minutes, the harpist was strumming a classical tune "Clair de Lune" and the atmosphere of the yummery softened. Jeannie counted out the change to an appreciated guest and thanked the man. Frederick slid the package across the counter and the man moved over to the Gift Corner to watch the harpist.

Rusty walked in from the kitchen carrying a stack of foldable cake boxes. He stopped and stared at the pretty musician. "I've never seen a harp player before except on TV," he said quietly. "Sure beats modern music with all its cussing."

Nick was in the process of reloading a cookie tray. "Yeah, it's totally different."

BB stepped out of the kitchen to investigate the melodic tones of the stringed instrument. She stood at the counter, her pink apron dusted with flour and jam and chocolate splatters. The sometimes-talkative young woman was silent. Even Suzy stepped away from her macaronage to look at the new addition to the yummery. "As long as she doesn't play 'Feelings' then I'm good." She glanced at her watch and rushed back into the kitchen.

As appreciated guests put down cellphones and ignored laptops and tablets, the constant noise of talking and the sounds from the electronic devices had been silenced.

The magical moment disappeared when the door opened and Detective Churchill and his boss, Detective Rodman, walked in. The balding older man with the blue baseball jacket and jeans was as casually dressed as Churchill with his khaki cargo pants and burgundy sweatshirt. "Oh, darn, I forgot my tux," Rodman said. "This place is getting swankier than Rodeo Drive!"

Churchill smiled and stared at the unusual sight in the front corner of the yummery. "I love it. Yolanda sure knows how to celebrate an anniversary!"

Yolanda rushed over and greeted the men. "So nice you could make it, Churchie. And hello Detective Rodman."

He gave a slight wave. "Just call me Tom. I gotta say, what a great setup you got here, miss. I mean, even without the harp music, it's so classy. And I, for one, am craving some of your chocolate walnut brownies."

"Is she playing Debussy or Vivaldi?" Churchill asked.

Jeannie chimed in. "Hello, gentlemen. So nice to see you today. I think she's playing Debussy. But whatever, it's so beautiful."

"That it is, ma'am," the older detective said. "This place is one in a million."

Teagan cheerily pushed the pink cart over to the men, smiling and bending down to retrieve a tray half full of pie slices. "We've still got cherry and apple pie samples and BB's just pulled a dozen French apple pies out of the oven."

The men were smiling at her as she handed them the samples.

Yolanda's parents came out of the kitchen carrying two large cardboard boxes. Frederick opened one of the boxes to show it was filled with smaller pink boxes from the yummery. "Look, you guys have the toughest jobs out there. We thought you'd appreciate some macarons, cookies and brownies to have on hand."

Churchill was astonished as he gazed at the amount of sweet treats that open box contained, along with the second unopened box. "Really, that's not necessary, we were just here to stock up on some macarons and brownies."

Frederick smiled. "Look, you folks deserve this. It was our idea, all of us. It's a great way to sweeten up your Sunday."

Rodman laughed and shook Frederick Carter's hand. "Thank you. It's not just us, we have a pretty large staff that's going to be enjoying your yummery's yummies, you can count on that."

The men left the yummery and Frederick brought out his camera. "We need to celebrate the first anniversary the old-fashioned way."

"Oh, Dad, not that old film camera!"

He picked it up with one hand. "It's digital. I just got it last week. It's better than my phone camera. And it beats waiting for the prints! Now, let's get a group portrait over in the scenic Gift Corner."

The End

THE RECIPES

Pink Lemonade Macarons

Pink Lemonade Macaron Shells
- 1 cup powdered sugar [confectioners' sugar or icing sugar]
- ¾ cup almond flour [sift 3 times]
- 2 egg whites [room temperature]

- 2 drops pink gel colorant
- Pinch of salt
- Serving size: 52 shells or 26 macarons [approximately]

Equipment:
- Stand or hand mixer with whisk attachment
- 2 – 4 large baking sheets
- Parchment paper or silpat mat
- Large sieve or flour sifter
- Pastry/piping bag with large round tip
- Measuring cups/spoons/stainless steel or glass bowls
- Silicone or rubber spatula
- Piping/pastry bag
- Large cup or glass to hold piping bag

* Line two baking sheets with parchment paper or a silpat. If the sheets are thin, double them up. Macarons are sensitive to heat, so they need to be baked on a durable tray that has lots of insulation. You'll also need a pastry/piping bag with a large round tip ready before you begin.

* Sift powdered sugar with the almond flour. Large grains that don't make it through can be thrown away or used as a skin exfoliator. I discovered this when I washed the equipment by hand the first time!

* Whisk the sugar and flour to make sure it's fully blended.

* In a stainless steel or glass bowl, beat the egg whites until foamy like a bubble bath before adding the salt. Then add granulated sugar in 3 batches. Start at a low speed and gradually increase the speed. When finished, the mixture should have stiff peaks. Add color last, but only whip for the briefest amount of time to mix in the color.

* Add dry ingredients to the meringue in 2 batches using a spatula. Fold until the mixture comes together, scraping the sides and flip batter over. When the sugar/flour mixture is blended, the batter will be easier to mix and will look shiny. Lift the spatula and see how quickly batter falls in "ribbons" from the spatula. A ribbon of batter dropped into the bowl should merge with the rest of the batter in 20-30 seconds. Another test is to "write" the number 8 with the batter.

* Add tip to piping bag and then twist near the bottom to prevent any mixture from escaping. The tip should face upwards and that also helps keep the mixture in the piping bag as you place it in a cup and form a cuff over the rim so it's easy to add the batter.

* Spoon batter into piping bag. Twist the top of the bag and untwist the bottom, gently pushing the just-poured batter

toward the bottom. You'll remove any excess air that way.

* Pipe the batter onto the parchment or silicone mat. With parchment, you can use a template.

* Pipe batter on the parchment-lined baking sheets in 1.5-inch circles. Keep the batter inside circles if using a template.

* Rap baking sheet several times on the counter. This will further flatten the macarons, and remove air bubbles.

* Preheat oven to 300 degrees Fahrenheit.

* Allow macarons to sit for 30-60 minutes until a film forms. Lightly touch a macaron and if no batter clings to your finger then it's dry and ready to be baked.

* Bake for 16 -18 minutes. The tops should be firm and glossy and the bottoms of the shells should have formed "feet" or frills at the bottom. The risen macarons should be firm with the slightest amount of give. If it wobbles, they require another minute or so. When done, the cookies can easily be removed from the parchment.

* Remove from oven, place cookie sheet on a wire rack or flat surface and let cool completely.

Lemon Curd Buttercream Filling

- 1/4 cup softened butter [use a high quality butter like President or Kerrygold]

- 1 1/2 cups powdered sugar [confectioners' sugar or icing sugar]
- 2 Tablespoons heavy cream
- 3 Tablespoons lemon curd
- 1 teaspoon vanilla extract or vanilla bean paste
- 5 drops yellow gel color [optional]

Whip butter for about 2 minutes before adding some of the powdered sugar. Add the cream, lemon curd and vanilla. Gradually add the remaining powdered sugar until the filling is the desired consistency. Add colorant last.

Pair the shells according to size. Spoon or pipe filling onto one side. Gently add the other side. If using a piping bag, start in the center by doing a swirl until you reach near the edges but not right at the edges. You don't want to overfill them and make a mess with leaking buttercream filling. Gently add the top shell and give it a twist of about a quarter turn to make sure the shells are nicely lined up.

Store your macarons in an airtight container and put in the refrigerator. They should last about a week. Macarons taste best at room temperature, so remove from the fridge about an hour beforehand.

If you don't have the time or patience to make macarons from scratch, you might want to try to make some Raspberry Chocolate Cupcakes. The black specks you see in the frosting are from the vanilla bean paste.

Raspberry Chocolate Cupcakes

Yield: 12 cupcakes Bake time: 17-19 minutes
Oven Temperature: 350 degrees Fahrenheit

Ingredients:

- 1/3 cup dark chocolate, finely chopped [Divine's dark chocolate with raspberries] [3 oz.]
- ⅓ cup Dutch-processed cocoa powder
- ¾ cup hot water
- ¾ cup all-purpose flour
- ¾ cup granulated sugar
- ½ teaspoon salt
- ½ teaspoon baking soda
- 6 tablespoons virgin coconut oil [melted]
- 2 eggs [room temperature]
- 2 teaspoons [fresh] lemon juice
- 1 teaspoon vanilla bean extract or vanilla bean paste

Equipment:
- Stand or hand mixer for frosting
- 12-cup muffin pan
- 12 Paper or silicone liners
- Large sieve or flour sifter
- Pastry/piping bag with large star tip
- Measuring cups/spoons/bowls
- Whisk or fork
- Piping/pastry bag
- Large cup or glass to hold piping bag

Directions:
Place the chopped chocolate and cocoa powder in a medium bowl. Pour the hot water over the mixture and whisk until smooth. Refrigerate mixture for 20 minutes.

Preheat oven to 350 degrees Fahrenheit. The rack should be in the center. Line 12-cup muffin pan with liners.

Sift the flour, sugar, salt and baking soda in a medium bowl; set aside.
In a small bowl, whisk the eggs thoroughly.

Whisk the virgin coconut oil, eggs, lemon juice and vanilla extract into the cooled chocolate. Add the flour mixture and mix until smooth. There will be small lumps from the raspberries in the dark chocolate [if using that type]. DON'T OVERMIX!

Fill cupcake liners ¾ full. Bake until the cupcakes are set and just firm to the touch, 17 - 19 minutes. Or, insert a toothpick into one and if it comes out without crumbs it's done. Cool cupcakes in the pan on a wire rack for 10 minutes, then remove the cupcakes from the pan and place on the wire rack to cool completely, about 1 hour.

Rockin' Raspberry Frosting

3/4 cup unsalted butter, [room temperature]
3 1/2 cups powdered sugar [confectioners' sugar or icing sugar]

3 Tablespoons heavy cream

1 1/2 – 2 teaspoons vanilla bean paste

1/4 cup seedless raspberry preserves
3 drops magenta gel color [more for a brighter shade]

Frosting Directions:

Beat softened butter on medium speed for about 3-4 minutes until completely smooth and creamy. Slowly add the confectioners' sugar, cream, vanilla bean paste and colorant. Increase to high speed and beat for 1 minute. Add the raspberry preserves and beat until thick and creamy, about 5-6 minutes, so it's very soft and fluffy.
Pipe onto cooled cupcakes.

ABOUT THE AUTHOR

AUTHOR'S NOTE:
Thank you for taking the time to read *Macarons and Murder*. Feel free to write a review at any of the online bookstores. Also, please tell your friends, family and local library about this book, along with any of my other titles. Thank you!

****

Lisa Maliga is an American author of contemporary fiction, psychological thrillers, and cozy mysteries. Her nonfiction titles consist of how to make bath and body products with an emphasis on melt and pour soap crafting. When researching her cozy mystery, she discovered the art of baking French macarons. When not writing, Lisa reads an assortment of books, takes photos, skates, and is working on a series of baking and soaping video tutorials.

You'll find more about her work at:

http://www.lisamaliga.com
http://lisamaliga.wordpress.com
https://www.youtube.com/user/LisaMali
gaCreates Soapcrafting & baking
tutorials

http://pinterest.com/lisamaliga
http://www.goodreads.com/LisaMaliga
https://truthsocial.com/@lisamaliga
The Discerning Readers' Newsletter
http://eepurl.com/UZbE9
French Macaron Baking Adventures:
https://lisamaliga.wordpress.com/frenc
h-macaron-baking-adventures

FICTION:

Diary of a Hollywood Nobody - Chris Yarborough is a Midwesterner as green as the corn back home in Ohio. This former bookstore employee moves out to Los Angeles to pursue a profitable career in screenwriting.

Hollywood After Dark: 3 Tales of Terror – [Paperback and eBook] This trio of horror novelettes takes place in Los Angeles and Hollywood. Titles include *Satan's Casting Call*, *An Author's Nightmare*, and *Hollywood Starz Storage*.

I Almost Married a Narcissist - Charlotte White falls in love with a younger Romanian gymnastics coach. Andrei Antonescu is a sexy and handsome foreigner who loves to have fun and flirt with the ladies. The more she gets to know him, the more red flags are unfurled. Once she's able to see past his good looks and muscular body, Charlotte is unprepared for some shocking revelations.

I WANT YOU: Seduction Emails from a Narcissist - Arlen J. Stevenson is a narcissist who uses his scant literary accomplishments to entice his online victims. Meeting and seducing vulnerable women is what drives this Alabama-born man. [Paperback and eBook]

Love Me, Need Me: A Narcissist's Tale is about a bumbling sexual predator, narcissist, and author of three insipid zombie books. Middle-aged Arlen J. Stevenson hails from Alabama. His relentless and often hilarious pursuit of women online leads him to our other protagonist, Los Angeles-based writer of term papers, Helena Hoffman. [Paperback and eBook]

The Narcissist Chronicles: The WHOLE Story – Contains two full-length novels about the adventures of an online sexual predator. *Love Me, Need Me: A Narcissist's Tale* and *I WANT YOU: Seduction Emails from a Narcissist.*

North of Sunset - Sherman Lee is a volatile action movie producer in search of critical acclaim. Best friend Wesley Barron stars in his hit movies and knows about the producer's troubled past. Emily Karelin is sent to work for Sherman due to her lack of show biz knowledge. Temping to support her figure skating habit, Emily works in his Beverly Hills mansion, unaware of how her life will drastically change. [Paperback and eBook]

Notes from Nadir - A California writer returns to her Midwestern home due to financial difficulties. Moving in with Mom, she lands a job at an online auction site. She deals with wacky coworkers, unsympathetic relatives, health issues, and the struggle with being in Nadir--the place and the state of mind. [Paperback and eBook]

Out of the Blue - Sylvia Gardner is a naïve library clerk who lives with her dysfunctional mother in Richport, Illinois. After being dumped by her first boyfriend, Sylvia falls in love with an English actor after watching him on a PBS drama. Researching Alexander Thorpe's life and career for two years, she saves her money so she can visit him in his Cotswolds village. She stays at the Windrush Arms Hotel, discovering they share a secret connection. [Paperback and eBook]

Satan's Casting Call - Duncan Smith-Holmes is a struggling young actor who is in desperate need of a paying gig or he has to leave Hollywood.

September Harvest - In this story set in 1979, we meet Laurie Caswell, a bookstore clerk at the Northbrook Mall. She goes to the movies with her boyfriend. Later, they go to her house and share some booze. Laurie has a nightmare of the dying mall in 2021, which resembles a prison. Will the nightmare come true, or will the old book she discovers the next day at a yard sale help change the course of humanity?

South of Sunset - Such a world-renowned name conjures up images of movies, sunglass-wearing stars, palm trees, plastic surgery, drug habits, the proverbial overnight success ... and the happy ending. In this collection of original short fiction, the author takes us into the minds of an assortment of losers, dreamers, successes, wannabes, and has-beens.

Sweet Dreams - Brenda Nevins is a successful romance author with a movie deal, a reality TV show, and a forthcoming bakery. Complications arise whenever any communication she sends or receives turns into fragments of a fantasy story. Will she find whoever is responsible for hijacking her career, finances, and even her fiancé?

NONFICTION:

12 Easy Melt and Pour Soap Recipes - Contains original recipes, 37 color photos, and several places to buy soap base, molds, fragrances and other necessary supplies. Learn how easy it is to craft your own melt and pour soap in less than one hour!

Fun Foodie Soap Crafting - You'll receive more than a dozen original and tested recipes, pretty packaging and labeling tips, 40+ photos, mistakes to avoid, and numerous supplier resources.

Happy Birthday Melt and Pour Soap Recipes - Say Happy Birthday with hand crafted soap! This unique book contains eight recipes for all budgets, along with melt and pour information, and birthday soap presentation tips. Contains 30+ color photos.

How to Make Handmade Shampoo Bars – Learn how easy it is to make natural handmade shampoo bars. This innovative eBook includes 25+ recipes for shampoo bars, hair rinses, and hair masques. Contains more than 50 color photos, step-by-step instructions, and a chapter on natural additives.

How to Make Handmade Shampoo Bars: The Budget Edition [Paperback only] – Same as above only with black and white photos.

Is the Long Island Medium the Real Deal? [Editor] - In this groundbreaking book, author and demonologist Kirby Robinson examines Theresa Caputo's claims of mediumship and what's on The Other Side. [Paperback and eBook]

The Joy of Melt and Pour Soap Crafting is written by someone who learned how to work with crafting glycerin melt & pour soap the hard way -- with only a single page of instructions to follow! If you've always wanted to make your own soap, here's an opportunity to learn just how easy it really is! Contains 40 recipes and MUCH more!

Maple Sugar Melt & Pour Soap Recipe FREE at Smashwords. Learn how to make a fun fall melt and pour soap recipe starring pure maple syrup—a healthy addition.

Matcha Green Tea Melt & Pour Soap Recipe – Learn how easy it is to make this luxurious melt and pour soap starring Matcha Green Tea. This soap is wonderful for all skin types. It would make a great addition to any bath and body or tea lover's gift basket! FREE eBook.

Monoi de Tahiti: Spa in a Bottle - What is Monoi de Tahiti and how will it benefit you? A bottle of this Polynesian beauty product has a variety of uses and will soothe your skin, hair, and nails. "Monoi de Tahiti: Spa in a Bottle" is a unique e-book focused on this fragrant and natural Tahitian beauty oil.

MORE Joy of Melt and Pour Soap Crafting - Two eBooks in one! You get *The Joy of Melt and Pour Soap Crafting* and *12 Easy Melt and Pour Soap Recipes* in one volume!

Nature's Beauty Oils: Monoi de Tahiti and Shea Butter – Two eBooks in one! Learn about nature's most versatile beauty oil and butter.

Never Mock God: An Unauthorized Investigation into Paranormal State's "I Am Six" Case - *Paranormal State*'s "I Am Six" episode is a perfect American horror tale -- for all the wrong reasons. It stars the ambitious founder of the Paranormal Research Society, an attention-seeking client, a bumbling group of paranormal investigators, a psychic-medium in search of ratings, and a rogue exorcist. [Paperback and eBook]

Nilotica [East African] Shea Body Butter Recipes [The Whipped Shea Butter Series], Book 1 - Learn the quickest and easiest way to whip Nilotica shea butter. Each recipe is easy to follow and includes the time it takes and amount it yields. Find out the secret to getting that incredibly light and airy texture.

Nuts About Shea Butter - The reader will discover shea butter's benefits, its numerous applications, and how to get optimal use from this healthy and natural nut fat. Learn about the differences between East African and West African shea butter. See photos of the various types of shea butter.

Organic and Sulfate Free Melt and Pour Glycerin Soap Crafting Recipes - If you want to make the most natural soap without using lye, here is a way to craft organic and sulfate free melt and pour glycerin soap at home. In less than an hour, you can craft lovely organic, sulfate free and eco-friendly Castile soaps with these carefully tested recipes.

Paranormal State Exposed [Co-Author] - Explore the rumors of staged scenes, questionable evidence, misleading editing, and duped clients. As other paranormal programming comes along imitating this style of presentation, it's vital that the problems are investigated.

Paranormal State: The Comprehensive Investigation [Co-Author] - Includes the eBooks *Paranormal State Exposed* and *Never Mock God: An Unauthorized Investigation into Paranormal State's "I Am Six" Case.*

The Prepper's Guide to Soap Crafting and Soap Storage - Be the cleanest prepper around! Create your own lye-free soap or find the best type of soap to store in the coming years. Informative book shows the best ways to craft your own soap. You'll receive original recipes and valuable storage tips to get the most out of your soap.

Rooibos Tea and Pink Kaolin Shampoo Bar Recipe - Discover how to craft rebatch/hand-milled soap base into a unique and versatile shampoo bar for most hair types. Also includes a recipe for Rooibos tea and apple cider vinegar hair rinse.

The Soapmaker's Guide to Online Marketing – This handy eBook is packed with detailed information on designing, building, and promoting your website. Learn how to write a press release. Get loads of free promotional ideas. Learn easy search engine optimization techniques and much more.

Squirrels in the Hood - When Sunshine the cat departs in 2006, the second story balcony she occupied is very empty. Now that birds can be fed, the author does so, also attracting an array of hungry squirrels.